ALL THE NATURAL BEAUTIES

JOHN DEAL

DARK LAKE
PRESS

DARK LAKE
PRESS

ALL THE NATURAL BEAUTIES
ISBN-13: 978-1-7375382-0-2 (paperback)
ISBN-13: 978-1-7375382-1-9 (ebook)

Cover design by Danna Mathias, Dearly Creative

Dedicated to the wonderful people and places that make up the Lowcountry, a place I lived and worked for nearly ten years. I can still hear the tide coming in, smell the salty air, and taste the great food at Poogan's Porch, the Wreck, the Boathouse, Coconut Joe's, and many more. There's nothing better than a Sullivan's Island oyster roast, boiled shrimp fresh from Shem Creek, and afternoons at Dunleavy's or on the deck at the Windjammer with Jimmy, Doc, John, and Bobby.

PROLOGUE

Thursday, April 1
The Business District, Charleston, South Carolina

Mandy McCarthy dropped to the sofa in the break room. Her legs ached, and her feet were sore. Her neck was an overwound rubber band. The end of her brutal twelve-hour shift at the Medical University of South Carolina (MUSC) hospital had mercifully arrived—eight p.m.

She rubbed her temples and stretched her arms. A drink wouldn't hurt. Another shift loomed, so she promised herself she'd make it brief, get home, and under her warm blanket. She hustled to the staff changing area and switched her scrubs for a pair of old faded jeans and a simple white T-shirt. Her casual appearance would be glamorous enough for a short night out. Mandy pulled her shoulder-length blond hair into a ponytail and applied a hint of makeup. She glanced in the mirror. She wasn't smoking hot, but naturally appealing. After a few more touch-ups, she flew down the stairs and into the night breeze.

Charleston, the Holy City, provided Mandy with life and work advantages. Her job at MUSC and apartment were close by, and bars and restaurants littered the scene. A few steps would get her anywhere she needed. She had a car but rarely used it.

She zipped up her jacket and drifted along the stone pathway on Calhoun Street. The night air was cool on her face. The streets glistened from the mist. The lights twinkled, giving the sky a yellowish shine. Shadows from the magnolia trees and palms, abundant at the College of Charleston, fell across the sidewalk. The tension in her neck eased, and the fog of the day lifted.

Mandy chose the King Street Bar, across from her apartment. Local hangouts didn't draw the masses this early on a weeknight. The college-age crowd wouldn't crank up for at least another two hours, and her eyes would be shut by then.

She winked at the doorman and took two steps at a time to the second floor, where there were fewer people, and it was away from the live music. She wouldn't have her eardrums rattled tonight. She settled at a small corner table and savored the tartness of lime and a hint of salt in her margarita. Mandy smiled at a tall, well-built man. He smiled back.

Her eyes fluttered open . . . blackness. Sounds of her breathing disrupted the silence, but nothing more. She attempted to move, but her arms and legs were frozen. Her shoulders were numb from her arms being extended over her head, there was a cold hard surface beneath her, and something covered her mouth. *Where am I, and how did I wind up here?* Mandy's mind raced. How many drinks did she have? Her head pounded, and she shivered.

Don't panic! What else happened? Wait a minute. There was the handsome stranger. Her memory skipped recalling his name. *Jim . . . I think.* She pictured his kind smile, charm, and sense of humor in her mind. *We were talking and then—*

Footsteps. Mandy heard scraping, and a sudden bright light blinded her. She blinked and worked hard to focus. She felt a flash of terror when she saw the ropes entwined around her wrists and ankles and her naked body. Fear consumed her.

The handsome man peered down at her. His lips curled into a smile as he glared into her shocked baby-blue eyes. "You had quite an evening." His face shrunk the distance between them as he whispered, "Perhaps next time you should watch your tequila . . . if only there would be a next time."

He crawled on top of her. His face was wicked and his breath hot. The stink of alcohol filled her nostrils. She couldn't stop his violent attack or the horrific pain. A sharp edge glided across her throat. Warmth spread down her neck as the life drained from her body.

Eyes fading back to blackness, she screamed, but only in her mind.

PART ONE

EMERGENCE

CHAPTER

ONE

Friday, April 2
Hyde Park neighborhood, Boston, Massachusetts

Where are you, Pete?

Boston detective CJ O'Hara slipped through the side door into the dimly lit warehouse where she and her partner, Detective Pete Jenkins, had responded to a possible burglary. While it was risky, they'd decided to split up, each moving into opposite ends of the vast space.

CJ had difficulty seeing with only two rows of overhead lights working. The bulbs flickered wildly, making the visibility worse, much like being under strobe lights in a warehouse bar. Particles of dust danced in the broken frames of illumination.

She couldn't see Pete, and her heart pounded. Her pulse rate had spiked, and she struggled to control her breathing. *Stay calm, CJ. You can do this.*

Where are you, Pete?

CJ looked for movement, which was difficult by the metal racks holding containers and boxes of various sizes that filled the building. She couldn't see across the warehouse and wondered if the perpetrators were lying in wait, ready to spring a trap.

She had to choose: stay silent and hope she had the drop on them, or announce her presence. She'd be stupid to think they'd come out and throw up their hands. A third option: wait for backup. But the backup wouldn't get there in time if Pete was in trouble. She crept forward and her eyes darted around as she rounded the next rack.

A gangly man with long blond hair and angry eyes stood at the end of the row with his arm wrapped around Pete's neck, a gun to his head. He sneered at her. "Look who it is. Another one of Boston's finest." He stepped toward her, keeping his grip tight on Pete. "Tell you what, babe, you need to give me your gun."

CJ eased forward with her gun trained on the man. Forty feet away, she stopped and stood her ground. Pete's life depended on how she handled this. "Boston PD. Drop your weapon!"

The man howled. "Here's my counteroffer. Drop your gun, or this piece of shit is dead meat."

Pete's eyes were wide and frantic. "Don't do it! He'll kill us both."

The perp struck Pete with the butt of his pistol with a dull thud. "Shut up, asshole!"

Blood trickled down Pete's face. His consciousness waned, but he flashed his eyes up, then quickly down.

What is he signaling? CJ didn't understand the movement.

"Honey, I'm losing my patience. I'll count to three, and if your gun isn't on the ground, I'm putting a bullet in his head."

She shook her head. "I can't."

"Have it your way."

Through the blinking lights, Pete mouthed "down," and she suddenly understood!

"One, two . . ."

Pete jerked his head down, exposing his captor's face. The explosion was deafening, rattling the walls of the metal structure. Pete and the perp fell forward with the man's weight forcing Pete face-first into the concrete floor, where both men lay motionless.

CJ sprinted to him as a second man slammed into her, knocking her off her feet. A knife flashed, and she sensed a sharp pain in her left shoulder as she crashed to the floor, losing her weapon. She scrambled after the gun, grabbed it, and spun into a sitting position. The second man came at her with a knife until he stared down the barrel of her Glock. Shock showed in his eyes as he froze.

"I surrender! You got me. Don't shoot."

She kept her eyes fixed on him as she slowly got to her feet. "Drop the knife and put your hands up!"

The man's fingers squeezed the knife, but he didn't move.

"Do it now! Drop the damn knife and put up your hands. Now!"

He lunged at her. She fired, hitting him in his upper torso, and he went down whimpering. CJ kicked the knife away and ran to Pete, where she saw the perp's dead eyes and a gaping hole in the center of his forehead. Blood covered her partner's face. Oh, God! Had she hit him, too?

"Pete! Can you hear me? Pete!"

Pete moaned, and he blinked. She realized the blood was coming from his broken nose and a gash on his head. She cradled his head as the sirens grew louder. "Hold on."

Moments later, four officers burst into the warehouse. One sprinted to CJ, horrified by the blood. "Are you hit?"

"No. I banged my shoulder when I fell, and the perp nicked me with his knife. Pete needs help, and I think one asshole is still alive."

The officer frantically radioed for medical help. "Two down. One of our own. We need a rush on a bus!"

CJ sat planted on an overturned five-gallon bucket when the paramedics arrived. Her shoulder throbbed, and the gash stung.

Kneeling in front of her, the paramedic said, "Any wounds besides your shoulder?"

"No. But I'm sure I'll be sore all over tomorrow."

The paramedic cut the sleeve of her blouse open and applied a dressing. "We're loading the others up for transport to Boston Med. I've patched you up so you can ride with an officer and follow us."

CJ watched as they loaded Pete, who bitched about not being able to ride with her.

"Why can't I ride in a cruiser?" he asked.

She smiled at his stubbornness. "How about you cut the crap and let these guys do their job? They say the ambulance, you get the ambulance."

Pete rubbed his forehead. "Bossy woman."

The paramedic grinned. "Not a bad-looking woman to be bossing you around, though."

"All right, boys, remember, I'm still packing."

Pete feebly smiled at her. "Good thing Harry taught you to shoot."

Shoot. A sudden wave of nausea hit CJ, and her head spun. She'd killed a man, having never discharged her firearm in the line of duty before. The fingers of torment seized her. The perp had given her no choice, but this didn't help the pain in her heart.

———

Boston Med was a beehive, with medical staff bustling in all directions. The smell was antiseptic, the air stale, and the walls glared stark white like freshly fallen snow. CJ hated hospitals—being in one always flooded her memories of her sister lying comatose.

The doctors argued with Pete about staying overnight for observation. His sensitivity to light, dizziness, and disorientation concerned them. Pete complained the whole time, something about date night with his wife, who stood at the foot of his bed laughing. "This is a hell of a way to avoid taking me to dinner."

CJ's shoulder was sprained, and she needed stitches. The doctors agreed to let her go home, provided she kept the sling on and used her painkillers if necessary. They said it would take a week or so for the soreness to dissipate.

Captain Frank Wilkins wove through the doctors and nurses, looking for his officers. He towered over the hospital staff, his dark brown eyes searching the crowd and his jet-black hair a mess. CJ saw him coming and gave him a halfhearted smile.

"I'll be fine, Cap. I have a mild sprain of my left shoulder. No surgery's needed. I've added another scar to my collection. Pete has a concussion, and as usual, is raising hell. He doesn't want to stay overnight. The doc says he should be fine and ready for duty in ten days."

Frank patted her uninjured shoulder. "Glad you two weren't badly hurt. I get a lump in my throat every time I hear 'shots fired' and 'officer down.' I understand one bad guy is in the morgue and the other is here."

"Yes, sir."

"Fair enough. I need your gun until we review the shooting to document the justifiable use of lethal force. Internal Affairs will come get your statement. After that, go home. Take next week off, so your shoulder heals."

"I can work," CJ said.

He shook his head. "No. Let's allow time to complete the review of the incident and for that shoulder to mend."

CJ sighed. "Yes, sir." She suddenly felt nervous. *Incident review.* Her actions shouldn't be an issue, but even so, it was scary. Politics always loomed in these types of assessments.

"I'm going to head off, but I want you to go home after you provide your statement. Take it easy. Are you okay driving? Got any painkillers?"

"I'm fine to drive. An officer brought my car here. The doc gave me a prescription for some Oxy, but I won't take them unless necessary."

Frank thumbed at his phone. "Depending on how your shoulder is doing, let's meet in my office next Friday afternoon at three." When she nodded, he turned and wound his way back through the crowd.

CJ couldn't decide whether to be excited or worried. A decision on her promotion was past due, so was this it? Would it be delayed because of the shooting? She was frustrated she'd failed to ask for details.

———

An hour later, CJ exited the hospital and walked to the parking lot. Ice crystals stung her face, and she threw her hood over her head. In early April, snow in Boston was unusual. CJ closed her eyes and imagined the warmth of St. Patty's Day only a couple of weeks earlier when she'd been able to wear shorts and a T-shirt.

Traffic was a nightmare. She had a forty-five-minute drive to her Allston-Brighton neighborhood condo. *I guess I'll have plenty of time for my thoughts.*

CJ headed north on Massachusetts Avenue, weaving around cars. She flipped the radio off as she thought about how she'd progressed to this point in her career. She had been with the Boston Police Department ten years, the last three as a detective in the Bureau of Investigative Services (BIS).

She had followed in the footsteps of her uncle Harry O'Hara, who'd served with the Boston PD for thirty-five years. He had been the rock in her career and, to be honest, her life. He was the only family she had left. With his move to Charleston, she had lost him, too.

All CJ did was lose people she loved.

TWO

Saturday, April 3
The Boroughs, Charleston

The predawn air was crisp, quiet, and still. He silently wove through the chokeberries that lined the yard's boundary, carrying his precious package, and was careful not to disturb the contents until he found the right spot, a perfect resting place.

He brushed the hair from her face and folded her hands over her chest. "There you go, sweetheart. Now you look beautiful." She looked so peaceful that he hated to leave her, but the sun's rays were now peeking over the horizon. What a splendid time he'd had with her, and oh, how he had enjoyed himself. It had taken thirty years, but he'd finally acted on his urges. He hadn't expected it to be so easy, but she'd practically walked right up to him and begged him to take her.

She was the kind of girl who caught his eye. Naturally attractive, without too much war paint. Her silky blond hair and baby-blue eyes had made his heart swell. He hated fakes like those overly dolled-up girls who strutted around everywhere. Give him a natural beauty any day.

Meeting her had excited him. It was a bit risky, but fortunately, the bar had held few people, and the sparse lighting had made it a bit dark inside. She had smiled at him, and he'd returned the gesture, offering to buy her a drink. She had said she planned on an early night and told him just one. With a little convincing, he had talked her into another round. He'd picked it up from the bar himself and added a roofie that he got from a younger dealer on Dorchester Road in North Charleston. He'd wanted to do his part to help her get to bed early.

The delights that had followed their meeting were the best. The morning after, when she realized she was in real trouble, her wide eyes had pleaded for him to let her go. Then, the thrill he had felt when having her a second time, while she squirmed and cried in pain, was indescribable. His ultimate joy, though, was the blood—so much blood.

As he looked at her, his urges started building again. One last gaze, and he'd be gone before the sun revealed him. The mementos he had taken would remind him of her. He blew her a kiss.

"Goodbye, sweet Mandy."

Gavin Morris was going to be late again. This wasn't good since he was already in the doghouse with his boss. He sped along the asphalt of Concord Street, hitting potholes, crunching gravel, and then parking so he was hidden behind some dense bushes. So far, his plan had worked.

He quietly scampered along the thick foliage lining the building toward the back door. He ducked as he passed under a window. *What is that stink—rotting meat and dirty kitty litter?*

Gavin saw her and froze. His stomach flipped upside down at the sight of the pale, mutilated body of a young woman. He flung the back door open and screamed for help. He fell to his knees and lost his breakfast.

Charlie Mills, the owner of the Charleston Boat Shop, called 911 after he responded to Gavin's scream. He and Gavin made sure not to get too close to the young woman lying on the plastic tarp in the shop's outdoor storage area. Someone had cut her throat and sliced her open.

Officer Ben Parrish of the Charleston Police Department arrived at the scene within twenty minutes. He wasn't sure what he'd find, but he knew a boat shop owner had found a body. He was barely out of his cruiser when a middle-aged, pear-shaped bald man ran up to him.

"We found her in the back. It's terrible. She's so young," the man said.

"I'm Officer Ben Parrish. Let's go."

The man pointed toward the building. "I'm Charlie Mills, the owner of the business. This way."

"Were you the one who found her?"

"No, one of my employees, Gavin, found her. He's sitting around back, really shaken up, and you'll see why soon."

Gavin was sitting on the ground, legs pulled up, and his head rested on his knees. On wobbly legs, the thirty-something, skinny man slowly stood when they approached him.

Ben caught his eyes. "Sorry for the terrible start to your day."

Gavin shook his head. "This is an awful thing. I'll have nightmares for a year."

"How about you guys wait inside while I inspect the scene? I'll need your statements before I leave."

Ben approached the body as he pulled on booties and surgical gloves. Horrific was the best word to describe the scene. Ben had witnessed some ugly things in the military and as a police officer, but nothing like this. The young woman was lying on her back with her hands folded across her chest. Her pale nude body had dark red, purple, and yellow splotches from the wounds on it.

Ben squatted his six-foot-four body next to her, careful not to touch her. The young woman had a gash across her throat and another from her sternum to below her belly button. Her midsection was sewn up. *Is that fishing line?* Whoever had done this was ruthless, but loving, in a sick way for trying to repair the damage. Like a mangled *Sleeping Beauty*, she appeared to be napping.

Ben reached into his pocket for his phone and called dispatch. "Hey, it's Ben. I'm here at the Charleston Boat Shop. We have a dead body of a young woman—I'm guessing in her early twenties. I need the Crime Scene Unit and the medical examiner here ASAP. I'll secure everything, but we need to process the scene before the day gets too warm."

He unwound the bright yellow police ribbon to secure the location. The only way in and out of the chain-link-fenced area was on one side. Ben decided to wait to take witness statements until backup arrived. He didn't want to risk losing any evidence.

———

The three-person CSU team, led by Crime Scene Investigator Eddie Rodriquez, arrived within thirty minutes. Eddie was about Ben's age, thirty-one, and stood only five eight. He had a slim build with short brown curly hair and attentive hazel eyes.

Medical Examiner Thomas Whitehall from the Charleston County Coroner's Office arrived for his field examination and to take the body back to the morgue for a complete autopsy. He was a slim man, rather plain, with receding silver-gray hair. He had kind eyes and was nearing sixty.

"Good morning, everyone," Thomas said. "I'll wait until you see what we find around her before I look. What time was it called in?"

Ben eyed his notes. "Dispatch got the 911 at seven-fifteen a.m. I got here twenty minutes later."

Thomas nodded. "I'll estimate the time of death after a closer look, but at first glance, it seems she's been dead for a while."

Ben went inside to take statements. He couldn't rule either Charlie or Gavin out as the murderer, but his instincts told him neither was the culprit. There was no way Charlie would commit the murder and leave the body on his property. Likewise, Gavin was too distraught to be the killer.

He started with Charlie first, who sat at his desk and absentmindedly fidgeted with a boat propeller. Ben asked him to begin with what happened when he first arrived.

"I arrived here a little before seven and came in the front door. I unlocked the back door but didn't go outside. I started reviewing the paperwork of repairs and equipment on the day's schedule. Saturday is a busy day since the shop is closed on Sunday."

He sighed. "I was at my desk, and Gavin screamed for help. He was doubled over by the back door, puking his guts out. I saw the dead body and called 911 from my cell."

"Was anyone else around?"

"No. Just Gavin."

"When was the last time you were out back?"

"I was in the storage area late yesterday afternoon, making sure we had what we needed for today—no body then."

Someone had clearly placed the body there late last night, or early that morning, Ben reasoned. "Can you provide anything else?"

Charlie thought for a minute. "I have an alarm, but no video surveillance. A neighbor owns video cameras, and he may have views of the back area."

Ben scribbled notes on his pad.

Ben found Gavin sitting in a folding chair in a storage room—bent over, head in hands. He was still shaken up, but he said he'd tell Ben everything he could remember.

"What's your last name?" Ben asked.

"Morris."

"Okay, please start at the beginning and try not to leave out any details."

Gavin rubbed his temples. "I arrived for work at 7:10 a.m. I know the exact time because I looked at my cell phone. I was late for work and figured I was going to be fired, since that's been an issue for me."

Ben tried to reassure him. "I think under the circumstances, you won't lose your job. Tell you what, I'll talk to Charlie for you and put in a good word. What happened next?"

Gavin wiped tears from his eyes. "I parked in the lot next door and planned to sneak in the back. I was gonna play off being late by saying I had been in the back when Charlie arrived. Charlie doesn't go out back much. I'm the one who usually fetches supplies and equipment from the outside storage area."

Gavin's hands shook as he lit a cigarette and took a long drag. "So, I went around back, and her body was there. At first, I didn't realize it was a real body, but once I . . ."

"Was anyone else around?"

"No, no one. We always start work at seven on Saturday, but no one is around until we open for customers at eight."

Gavin started sobbing. "Poor, poor girl. She was dead, so I didn't go near her. Her eyes were all glassy looking and . . ."

Ben patted him on the shoulder when he trailed off. "I appreciate your help. Here's my card if you think of anything else."

"Okay. I hope you catch whoever did this."

Ben told both men he would contact them with any other questions. "I'll get one of the CSIs to collect your fingerprint and DNA samples. This will help us rule you out." Ben headed outside to wait on the CSU and ME to finish. As he pushed the back door open, he looked at Gavin. "Once we finish up and take her body, the area will be clear."

Gavin shook his head. "I'm not going out there for a while."

The CSU and ME indicated they'd finish in less than thirty minutes, so Ben postponed checking on the neighbor's video cameras until they cleared the body. He was anxious to receive a preliminary report of the findings before everyone left.

Their fieldwork completed, Eddie and Thomas joined Ben in the shade of the building. Eddie reviewed his notes. "I'm struck by how clean the area is—no fibers, fluids, or residues. Whoever left her here was careful not to leave anything behind. We'll take the tarp back to the lab and see if we can find anything, but I'm not hopeful."

Thomas echoed this. "I found no visible residues on the body or any residue under the fingernails. It appears she didn't fight her attacker, or they cleaned her up. We've bagged her hands, so I can examine them during the autopsy."

"What about a time and cause of death?" Ben asked.

"My best estimate for the time of death is twenty-four to thirty hours ago based on the body temp, lividity, and state of rigor," Thomas said. "Her blood has pooled. The crimson and purple areas indicate she has been lying on her back for several hours."

Thomas pointed to her neck. "The most likely cause of death is the laceration across the throat. I believe the cut down her midsection was done postmortem. She was probably killed elsewhere, as evidenced by the lack of blood at the scene. Whoever did this is extremely skilled with a knife or cutting instrument. Other damage to the body includes ligature marks on the wrists and ankles. I think he tied her down at some point."

"Was she sexually assaulted?" Ben asked.

Thomas exhaled. "Sadly, yes. I didn't find any signs of semen, so my guess is he used a condom. We'll know more when I do the autopsy."

Ben scanned his notes before asking, "Any other identifying marks or anything unusual?"

Thomas pointed to her right ankle. "She has a small seahorse tattoo. The tattoo and her fingerprints should help us identify her. She took excellent care of herself. She had a recent manicure and pedicure. Her teeth are perfect—no caps or crowns, only a couple of small fillings."

Ben watched as the body was loaded into the truck. The Live 5 News van had arrived, as well as numerous on-lookers. Ben ignored their questions. "We'll release a statement later," he told them briefly.

He went to the neighboring property and searched for surveillance cameras, but they seemed too far away to catch anything. Ben spoke to the owner, who confirmed they only captured the area near his front and back doors, so there was no video of the boat shop's back area.

Ben reviewed his notes, and a wave of sadness washed over him. Somewhere, the family of a beautiful young woman was about to have their world turned upside down.

THREE

Sunday, April 4
Wando, South Carolina

Harry O'Hara started his morning as he did every morning since moving to Charleston from Boston nine months ago: he got up at five and had a cup of coffee on his back deck overlooking the tidal creek to the Wando River. He loved mornings in the Lowcountry. The yellow and orange fingers of the sun reached over the marsh. The birds sang, and the salty odor filled the air.

He stood up and stretched his six-foot frame. At sixty, Harry was still in great shape. His salt-and-pepper hair, more salt than pepper, was close-cropped. His hazel eyes, more green than brown, were still sharp as an eagle's.

Harry carried the new trolling motor to his boat. He'd need to try it out, but he knew it would make fishing much easier in the shallow creeks. He pulled the motor's receipt out of his pocket, and a card dropped at his feet. Harry stared at the card and exhaled. *I need to call and confirm my appointment.*

Harry went back to the deck and stretched out in his chair. He'd wanted a quieter life. Boston was all hustle and bustle. Now he started his morning slow, spent part of the day fishing or riding around in his boat, and had dinner at one of the many excellent local seafood restaurants. Harry loved fresh fish and all seafood, for that matter. If fishing went well, he made dinner and marveled at the sun going down. About the only negative were the tiny biting flies the locals called no-see-ums. They bit the worst at sunset.

Harry's life only had one potential complication. His friend, Charleston Police Chief Walter Williams, had just asked Harry to work as a consultant on homicide cases. Harry had been a detective in the homicide unit of Boston's Bureau of Investigative Services for twenty-five years. Walter had told him, "You have more homicide investigation experience than all my people combined." Harry had said he'd consider it. He was missing the mental challenges of solving cases, but it was a welcome change not to see people committing horrific acts.

The morning was too beautiful to make any big decisions, so Harry decided to go fishing and try out his new motor. He wanted the sun and wind on his face. *I only said I'd think about the job offer, after all. There's time.* Harry would be more inclined to act as a consultant if his niece, CJ, accepted the offer to join the Charleston department. He'd missed her since he'd left her in Boston.

Harry sat in the boat and punched numbers into his cell. After the beep, he said, "Hello, this is Harry O'Hara. I'm confirming my ten o'clock appointment with Dr. Mitchell for Tuesday morning."

FOUR

Friday, April 9
Hyde Park neighborhood, Boston

The numbers on the clock were brighter than usual—5:35 a.m. CJ was sure time had slowed to the pace of a glacier. She flipped her blanket off and left her soft bed. She couldn't sleep; the thoughts of if she'd be a sergeant or if she still had a job troubled her.

CJ dreaded her morning appointment.

———

Three hours later, Dr. Matthews asked CJ to take a seat on the black leather couch across from him in his Boylston Street office. He looked odd, with his beady eyes and crooked nose. His glasses were too large for his face, and his gray hair stuck out like quills on a porcupine. CJ anxiously shifted and the couch squeaked. She knew this session was required, and she hoped it would help, but wished she were anywhere else.

"Detective, have you ever seen a psychiatrist before?" Dr. Matthews asked.

CJ cleared her throat. "Yes. I saw a shrink when I was young." *Jeez, shrink. Way to start, CJ.*

"For what purpose?"

A bead of sweat formed on her forehead. She flashed back to her earlier sessions. "My parents and sister died, and I was having a hard time coping." *Please don't ask for more.* She watched as the doctor made a note on his pad.

"How did they die?"

CJ shifted—squeak. She hoped the bead of sweat wasn't visible. "They were killed in a car accident when I was eleven."

"Tell me about your family and the accident."

"I had great parents and a wonderful family. My parents, Sean and Catherine, met at church and married right after high school. I had a sister, Chloe, two years older, who was my best friend. My life was perfect until a drunk driver killed them on the way to pick me up after a church potluck. The guy had been drinking all afternoon, ran a red light, and broad-sided my parents. My dad and mom were killed instantly. Chloe survived the crash, only to die after a week in the hospital." *I'm the reason they died.*

"I'm sorry. That must have been devastating for you. What are you not telling me?"

CJ slowly exhaled. "I felt guilty since I made them come to pick me up. If they hadn't, they wouldn't have been killed."

"Felt or feel?"

"Excuse me?"

"Do you still feel guilty?"

"I'm better . . . but I still struggle with it."

CJ still had survivor's guilt. Counseling helped, but she had always carried the responsibility for her family's death. It was almost unbearable the week after the accident. The three funerals over ten days were nothing but a blur. The excruciating pain had never left.

"I'm sure everyone has told you the death of your family was not your fault."

She just nodded.

"Okay, so after your parents died, where did you live?"

"My uncle Harry took me in. He was my dad's oldest brother and close to us. He never hesitated, but it couldn't have been easy. He was a bachelor and had never married or had children. Harry worked long hours with the Boston PD." Tears ran down CJ's face. *Please move on.*

"Any other family?"

"No. My grandparents died when I was five, and I never met my other uncle, Craig. He moved to Charleston, South Carolina, over thirty years ago to work in the fishing industry before I was born."

"How was life with Harry?"

"He was a father to me, and I didn't always make it easy."

"How so?"

"I started drinking in high school, sometimes lots of drinking. Cosmos, Pink Passions, and Kamikazes. My lowest point came early in my senior year when I got stopped for DUI. Uncle Harry stood by me, and I made it through the incident."

"Do you still drink?"

CJ's heart rate picked up. She wiped her face.

"Do you?"

"Yes. Only occasionally, though."

He leaned forward. "Is alcohol a problem for you?"

"No," CJ lied. Truthfully, she didn't drink every day, and the DUI had taught her not to drive if she did. She stayed away from hard liquor, but there were times she drank to excess to escape.

Dr. Matthews scribbled more notes, stared at her, and then moved on to the shooting.

The hour seemed to take days. CJ described how she felt about shooting and killing a man. She broke down more than once. She wasn't fragile, but her grief and remorse over the death was genuine. Dr. Matthews told her he believed the incident was unavoidable. This didn't make her feel any better. She added the demon of killing a man to her survivor's guilt—three scars and two demons.

CJ sat in the precinct after the interview, which was buzzing with activity. She was uneasy, and her nerves were frayed. Pete watched her as she checked the time on her phone.

She fretted and fidgeted. She checked it for the third time and jumped up. "I have about thirty minutes before I go see the captain. I'm wandering down, so I'm ready."

Pete smiled at her. "Promotion's gonna happen. I'll be here, ready to celebrate. Drinks on me!"

"We're not going out drinking. You're supposed to be home, not here."

"Spoilsport!"

CJ shifted from foot to foot outside Frank's door while he talked on the phone. It only took him a few minutes to end his call, but to her, it felt like hours passed while she waited. She stood there sweating, hoping the sheen on her face wouldn't be noticeable.

"Come in, CJ. Sorry to keep you waiting. How's the shoulder?" Frank finally asked when he hung up.

"Shoulder's fine, Cap. A little sore, but I can lose the sling. I'm ready to work."

"Happy to hear it. You can return to work on Monday." Frank wheeled around and grabbed a report from his credenza. He spun back and looked squarely at her. "Let's talk about the incident review. The positive news is you've been cleared of any wrongdoing—the shooting was deemed justified. We had one small hiccup, but it's been addressed."

Her heart rate increased. "Hiccup?"

"Yes. The second perp said you shot him for no reason."

Her face went red. "What the hell! He's a lying son of a bitch!"

Frank extended his bony hands in a stop position. "Hold on. The perp said he put his hands up and surrendered, but you shot him anyway. He hired a lawyer and was squawking about filing an attempted murder charge. Pete was on the ground, so he wasn't a witness and couldn't clear you. However, the building owner had a surveillance camera. The video clearly showed the man surrendering, putting his hands up, then lunging at you with a knife. Your shot came in self-defense after he lunged at you. His attack caused you to shoot, so case closed."

CJ sat, breathing hard. She feared she might hyperventilate and pass out.

Frank chuckled at her, sensing she had worked herself up. "His only response when his lawyer showed him the tape was, 'It was worth a try.' Needless to say, the lawyer walked away with no case."

"I'm fortunate there was a camera, or I guess I'd be fighting for my job."

Frank nodded. "Yeah. Maybe. This time, everything is clear, and this review is in the books."

Okay, so I still have a job. What about the promotion?

He leaned forward. "Now, about your promotion."

She held her breath.

"The BIS has been running behind in determining promotions and filling our open sergeant slots. The process is taking forever this year."

CJ squirmed. *Stop stalling. Spit it out!*

He sighed. "I regret it, but your promotion wasn't approved."

She couldn't respond. She sat, numb.

Frank broke the silence. "I know this is crushing news for you. You're a damn good detective, and from my perspective, you'd be a great sergeant. All I could obtain from the selection committee was that you need more time to demonstrate the 'judgment expected of a sergeant.' I'm sorry."

CJ mumbled, "Thanks for your help," and left his office. She marched straight down the hall, past her desk, and left the building. By the time she reached her car, she was no longer numb. She was pissed. She sat in her car and screamed. "How can they pass me over? I've done everything expected, and there are open spots. What is this 'judgment expected of a sergeant' crap?"

She pounded the steering wheel, put her car in gear, and whipped onto Hyde Park Avenue, heading north to her condo. She didn't answer Pete's call. She was too disappointed and pissed off to talk to anyone.

She got to her condo, stripped off her clothes, dropped them in a pile, and turned on the shower. The warm water helped calm her anger and disappointment. She dried her hair, dressed, and aimed for the nearest bar. She needed a drink, maybe several, to escape.

FIVE

Friday, April 9
Goose Creek, South Carolina

She was a natural beauty. Not fake at all.

He watched her as she filled the gas tank of her Honda Civic. She was cute in her tiny shorts and bare feet as she washed the front and back windows. She opened the hood and checked the oil level. She appeared to know what she was doing around a car. He couldn't take his eyes off her.

She finished filling her tank and went to pay for the gas and grab snacks. As she crossed the parking lot, he watched her. He wondered if her sandy blond hair was natural. He liked the way it blew in the late afternoon breeze. She wasn't wearing much makeup, but she didn't need it. Her face was captivating, and her blue-gray eyes shone in the afternoon sun.

Once she went inside, he approached her car, which had a North Carolina State University decal on the back window and a parking sticker on the bumper, indicating a college student headed south for a break. He bet she was meeting a bunch of girlfriends for fun on the beach. He visualized a bunch of tanned coeds frolicking on the sand, their toned bodies . . . *Focus!*

Her car appeared fine. No, wait, what's this? Did her back right tire need air? He chuckled to himself. Well, he'd make sure the tire was too low to drive far.

He acted quickly and slipped the screwdriver back in his pocket as he smiled and walked away. Would this natural beauty be able to handle a flat tire without help? He'd soon see how well she understood cars, and he'd be sure to be there to rescue her. He leaned his head back and sucked in a deep breath of the moist air—a thunderstorm was coming.

SIX

Friday, April 9
Kiawah Island, South Carolina

Laura Perkins was excited she was on the last leg of her trip to Kiawah Island. Her car's navigation showed she had less than sixty minutes from the beachfront condo she and some of her sorority sisters had rented for the long weekend. She was happy to get away from the campus. Her classes weren't an issue, but she needed a break from her boyfriend. She had to decide whether she would break things off with him. Their relationship was too inconsistent. One day it was good, the next, terrible. *Why are some guys such jerks?*

Loud music was at the end of the line when she called. No doubt the party had started.

"Hey, girls! Sounds like a party. I got off Highway 17 on Main Road, so I'll follow the road to the island. Be there soon!"

Laura hung up laughing. She'd taken a critical exam that morning, or she would have gone with the rest of the group yesterday and not driven by herself. But since she had her Honda, she'd swing through Charlotte and visit her parents on her way back to school.

Her path wound back and forth across marshes, creeks, and the Stono River, and got less traveled as she got closer to Kiawah Island. The reddish-orange sphere of the sun dropped into the horizon in her rearview, and flocks of seagulls hurried to their nightly resting place. The salty odors of the ocean increased. Kiawah River Bridge was ahead!

She sang along with Jason Aldean's *The Truth* when her car shook. Had she run over something, or was there a rough spot on the road? The shaking grew worse, and slowing down didn't help. When she stopped at the gas station, she'd checked everything. She frowned, and pulled over to the broad shoulder, making sure she was entirely off the pavement. Hopefully, this was a quick check, and she'd be back on her way.

She inspected the front and back tires on the driver's side. Both were fine, so she rounded the back and saw her right rear tire was low. *Crap, a flat.* Should she call AAA? If she called them, she'd need to wait. There would be no telling how long it would take out here in the middle of nowhere. She could call her friends, but they'd be no help. Her dad had shown her how to change a tire, so doing it herself was best. She opened her trunk and found the jack. *How do I do this again?* She had just determined how to put the jack together when a black SUV pulled up behind her.

He sat in his Ford Bronco and stared at her. It was such a shame she was stranded on the side of the road. Bad luck for her. He looked around, but there was no one and no other cars. He opened his door and stepped out. "Excuse me, young lady. Do you need help?" He gave her his best smile.

She smiled back. "My tire is flat. It was fine when I stopped for gas in Goose Creek. Maybe I picked up a nail or something." Laura hoped the tall man would offer his help. She was sure he could change a tire faster than her, and he was handsome. She pointed at her tire. "I think I can change it, but it'll be a new experience for me."

He approached her, still smiling. "Not to worry, I've changed lots of tires. I'll help you."

She exhaled. "That would be great, if you wouldn't mind. I'll pay you."

He laughed as he slid on his leather work gloves. "I don't mind at all, and you don't need to pay me. You'll be my good deed for the day!"

She couldn't believe her luck. This was great. She'd be back on the road in no time. "Thank you so much. I owe you."

He kept smiling and thought, *Yes; you do.* Fighting the urge to grab her, he stuck out his hand and introduced himself with a lie, of course. "I'm Jim."

She took his hand. "Hello. I'm Laura."

"Nice to meet you." He started setting up the jack. "Where you headed?"

She grinned. "I'm going to Kiawah Island for a girl-friend's bachelorette party weekend."

He nodded. "Kiawah is beautiful. You're not far away, and I'll have you back on the road in a jiffy." Once the jack was in place, he stood. "You're lucky I was going your way. I haven't seen another car go past."

"Yeah, since I got off I-526, the drive has been pretty quiet. I'm glad I don't have far to go since it's getting late."

He looked at the darkening sky and smiled. "Let's change this tire and get you on your way. How about you come round and watch?"

She had no concerns. Jim seemed like such a gentleman, unlike her jackass boyfriend. "Perfect. You can teach me."

As she kneeled in front of him, he lunged and grabbed her. He ran his hand under her jaw and yanked backward, so she couldn't open her mouth. She struggled and fought him, but his grip was tight. He was much taller and stronger than she was, and he had the element of surprise.

He whispered in her ear, "This is the time for you to cooperate, and you'll be fine. If not, I'll hurt you badly."

She was confused and scared. She ceased struggling as her mind raced. She cooperated until he got her near the back of his truck, and then she started to fight again. But when the knife's edge touched her throat, she froze.

He growled. "Easy way or the hard way; it's up to you."

She began to cry as he taped her mouth with heavy duct tape and also used it to tie her wrists behind her back and her feet together. Then he picked her up and threw her into the back of his SUV. He wrapped a rope around her neck, and she struggled to breathe. He pitched a heavy tarp over her, and blackness enveloped her.

Laura lay still in the back. The tape on her wrists and ankles stung, and the rope cut into her neck. She still couldn't breathe without difficulty. Where was he taking her?

He looked in his side mirror and smiled. His plan had worked to perfection. The small hole in the tire had allowed her to drive far enough off the freeway when the tire went flat to an area where passersby were few. He was surprised not one car had passed while he was with her on the side of the road. It had been the ideal spot.

An hour later, he pulled off the road to his safe place. Gravel crunched under his wheels, and tree limbs slapped at his truck. When he had parked inside an old building, he got out and yanked the tarp back. Laura stared at him, and fear gripped her throat.

He untied the rope and pulled her out of the SUV. His arm was tight around her neck, and her feet could barely touch the floor. He carried her to an adjacent room, dimly lit and cold, and threw her on a metal table. She groaned in pain, and he laughed loudly. "I'm so sorry. I didn't mean to hurt you."

He removed the tape from her ankles and tied each to the bench with ropes. Once her feet were tied down, he rolled her over and took the duct tape off her wrists. She immediately tried to hit him, but he pinned her hands down and laughed at her again. "Now, now, play nice."

One by one, he tied the ropes around her wrists and to the bench. She was stretched out on the table face-up, unable to move. The tape was still tight on her mouth, so she couldn't scream. He smiled sinfully at her. "How about I make you more comfortable?" He ripped her shirt off, and using his knife, he cut off her shorts and bra. She was left wearing only her panties. "You should be comfortable now."

Her breathing was ragged, and tears streamed down her face.

He leaned over and stared into her eyes. "It's no time to cry. That time will come later. Are you cold?"

She stared at the ceiling, trying to transport herself elsewhere.

"How about I turn on the heater for you?" He went over to the side of the room and grabbed an electric heater, and pulled it close so the heat lashed at her. He chuckled. "Let me know if you get too hot." He stroked the side of her cheek. Licking his lips, he ran his hand across her breasts and stomach and down her legs. "Such a beautiful young woman. I'm so happy we met."

She was repulsed, but she couldn't avoid his touch. She could only cry.

He clapped his hands. "Okay, I'll be back, and the fun can begin."

He left the room, flipping off the lights. The only light was coming from the red glow of the heater. All Laura could do was wait in the musty-smelling cavern. She only hoped someone had seen him bring her here—wherever here was.

SEVEN

Saturday, April 10
Allston-Brighton neighborhood, Boston

CJ bolted upright in her bed, startled by the commotion. "Who in the hell is banging on my door?"

She sat up too fast, and stars floated around in her vision. Her temples throbbed, and her head felt like it was exploding. The top of her skull was on fire. She rubbed her eyes and gently twisted her head to see her clock, as she knew moving too quickly might cause her to pass out.

"Jeez—7:38 a.m."

Someone was rattling the door off the hinges.

"Okay, okay, I'm coming. Stop banging on my damn door."

She dragged her aching body out of bed. She was only wearing a T-shirt, so she went to her closet to find her robe. Where was it? More banging. Whoever was out there was determined to force CJ out of bed.

"Kill the racket," she yelled. "I'll be there as soon as I can."

CJ couldn't find her robe in her closet, so she trudged to the bathroom. Her robe was in a heap in the corner. Finally! She pulled on the fluffy garment, tied it tight, and stumbled down the steps. *Stop banging on my door!* She'd planned to sleep late on her day off, but here she was, up at the crack of dawn. She peeped through the hole, removed the chain, and opened the door. "Hey, Pete," she greeted him hoarsely.

Pete stood there with a worried look on his face. "Jesus, you don't answer your phone, and I knocked for almost thirty minutes. I was about to call SWAT."

"I needed a break from life."

Pete frowned. "I brought coffee. Let me in so we can talk. You may not want or need it, but I do."

"Fine, come in. If I say no, you'll try to break down my door again."

Pete headed to the couch and put down a to-go coffee he'd brought for her. "No, I'll call SWAT. They're great at breaking down doors."

CJ slogged after him. She thought the world of Pete, but she wanted to be left alone. He wasn't interested in her desires, though.

"I knew you didn't get good news when you didn't come back after your meeting," he said.

No response.

Pete paused a bit, looking around her condo at the disarray. "I tried calling you."

"I appreciate it. I was too hurt, pissed, and to be honest, embarrassed to talk to anyone. I haven't even told Harry yet."

"CJ, we both know you should have been promoted. I've watched you, and you're more than qualified."

She was numb and sat in silence. *Please leave me alone.*

Pete looked at a broken beer bottle on the floor. A man's plaid shirt was hanging on the chair. "What the hell happened here? It wasn't him, was it?" he asked softly.

Her eyes flared at him. It wasn't any of Pete's business if she had a guest, and no, it wasn't the lieutenant. He'd told her he was separated. *You're a dumbass, CJ!*

Pete stood. "Okay, okay. I'll leave you alone." He was worried about her and made one last effort. "I'm taking Nancy and the kids out for the day. I promised them. They'd be happy if you came with us."

I want to be alone.

Pete read her face and walked to the door. "Okay, I understand. Give me a yell if you need anything."

CJ watched her friend with the dad-bod paunch walk toward his car. The cocoa-colored spikes of his crew cut held firm in the morning breeze. She locked and chained the door. She wasn't happy Pete had woken her up, but she was touched he'd gone to the trouble of stopping and checking on her. If she hadn't stayed out way too late drinking and felt like death warmed up, she might have considered spending the day with him, Nancy, and the kids.

Her stomach gurgled. She needed to eat something, although she might barf. The coffee Pete had brought helped wake her up, but it didn't calm her queasy stomach. She went to the kitchen and found a couple of bagels that weren't too moldy. She didn't eat at home that often due to her work schedule, so her cabinets were a little bare. Who was she kidding? Her kitchen was empty. It looked like she'd never moved in.

After she choked down part of a bagel and four aspirin, she took a shower. She smelled like the bar: smoke and stale beer. The hot water pounded on her head and shoulders, somewhere between water massage and water torture. Either way, her headache was better. She tripped getting out of the shower and slammed her toe into the wall—*Shit!*

She dropped to the bed and exhaled as her shaky fingers punched at her cell to make a call. "Hey, Uncle Harry," she sighed when he answered. "Listen, I have some news, so I'll jump right to it." Her heart joined her head and started pounding. "I didn't get promoted."

On the other end of the line was silence, at first. Then Harry exploded. "What in the hell is the department turning into? This is bullshit. It used to be if you met the qualifications and a role was open, you got the job. Now politics fucks everything up." He drew a deep breath. "I'm so sorry. How are you handling this?"

"I'm devastated, but I'll be okay. Eventually. I'm not sure why I failed to make the cut—"

Harry interrupted. "You didn't fail to make the cut. The cut failed you. You deserved this promotion. The Boston PD's gone to hell in a handbasket." He exhaled. He knew he wasn't helping. "I'm sorry I'm down on the department. You still work there. This isn't right, and I've never been afraid to speak my mind. I'm glad I'm retired, or I'd shoot off my mouth and get tossed out on my ass."

She tried to maintain her composure. She didn't want to cry. "I'll be fine. It may take me some time, but I'll bounce back."

Harry sighed. "You will, honey. It shouldn't be this hard, though." He didn't want to push it, but he added, "You still have an open job offer in Charleston. The chief would be ecstatic if you accepted. He keeps asking about you."

"I enjoyed meeting Chief Williams, seeing the department, and Charleston is beautiful. I'll give it some thought."

Harry tried to be upbeat. "Your call. You can never go wrong with options . . . and being wanted is a great thing."

CJ smiled. "Yes, that's true. I'll let you go, but I'll call you soon. I love you, Uncle Harry." She hung up the phone. She was still upset, but she smiled, thinking about him. She'd been through a lot in her life and didn't know where she'd be without him.

She spent the rest of the day in a daze. The overcast sky darkened, and the night mist streamed down her plate-glass window. Staring out, she decided it was time to list the pros and cons of staying in Boston versus going to Charleston.

CHAPTER

EIGHT

Saturday, April 10
Shem Creek, Mount Pleasant, South Carolina

Ben didn't mind working on Saturdays, the last workday of his four-day-per-week schedule. He usually got off by six p.m., so his Saturday nights were free. Ben was up before the rooster crowed. His black Lab, Jake, was stretched out, wagging his tail and watching him.

"I guess you're ready for breakfast, eh, pal?"

Jake was up in an instant. His tail wagged faster.

"Here you go, boy. Chicken-flavored kibbles."

Ben gave Jake one last pat on the head and started off for work well before his shift began at seven a.m. As usual, he swung by Sand Dollar Sweets and grabbed some doughnuts. Everyone at the precinct was always excited to get their delicious treats on Saturday morning.

He pulled off Lockwood Drive into the Charleston PD headquarters, housed in the Chief John Conroy Law Enforcement Center commonly known as the LEC. Careful not to drop the boxes of doughnuts, he swiped his key card and took the stairs.

Helen motioned to Ben when he came through the door. She was on the phone with a serious face. "We have another one."

Ben was confused. "Another what?"

Helen, who always took her dispatch job in stride with little emotion, was close to tears. "Another dead young woman, like last Saturday."

He dropped the boxes on the desk and exhaled. "Where?"

She handed him the paper where she'd written her notes. "Over at the docks near Sawgrass Marina in Mount Pleasant. Shem Creek is Mount Pleasant PD's jurisdiction, but the call got routed here. I called them."

Ben turned for the door. "Let the sergeant know where I'm headed when he arrives. Tell him I'll call him as soon as I determine the situation. Put the CSU and ME on alert. I'll be at the site in fifteen minutes, and if it is another body, I need them there ASAP."

Ben went out to his car, jumped in, and hit the lights. He usually avoided using his siren for calls like this, but he needed to move fast. He hoped the caller was wrong, but

his instincts told him otherwise. Ben jammed the pedal
down as he crossed the Arthur Ravenel Jr. Bridge. He veered
onto Coleman Boulevard over the Shem Creek Bridge before taking a left on Mill Street. The yellows, browns, and
greens of the grasses and light blue waters combined into a
strange palette for a murder victim. He was glad he was familiar with the surroundings, as the site was off the beaten
path. Only a local would find the dirt road leading to the
boat slip number Helen had provided.

Ben could see no Mount Pleasant PD car there when he
arrived. He jumped out of his cruiser and the frantically
waving arms of a sweating man greeted him, who looked
to be in his mid-forties.

"I'm Lee Calhoun," the man said. "The girl's down by
the start of the dock in the marsh. Oh, God! This is terrible."

Ben shook his hand. "I'm Officer Ben Parrish."

The two men headed down the dock and Ben asked
Lee for details about how he found the body.

Lee looked pained. "I was taking my boat out this morning, as I wanted to start early. There were lots of seagulls,
and I thought they were eating some fish guts someone had
tossed. On the way to my slip, I passed by . . . there was a
foot. I got closer and found the poor woman. She's on dry
land now, but the tide's turned, and she'll be wet soon."

The two men passed boats on racks and through thick
foliage until they arrived at the spot where Lee had found

her. He motioned to a young man. "This is my son, Adam. The only thing we could do for her was to keep the seagulls away. The damn birds made a mess."

Adam appeared to be in his mid-teens. He was pasty white and looked uncomfortable.

Ben stepped off the walkway into the grass. He tried not to curse when the mud sucked at his shoe and his foot got wet. "Did either of you touch the tarp or the body?"

Both answered at the same time. "No, sir."

Lee added, "I got close enough to see the lower half of her body and knew it was real. I told Adam to stay back but to do his best to keep the gulls away." Lee waved to Adam. "Okay, son, let's leave the officer to do his job. Your mom will have my ass for having you stand guard, but the young woman at least deserved some respect."

Ben thanked them and asked them to wait to provide a statement after the crime scene team arrived.

"No problem. We'll walk down and grab a coffee at the snack shack. They should be open soon. Most days, we grab breakfast before we launch, but I doubt this will happen today." The father put his arm around his son. "Come on."

Ben peered at the body. *Jeez, just like last Saturday.*

The young woman was lying in knee-high sawgrass. Like the first victim, she rested on a tarp. The seagulls had partially uncovered her, and they had been picking at her body. This wouldn't help the forensics folks' investigation. Neither would the rising tide. Ben called Helen and let her know he needed the CSU and ME there ASAP.

Ben tried to focus, but the sight of the young woman made it difficult. His stomach was doing backflips, and he was fighting the urge not to puke. It had been tough last week, but at least the body had been in an area protected from the added destruction the seagulls had caused. The damn birds had picked at her midsection and opened it up. Part of her intestines were pulled out—splotches of red, purple, and yellow painted her stark-white naked body.

Ben pulled on a pair of surgical gloves, took a deep breath, and lifted the tarp. A young woman's dead face appeared. She looked in her early twenties, with matted blondish hair and glassy blue eyes. The mixed odor of death, salt water, marsh mud, and seagull crap didn't help his stomach.

The scene reminded him of the first victim: a dead young woman with her throat and midsection sliced open and left on a tarp. Whoever had left her had taken care to lay her out with her hands folded across her chest. *What was this? Remorse or simply posing?*

Ben stretched some crime scene tape across the trees leading to the walkway. He didn't want to let onlookers or the press get too close. He wasn't sure how to keep the boaters moving down the creek away. He might need a boat to block the area.

He stood near the body to keep the seagulls from causing further damage. They had already returned while he put up the tape and were fighting over her body. "Keep it up, guys, and I'm gonna start shooting."

A stocky man in his early forties in a wrinkled gray suit approached Ben. "Detective Jack Metcalf with Mount Pleasant PD. A little far from Charleston, aren't we?"

Oh shit! Here we go. "Ben Parrish. The call came to our dispatcher, so I responded. We had a similar crime downtown last Saturday."

Jack stared at him.

Ben wasn't sure whether a turf war was about to break out, but he didn't give a damn. He was holding his ground.

"What's the story?" the man asked.

Ben briefed him on his initial evaluation as the CSU and ME arrived. Ben was happy Eddie and Thomas were on duty since they had processed the first victim. Jack and Ben stepped away to let them work.

"Detective, I told the two witnesses to wait at the snack bar. I can interview them unless you want to do it," Ben said.

"Tell you what, if you want to do it, I'll wait here with the forensics guys."

"Sounds fine."

Ben left to take the statements, first making sure everyone had his cell if they needed him. As he walked off, he called and left a message with the dockmaster to check if he had video surveillance in the area. He hadn't seen cameras but hoped there was some parking or dock area coverage. Ben thought about going boat-to-boat to determine whether anyone else was around. This might give him a break, and if someone had spent the night on their boat, maybe they'd seen something.

Ben found the father and son sitting at a picnic table drinking cups of coffee. Adam was still pale as a ghost and not interested in his drink. *Poor kid.*

"Hey, guys. Oh, shit! I'll be right back." He had just seen the media and several onlookers coming around the side toward the scene. Ben intercepted them. *All we need is a bunch of lookie-loos.* "Okay, everybody, the dock is closed for now. I need everyone to go back to the parking lot until we clear the area." Ben ignored the questions and bitching. The press was a royal pain in the ass. "Please, come on now, to the parking lot."

He chased the crowd out, strung more crime scene tape between some trees, and returned to the witnesses. "Sorry for the interruption, guys. We don't need the crowd's help."

Lee tried to smile, but Ben could tell his heart wasn't in it. "I watched the coroner's truck arrive. Sad day."

Ben nodded. "Yes, not the way to start a Saturday, or any day, to be honest. How about I take your statements?"

"Sure."

Ben sat down across from them and pulled out his pad. "I assume Adam is under eighteen, so I'll talk to you together."

"Yes, he's sixteen. He's still pretty shaken up, so talking to us together is best."

Ben smiled. "How about you tell me what you remember, starting from the beginning?"

Lee folded his hands and leaned forward. "Adam and I arrived here a little after six. We've been working on the boat engine and wanted to take it out to check it out. I wanted to start early, before all the weekenders filled the creek with boats. The last thing you want is engine trouble in the middle of a flotilla."

"When you arrived, was anyone else here?" Ben asked.

Lee thought for a minute. "No. A few trucks were in the parking lot, but no people."

"Adam, do you remember seeing anyone?"

"No, sir."

"Lee, were there signs of anyone on their boat, any overnighters?"

"No. You aren't allowed to stay overnight on your boat here."

Excellent. There goes a chance at other witnesses. "Okay, so what happened next?"

"Well, we got our cooler out of the truck and my tool-box. We locked the truck and started down to our boat. We were near the end of the walkway, and there was a flock of seagulls. There were at least a couple dozen flapping and squawking away. I thought someone had cleaned some fish and tossed the guts off the dock, as I said before. You're not supposed to do that as it draws the gulls, but it happens all the time. Damn rats with wings will eat—"

He stopped and took a deep breath. "I decided to get closer after I saw the foot, so I leaned over the edge of the walkway, and there was the lower half of a body sticking out from under a tarp. She was visible from her chest down."

Lee shook his head, his eyes lowered. "I told Adam to stay back. I didn't want him to see a dead body or the girl since she was naked. I chased off the gulls and told Adam to stay on the dock but to keep them away while I called

911. I only went out to the parking lot when I heard your siren."

"Adam, do you remember anything else?" Ben asked the young man.

"No, sir. I tried to keep the gulls away. Seeing the foot made me feel sick."

Ben made a few more notes. "I think you provided what I need unless you can think of anything else. Do me a favor and write down your address and phone number if I need to reach you. Here's my card, so you can call me if you remember anything we didn't discuss."

Lee wrote down the information. "I'll call you if we think of anything else."

Ben shook his hand. "Thank you both for your help. Adam, thank you for protecting the young woman from the gulls."

Adam smiled feebly. "You're welcome, sir."

Ben headed back to the scene. His cell phone rang, and he recognized the dockmaster's number from his last call. "Officer Parrish."

The dockmaster told Ben there was no surveillance camera coverage at the marina. Ben explained they had found a dead body and the dock would be closed for at least the next hour and hung up. "Damn it!" This perp is either lucky or brilliant. Hopefully, not both.

———

Ben and Jack stood in silence while the body was loaded on the gurney and moved to the shade of a large magnolia tree.

Eddie eyed his notes. "Other than the dump location, this mirrors our first case. We've collected what we could find, but I'm not hopeful we'll find much. The damn seagulls didn't help either. We have bird shit everywhere."

Ben sighed. "Thomas?"

"My report sounds similar. The only difference is this vic has been dead less than eight hours."

"Any identifying marks?"

"No. No tattoos or beauty marks. Nothing."

Jack shook his head. "So, this makes a second healthy female in her early to mid-twenties raped and murdered in the Lowcountry since last Saturday?"

The others nodded.

Jack turned to Ben. "Thanks for getting the CSU and ME here so quickly. I'll ask our chief to call yours, so we can coordinate. I am curious why one of your detectives didn't come, though. No offense."

"None taken. We're shorthanded, but we hope to get a detective from our Central Investigations Division assigned soon. I may be his or her partner."

"Her? When did you guys hire a chick in the CID?"

"We haven't yet, but the rumor is we may hire one from Boston."

Jack laughed and tried his Boston accent. "Baawston."

Ben smiled at him. *I hope this "chick" knows what she's doing if she comes here. She'll get a ton of shit.* But he was glad Jack wasn't a prick about the jurisdiction thing. One positive thing about smaller law enforcement agencies was that they worked together without too much politics.

Charleston PD had more resources than neighboring law enforcement agencies, and often other departments were happy for the help.

Ben and Jack walked out with Eddie and Thomas. The two officers waited until Eddie and Thomas had left the parking lot, and Ben headed back to remove the crime scene tape and reopen the dock. The crowd had grown more extensive, and several media vans were present. Reporters were screaming out questions. Ben cursed under his breath at the sight of Wendy Watts, a reporter for News 4. "Crap, she's all we need."

Ben reached for his cell and called his sergeant as he walked to his car to give him a summary. His sergeant told him he'd give the captain and chief a call and advise them as the mayor and the press would be all over it. He asked Ben if the press was present and whether they'd seen the body.

"Yes, I'm sure the press will splash this everywhere," Ben said. "Vans from all the majors are here, and so is the *Post and Courier*. Detective Jack Metcalf of the Mount Pleasant PD and I made no statements. As the press usually does, they'll make up a story—especially Wendy Watts."

CHAPTER

NINE

Sunday, April 11
Allston-Brighton neighborhood, Boston

Everyone wore drab clothes and was crying. No one was happy. The man standing by the coffins was saying nice things, but how did he know? He'd never understood them. They could have been Bonnie and Clyde, or maybe the man was a serial killer and the woman a prostitute, both sneaking around in the twilight. Someone took her hand, who she recognized, and he walked with her to the front. The people in the box looked familiar, yet fake at the same time. *I'm the reason they're in the box . . . I killed them.*

CJ bolted upright. The sheets were tangled and wet from a restless night, another realistic and horrible dream. Her heart beat fast, and her mind was foggy. For several minutes, she sat perfectly still, staring at the reddish-orange digits of her alarm clock and taking deep breaths, working to bring herself under control: 4:46, 4:47 . . . 4:48. *Jeez, get a grip on yourself.*

After she got out of bed, she put on her robe, and went down to the kitchen. She started the coffee and toasted one of the fresh bagels she'd bought the afternoon before. She sat by her window, watching the last raindrops fall. The bagels were fresh but dry, creamy but tasteless. *At least my coffee is hot.*

After her wearisome breakfast, CJ headed out the door to honor the family's Sunday tradition. The streets shone in the morning sun, almost as if the drizzle served as a coating—the tan and sand-colored stones reaching to the heavens, towering arches, and boldly colored glass. She entered the Cathedral of the Holy Cross, as she and her family had done until their death. She and Harry had carried on the tradition until his move. *I need to keep something normal in my life. I don't recognize any faces in the chapel.*

The robed priest droned on about heaven and hell, and CJ stared at the photo of her mother she carried with her. She missed her. CJ resembled her mother. She had the same naturally wavy auburn hair, unusually large round emerald-green eyes, and a heart-shaped face with a slim, small nose, and smooth chin. Anyone who met her couldn't help but be taken with her, especially her eyes, which looked unnaturally green, with tiny flecks of yellow that caught every ray of the sun.

After the service, CJ stopped and picked up some Thai food for lunch. She sat eating at her dining room table, thinking how Sunday lunches after church weren't the same without Harry. He was right. It was always good to be where you were wanted.

CJ finished her list and made a significant decision; she would call Chief Williams tomorrow morning and take the job in Charleston. She picked up the phone and punched in Harry's number. She thought about telling him after talking to Chief Williams, but she was too excited to wait. Plus, he'd never forgive her if he found out before she told him. As expected, he was thrilled she was coming south. A massive weight was lifted, and while she was nervous about the change, she was more confident than ever she was doing the right thing.

Harry hung up his phone after talking to CJ. He grabbed a beer and sat on his deck, watching the golden grass and white puffy clouds reflecting on the water. He stared at the doctor's diagnosis, crumpled it up, and tossed it in an orange five-gallon bucket.

CHAPTER

TEN

Monday, April 12
Allston-Brighton neighborhood, Boston

Today was an important day for CJ, and she was excited. She jumped out of bed and raced for the hot soapy water of her shower. Then she dried her hair, pulled on her robe, and scampered down the stairs.

She gobbled down a bagel with cream cheese. It tasted much better than yesterday. She hustled back up the steps, dressed, grabbed her credentials and gun, and headed for her truck. Her shift started at nine a.m., but she planned to call Chief Williams at eight and then turn in her resignation.

She pulled into the precinct parking lot at 7:25 a.m. She went down the street, grabbed a coffee, and found a quiet table under an awning. The morning breeze nudged a napkin with half a muffin to the ground. Three pigeons came out of nowhere and began eating it for breakfast. CJ watched as the pigeons took turns grabbing bites of their sweet treat. She smiled at how they waddled around, nibbling at the crumbs. The smallest pigeon darted in and out of the others, grabbing bites before his bigger buddies chased him off.

CJ's mind flooded with the face of the man she'd killed, the roar of her Glock, and the red spray when her bullet found its mark. She struggled to calm her nerves and sat silently. She finally checked the time on her watch. "Let's do this."

He answered on the second ring. "Chief Williams."

CJ took a deep breath. "Hello, Chief Williams, this is CJ O'Hara in Boston."

"Hello there, happy to hear from you. I was thinking about you this morning and wondered if you're ready to join us here in Charleston."

Wow, let's get straight to it. "If the job's still open, I accept your offer."

"Wonderful! Our offer is still good, and we're ready for you as soon as possible. We have a multiple-homicide case that is going to need full-time attention, and as we've discussed, we're shorthanded."

"Sorry to hear about the case," she said. "If possible, I'll give you a start date after talking to my captain this morning. I'm anxious to start, but I want to leave my team here in the best shape possible."

"Commendable. Talk with your captain and tell us how soon you can start. Your uncle will be pleased, and he'll have a room waiting for you until you find a place. I'll have HR call you to work out all the details." He paused. "CJ, the sooner, the better."

After ending the call, CJ breathed a sigh of relief. In less than ten minutes, she had committed to putting her life on a whole new path. She smiled as she walked toward the station. CJ felt guilty about resigning, but happy. She needed to call Pete, who was off today. He had been a real friend, and she wanted the news of her leaving to come from her. She owed him that much.

The phone rang several times, and about the time CJ worried she was headed to his voicemail, she heard him answer.

"Good morning," Pete said and laughed. "Sorry, it took me a minute. I'm trying not to burn the toast."

She pictured him standing in the kitchen at the toaster and laughed.

"Are you on your way to the precinct?" he asked.

"I got here a little early. Listen, I wanted to tell you a couple of things. First, thank you for caring enough to come over and check on me on Saturday."

Pete laughed. "Yeah, waking you up at daybreak on your day off."

"The other thing I need to tell you is I'm making a change in my life."

"Oh?"

"Yes, I'll be moving to Charleston. I accepted a detective position with the Charleston PD."

Pete paused. "I understand you're disappointed about the promotion, but are you running from something or to something?"

She replied confidently, "I'm running to something I think will be a great move for me. I hate to leave Boston and so many people like you, but this is a perfect move for me, personally and professionally."

"I won't say I won't miss you, but I'm thrilled for you if this is what's best," he said. "I can only imagine how happy Harry is today."

"Yes, he's quite pleased."

"You tell Cap yet?"

"Not yet. I'm about to do it now. I wanted to tell you first."

"That means a lot to me. Let me know how it goes and if I can help in any way. Nancy and the kids will want to see you before you leave. My son will be heartbroken."

"Yes, but I'm sure he'll find himself a cutie soon and forget all about me. I'd love to see you, Nancy, and the kids before I leave."

The precinct was buzzing when CJ walked in. The building was always extra busy early in the day when shifts were changing, and most of the officers were in the building. All the bodies only added to the stuffiness of the bullpen. An open window and some fresh air wouldn't hurt.

Captain Wilkins stood outside his office, thumbing through a folder.

"Good morning, Cap. Can you spare a few minutes before I head out on patrol? Would nine-thirty work?"

He smiled at her. "Yeah, that time should work. I'm in a freaking budget meeting at ten."

"Thank you. I'll swing by. I only need a few minutes."

He nodded and headed down the hall.

CJ spent the next thirty minutes having more coffee and small talk with her fellow officers. Most of the talk was about the upcoming Red Sox season; would Big Papi have a good year, and could the Sox win the division over the Yankees? She enjoyed going to Fenway—dark green grass, the "Green Monster" in left field, and the aroma of peanuts and hot dogs. She'd miss that when she was gone.

At 9:25 a.m., CJ got up, took another deep breath, and headed to the captain's office.

He was on the phone but motioned her in. She began getting anxious. Her decision was correct, but she respected her captain, and he'd been good to her.

He hung up. "What's on your mind?"

CJ steadied herself. "First, I want to thank you for your support in my recent promotion request. And the chance to work with Pete, a good detective, has been a blessing. Second, with mixed emotions, I'm giving you my resignation. I've accepted a position with another department." She handed him her letter of resignation.

Frank sighed as he stared at the letter. "I hate to lose you. You're a key part of this team. Part of me wants to talk you out of leaving. The other part knows this is the right move for you."

She wasn't sure how to respond, so she just sat.

"Do you know who I just got off the phone with?" he asked.

She was confused. "No, sir."

"That was Charleston Police Chief Williams. He called to explain his situation and to beg me not to talk you out of leaving." Before she could respond, he continued. "Make no mistake, I need you here, but after talking to Chief Williams, I realize he needs you worse." He exhaled. "There may be a serial killer loose in Charleston, and some-one needs to bring him to justice. If you leave here, you go find him and drag his ass to jail. Trust your instincts—you don't do that enough."

Yeah, I know that's a weakness for me. "Yes, sir."

Frank smiled. "By the way, Chief Williams wants one more thing."

CJ was puzzled. "What would that be?"

"He asked me to let you start next Monday. This homi-cide case is bad. He will team you with another investiga-tor, but you will take the lead. I'll leave it to you."

She wasn't sure how to respond. "I'm not sure what to say except that if I'm needed more in Charleston than Boston, I'll pack and get there by Monday."

He smiled, got up, and reached out his hand. CJ took it. "Best of luck. I only ask that when and if you come back to Boston, you come by and let me know how you're doing."

Without thinking, she hugged him. Her face flushed bright red. "Sorry, sir. I appreciate all you've done for me."

He winked. "Now, go protect and serve."

CJ called Chief Williams and told him she would be in Charleston bright and early Monday morning. He apologized for calling her captain, but he told her the two had spoken before he had made the offer and her captain had nothing but high praise for her.

After speaking to Chief Williams, she dialed Harry. When she got his voicemail, she left a message. "Hey, Uncle Harry, I'm all set. I need to book a room at the O'Hara Manor for this weekend. I start work in Charleston first thing on Monday."

CHAPTER

ELEVEN

Monday, April 12
Downtown Charleston

Rumbles rattled the morning, and flashes illuminated the horizon before a torrential downpour of water and hail pelted the ground. Ben sipped coffee as he stared out at the early day. Jake sat at attention by his feet. "Nasty start to a Monday, boy." Jake wagged his tail and whined. "Nope. No treats. You ate your kibbles."

Ben scratched the black blockhead with both hands. Jake responded with tail thumps on the wood floor. "You're a good boy, aren't you? Too bad everyone isn't good like you. There are lots of evil people out there, and Daddy has to keep the good people safe." Jake whined and gave a little bark. "Okay, you win—one peanut butter biscuit."

Ben was usually off on Mondays. He and Jake almost always went to the beach, where Jake chased the seagulls and then his tennis ball. Ben had had no one significant in his life for a long time but had Jake to come home to—someone always happy to see him. "Sorry, boy, I have to go to work for a bit. We'll chase the ball later, promise."

———

It was 6:35 a.m. when Ben turned off Lockwood Drive and into the LEC. The rain had slowed to a drizzle, and the rumbles and flashes from the previous storm were gone. The sky was painted a light red with a few black streaks. Ben mumbled, "Red sky at night, sailor's delight. Red sky in morning, sailors take warning."

Ben bounded up the steps to the quiet second floor. He'd beaten almost everyone in and had more than two hours before his briefing with the brass. He wanted to be ready. Ben reviewed the autopsy and preliminary forensics reports in a small, partially lit conference room. So far, there were no reports of fingerprints, DNA, or anything useful.

Other than the individuals who'd found the bodies, they had no witnesses. Surveillance videos gave him nothing. Ben rubbed his eyes and said to himself, "Don't worry, Chief. I'll arrest the murderer any minute. Look at all this hard evidence!"

A voice startled him.

"Good morning. Thanks for coming today. The chief, captain, and lieutenant confirmed we're on for nine."

I hope he didn't hear me.

Ben's sergeant, Preston Cobb, was a stocky man of forty with broad shoulders and red curly hair. He chuckled. "Talking to yourself actually helps. Answering yourself is when you should worry."

Ben blushed. *Busted!* "I'm ready for the briefing. A summary is ready, along with copies of the available reports and photos of both crime scenes."

"Okay. I'll be back at nine."

Preston patted Ben's shoulder. "Stop fidgeting. You'll do fine."

Ben tried to be confident, but he was nervous. He knew he lacked the experience of a seasoned detective, and they needed significant help to solve this case. He reminded himself he was only expected to summarize the facts, not lay out a plan for the investigation. *You can do this.*

Chief Walter Williams, Captain Stan Meyers, Lieutenant Paul Grimes, and Preston entered the room a few minutes before nine. Ben was wired and anxious after his fifth cup of coffee. They acknowledged each other, and Preston started the briefing.

"As we agreed on Saturday, we're meeting today to assess where we are in the murders of two young women. Officer Parrish, who responded to both crime scenes, has compiled a summary for us. We can brainstorm where we go next to catch whoever committed these horrific crimes." Preston pointed to Ben. "The floor is yours."

Ben cleared his throat and stood near the whiteboard, where he had summarized the key points of each murder. He described the first victim, identified by her parents as Amanda McCarthy, and the boat shop's crime scene in downtown Charleston. He went through the key points from the work of the CSU and ME—cause and estimated time of death, mutilation of the body, rape, and the lack of forensic evidence. Then he paused, waiting for questions.

Stan was a thin-framed six-foot-one man in his forties with dark brown hair and penetrating brown eyes. He looked at Ben. "Do we know where she lived and worked?"

"Yes, sir. She worked as a nurse at MUSC and lived alone in an apartment on Calhoun Street."

"Who reported her missing?" Stan asked.

"Her supervisor called her parents on Friday, April second, when she didn't show up for her Friday morning shift. Her parents drove down from Greenville after they couldn't reach her and filed a missing person report. We matched the photo in the report to the body in the morgue."

Walter walked to the board and stared at her photo. He was a Black man standing nearly six-foot-six, balding, with dark brown eyes. He had a scar on his right cheek. Supposedly, Walter had been a hell of a basketball player in his days at the College of Charleston. "So, we can estimate a timeframe for her abduction, but not the location the person took her from at this point?"

"Correct, sir." Ben said.

Walter scratched his cheek. "No witnesses, forensic evidence, or leads, correct?"

Ben sighed. "Correct, sir."

The group sat in silence, staring at the crime scene photos.

"All right," said Walter. "Let's cover the second vic."

Ben described the second case of an unknown female in her early twenties. The crime scene was almost identical to the first, except she had been dead a shorter period before being dumped, and she had no markings on her body. Again, the group sat silent after he finished, staring at the crime scene photos.

Walter broke the silence. "It appears the first and second victims were abducted, killed, and mutilated in the same manner and dumped somewhere other than where the unknown subject killed them. At this point, we have no witnesses, forensic evidence, or leads in either case."

Ben nodded. "Correct, sir."

The chief exhaled. "We have two dead young women, and I pray I'm wrong, but I don't think these two women will be the last. I'm not sure why this monster started killing, but he will not stop until we stop him." He smiled at Ben. "I understand these are complex cases, but you've provided a good summary of where we stand. I'm going to assign a detective to this case full-time, but ask you to partner with them as we need more than one person to chase this guy. You up for it?"

Ben nodded. "Yes, sir, I'm up for it. I'd appreciate working beside someone to bring justice for these young women."

Walter turned to Preston. "Can you assign Ben to this full-time as part of the Homicide Investigation Unit?"

Preston nodded.

Walter then turned to Stan. "Stan, can we free up another investigator from the Homicide Investigation Unit or a detective from the CID? Both are shorthanded."

"I'll need to determine if we can shuffle cases around," Stan said. "Do you think assigning Jackson makes sense?"

Walter frowned. "No. He's struggling with the cases he has, and to be honest, the guy wouldn't get this solved. What's he got, three unsolved murders now?"

Stan slowly nodded. "You know he'll want it, though."

"Yeah, well, I want to win the lottery and retire to Hilton Head. He's a no." Walter smiled. "There's a third option. Someone accepted our offer to join the department this morning. She'd be a solid fit and assigned to the CID as our first female detective. The mayor will love that."

"The O'Hara girl from Boston, niece of Harry O'Hara?" Stan asked.

Walter nodded. "She's the one. CJ O'Hara. If this goes the way I'm afraid it will, we'll need lots of help, and we'll need to call the FBI. I'd like to progress the case before we call, though, so we don't look like fools." He stood. "For now, let's plan on CJ taking the lead on the case full time with Ben working with her. I'd like her to report directly to you, Paul, as part of the CID. For this case, I want her to report to Stan. We'll be highly visible to the mayor and the press. You two okay with that?"

"Yes, sir," Stan and Paul answered in unison.

Walter smiled at Ben. "Thanks again for your work. Please continue filling in what gaps you can. Help is on the way."

Ben sat alone in the conference room. *I sure hope O'Hara knows what she's doing.*

CHAPTER

TWELVE

Friday, April 16
Allston-Brighton neighborhood, Boston

CJ didn't need the electronic nudge to stir her. She was already awake before the sun came up. She pulled on her jeans and a long-sleeved T-shirt. Her hair went into a ponytail, and a Red Sox cap topped her head. Her last belongings were stuffed into a duffel bag.

She took one final walk through the condo. Everything was gone. She smiled and bounced down the steps into the driver's seat. Fourteen hours on the road lay ahead. Before she stopped for the night, she wanted to reach Richmond, Virginia. She would see Charleston on Saturday afternoon.

Once outside Boston, she gave Harry a call, so he'd know she was on her way. He had offered to fly up and ride down with her, but she'd convinced him otherwise. He'd agreed a "big girl" would be safe on the road by herself. Harry answered on the first ring.

"I'm on the road," she said.

"Did you check the car before you left?"

CJ laughed. "Yes, I did. The department's maintenance guy checked it out and made sure everything was ready to go."

Harry missed her and couldn't wait for her to arrive. "Will you call me every couple of hours and let me know how the drive is going?"

"I promise. Don't worry; I'll arrive by tomorrow afternoon."

"Okay, drive safe and call me every couple of hours. I'll be as nervous as a cat in a room full of rocking chairs waiting for you."

"What a visual!"

She said her goodbyes and turned up Hootie and the Blowfish. Darius Rucker was belting out the lyrics for *Time*. She remembered the video, which included various shots of Charleston. She loved Rucker's gravelly voice and how he whined. *I may as well get into Charleston mode.*

CJ thought about the briefing she'd received from her new partner, Ben Parrish. Her first assignment was a challenge, and she was both nervous and excited. Experienced detectives would find this case problematic. How about a third-year detective new to the area and the first female detective in her new department?

Ben had volunteered to copy the files and reports for her and take them to Harry's for her review on Sunday. She wanted to hit the ground running and seem confident, but she also wanted Ben to feel comfortable they were a team. She hoped she'd find fewer politics in a smaller department.

The road wound on and lay long in front of her. As she passed them, she said goodbye to the Statue of Liberty, the City of Brotherly Love, Monument City, and the Lincoln Memorial. She stopped for the night when she reached Richmond, Virginia—the River City.

THIRTEEN

Friday, April 16
Station 18, Sullivan's Island, South Carolina

He loved Sullivan's Island with its clean sand and broad beach. The best part was the remoteness. Only locals were around during the week this time of year. There were stretches where no houses backed onto the beach. He loved the solitude.

The day was warm and sunny, with slight humidity and a light breeze. He felt sticky. The grove of trees at the edge of the sand was perfect for his folding chair. A couple of families had built sandcastles, kids played at the edge of the surf, and sunbathers tanned themselves in the sun.

A small girl of about five was playing in the ankle-deep surf, her blond pigtails flapping. She reminded him . . . it wasn't his fault. He was only ten and simply curious. His dad had overreacted to the girl's nakedness and her cries. He hadn't hurt her too badly. She shouldn't have started screaming. He wouldn't have cut her up as he'd done to the animals. His mom should have protected him from his dad!

He leaned forward in his chair and lowered his sunglasses. One sunbather piqued his interest. His vision was laser-focused solely on her. The young woman was lying on her stomach, away from the others on the beach, reading a book. He couldn't stop staring at her as she rolled over. She'd given up reading and stretched herself out, worshipping the sun. Her tanned skin glistened with oil.

Beachgoers left as the sun dropped lower on the horizon. Soon vibrant pinks, yellows, and oranges would mix with the blue sky, and darkness would fall.

His interest spiked as she pulled on a pair of navy-blue shorts and a white T-shirt over her pale pink bikini. She slipped on her flip-flops and threw her towel over her shoulder. She grabbed her bag and walked toward the path that ran through the grove of trees where he sat. *I'm a lucky man.*

She smiled sweetly at him. "Hey."

He smiled and eyed her as she passed. He stood.

CHAPTER

FOURTEEN

Saturday, April 17
The foot of the Arthur Ravenel Jr. Bridge, Charleston

Bobby Pickens loved getting out on the water at daybreak, and the fish had bitten well all morning. He'd caught several sheepshead and a hefty red drum, so he headed in for the day. His wife would be pleased if he got a few "honey do" items completed.

Bobby knew his wife would also be happy he'd brought dinner with him. Sheepshead was her favorite fish, and she'd lightly fry them along with some potatoes and onions and make some of her sweet coleslaw. His mouth watered at the thought.

His dog, Rascal, was the only one who enjoyed a day of fishing on the boat more than Bobby. He'd adopted him about five years ago after finding him behind the store where he worked. The litter had included five puppies. Rascal was the runt. He had intended to see them all go to good homes, but his wife had fallen in love with Rascal. As it happened, though, Rascal became Bobby's dog, going with him everywhere. Bobby didn't know his breed, but he thought some Jack Russell was in him based on his energetic personality.

Bobby kept his boat in a small marina near Town Creek. He liked that he could get his boat in and out so quickly. As he neared his slip, he slowed so he didn't kick up a wake. The owner hated it when you came in too fast and rocked the dock with waves. Rascal stood on the bow, barking like crazy. The dog barked at everything—birds, people, other dogs, and sometimes the wind.

Bobby laughed. "I know, pal. I see the seagulls, too."

Rascal jumped on the wooden platform and raced to scare the seagulls as Bobby's boat kissed the dock. Rascal did what he always did: run around the pier looking for trouble. The crazy dog was a bundle of energy. Rascal had clearly found something new, covered in a tarp.

"What did you find, boy?" he called.

Bobby couldn't understand people sometimes. Why would someone leave a tarp with a load of trash? He'd go check it out as soon as he got his boat squared away. The dog shoved his head under the tarp, barking wildly.

"Rascal, don't go getting into the trash now."

After taking care of his boat, Bobby took the fish up to his truck. He grabbed some ice out of the ice machine and added it to his cooler. Until he got them cleaned, he wanted to keep his fish fresh. He thought about passing on dealing with the tarp, but decided to do the right thing and go back. He also had to go back for Rascal, who was still sniffing away at it, his tail going a mile a minute. Bobby grabbed one end of the tarp and dragged it toward the dumpster. An arm popped out.

"What the hell?"

He peeked under the tarp and staggered backward at the sight of the body of the young woman. Tripping, he fell flat on his back. Scrambling to his feet, he grabbed Rascal and ran for his cell phone in the truck.

"Hello, this is Bobby Pickens. I found a dead woman, and someone has badly cut her up. I'm at the Town Creek Marina south of the foot of the Ravenel Bridge. Please hurry!"

Bobby hung up, not sure what to do next. Reluctantly, he went back to make sure no one disturbed the body until the police arrived. Who could do such an awful thing? Who could kill a young woman and dump her like trash?

For the third Saturday in a row, Helen in dispatch called Ben at home to report another body of a young woman. Moments later, Ben got in his car and hit his siren. His nightmare was escalating.

Flying up East Bay Street and onto Johnston Street, Ben got to the Town Creek Marina within fifteen minutes. A man with gray hair who looked in his early sixties waved his arms and yelled to him from down by the water. "She's down here, Officer."

Ben jumped out of his car and ran to the dock. "Ben Parrish."

"Bobby Pickens," the man said. "I wish I could say nice to meet you, but not this way."

Ben gazed at the partially exposed body. He pulled on his booties and surgical gloves and gently pulled the tarp back, revealing the face of a young woman. He dropped the tarp back over her and turned to Bobby, who stood behind him with a sad look on his face.

Examining the drag marks on the ground by the tarp, Ben asked, "Is this where you found her?"

"No. She was over by the back wall of the building, about twenty feet away. My dog Rascal was snooping around it. I thought someone left some trash, so I dragged the tarp toward the dumpster until her arm fell out and I realized she was there."

"Did you see anyone dump her here?"

"No. Everyone is out on the water. I came in early to head home to do my chores."

"Can you show me where you touched the tarp?" Ben asked.

Bobby leaned down to the tarp. "I held the end here."

"Did you touch the body?"

"No, I let go of the tarp when the arm popped out. Scared the hell out of me. I lifted the tarp a bit to make sure my imagination wasn't playing tricks on me. I made sure not to touch the poor thing, though."

Ben thanked him, got his address and cell phone number, and told him he could leave. He gave him his card in case he thought of anything else, and the man turned and wandered toward the parking lot. Rascal ran back and forth in the cab of his truck, still barking.

Ben went to his car, grabbed the crime scene tape, and secured the dock entrance. He didn't want to make the same mistake as last Saturday and let people get too close to the scene.

Thirty minutes later, the CSU and ME arrived and began their work. Eddie and Thomas were on call so that Ben would receive a comparison of the first two scenes to this one. Ben liked the thoroughness of both individuals in processing a scene. This was critical in building a solid case for prosecution once they caught whoever committed the crime. Too often, sloppy work when collecting evidence led to issues in a trial.

Ben scanned around for video surveillance equipment. The marina included a small dock with maybe ten boat slips, no office, no snack bar, and he didn't notice any cameras. Calling it a marina was a stretch. Whoever was dropping bodies sure knew how to pick their spots.

Ben heard someone yell and turned to see a reporter for Live 5 News trying to get his attention. He waved them off. "No comments. Stay behind the tape."

A few minutes later, vans from News 2, News 4, and Fox 24 arrived and filled the small parking lot. Ben hated the brown, orange, and yellow swoosh logo on the News 4 van—its presence meant Wendy Watts was on the scene. He rubbed the back of his neck and tried to relieve the tension. The jackals yelling questions and fighting for camera angles would make his lousy day worse.

This location was only about a mile-and-a-half north of where they had found the first victim. Ben met with Eddie and Thomas for their preliminary report. As in the first two cases, the information was familiar: a fit young woman in her early twenties with blond hair had been raped and her throat cut, with the same postmortem cut down her midsection. A small rose tattoo on her left wrist was the only difference.

Ben escorted the group to their vans, ignoring the media. He went back and removed the tape while he continued to fend off angry reporters. "Come on, guys, no comments at this time. We'll have a statement for you later."

The fake-friendly smile of Wendy Watts caught Ben's eye. Her bleach-blond hair, sparkling white teeth, and fake breasts made him cringe. *Is anything about her real?* She was a thorn in the department's side, constantly criticizing them no matter what they did.

"Excuse me, isn't it true that the Charleston PD now has three vicious murders and no leads or suspects?" Wendy asked. "Can the young women of Charleston trust the killer will ever be caught?"

Ben smiled with clenched teeth. "No comments at this time, Ms. Watts," he said and kept moving. He sat for a minute in his car before he called Captain Stan Meyers. Ben was nervous about talking directly to the captain for the first time. When Stan answered, Ben cleared his throat and summarized the preliminary findings.

Stan said he would call the chief. He knew this would undoubtedly hit *The Post and Courier's* front page and be the lead story on all the news networks with headlines like,

"Lowcountry Killer Strikes Again!" Wendy Watts would have a field day bashing the department—facts be damned.

As Ben drove back to the LEC, he called CJ. The two had only briefly spoken when he called her to summarize the first two cases and agree on a meeting time for her first day. He wanted to tell her they had another murder, so she didn't find out about it on the news for the first time.

CJ saw the number on her phone and answered. "Hey, Ben."

"Hey. Hope your drive is going well."

"So far, so good," she said. "I passed through Santee a few minutes ago, and will be jumping on I-26 soon. If all goes well, I should be in Charleston within the next hour." She sensed he needed to tell her something. "How's your Saturday going?"

Ben exhaled. "We have another body."

CJ's heart sank.

"All three murders have the same MO," Ben said. He summarized the new case for her, and let her know a copy of the report would be in her email to print once she got to Harry's.

She thanked him for alerting her before they hung up. She wondered if he was always this welcoming.

The cloud of another dead young woman replaced CJ's excitement about being near Charleston. She'd hoped she and Harry could have a quiet dinner and Sunday to relax before her first day. Unfortunately, someone out there had other ideas.

CHAPTER

FIFTEEN

Saturday, April 17
Wando

It was early Saturday afternoon when CJ pulled into Harry's driveway. She'd made the two-day drive in under fourteen hours and was ready to get out of the car. She wished she could relax, but all she could do was think of the three murders. Captain Wilkins was correct. This would undoubtedly be a trial by fire.

Harry met her in the driveway. "Hello, sweetheart. Welcome to the Lowcountry."

The two hugged, and as he always did, Harry kissed her on her forehead. He told her to leave her bags for now and come in so he could show her around. They would unload the car after she took a break from her drive.

Harry's three-bedroom, three-bath home was friendly and straightforward. It was all one story, and two of the bedrooms had terrific views of Fogarty Creek and the marsh. He also had a clear view of the creek and marsh from his kitchen and dining room. The best part was the covered back deck, which also overlooked the creek and marsh. Right off the deck was a boardwalk to a boat slip.

It was no surprise to CJ that Harry had her room ready when she arrived. He even had a vase with fresh flowers. She had a clear view of the creek and marsh out of two windows. He had set the third bedroom up as an office, complete with a desk, computer, and printer. She noticed the file Ben had dropped off was lying on the corner of the desk. While she was tempted to grab it and start looking it over, she'd wait until later.

After the tour, Harry helped her unload her car. The movers had taken the larger items, so she only had a couple of suitcases and some hanging clothes. She'd unpack later. It was time to sit with Harry and relax.

Harry grabbed them a beer and announced his plans for dinner. "Here you go. A cold beer should help you unwind after the drive. Instead of going out for dinner tonight, I thought I'd cook some swordfish on the grill for us. I wish I could tell you I caught it, but I got it from a friend down at the docks."

She smiled. "Sounds yummy. Hanging out at home would be perfect tonight."

They sat and talked about her last few weeks in Boston and his recent exploits out on his boat. After a couple of beers, Harry fired up the grill and made dinner. They sat at a small table as the sun dropped out of sight. Finally, after dinner, they broached the subject of her first case.

Harry pointed toward the office. "I put the file Ben dropped off on the desk in the office. I didn't peek, promise."

CJ laughed. "Thanks. I'll look before I go to bed. I also need to print out a report Ben emailed me. Another dead young woman was found this morning."

Harry shook his head. "That's three, right?"

"Sadly, yes."

CJ stared out at the marsh at a pelican sitting on top of a post grooming its feathers. He was a funny-looking bird with his big bill. She muttered, "A serial killer right out of the gate."

Harry thought for a minute. "I'm afraid you're right, but I have confidence you're up for the challenge."

"I hope so. I do have an ace in the hole."

This puzzled Harry. "Ace in the hole?"

She smiled. "You." She told Harry good night, and that she needed some sleep.

Harry knew she was lying, just as he would have done, and would stay up and read the file Ben had left.

She headed to her room, grabbing the file as she passed the office.

SIXTEEN

Saturday, April 17
Downtown Charleston

Ben slid his key card in the slot and entered the LEC. He wasn't sure what to expect, but his heart was racing after the call from the captain that a suspect was in custody. Late Saturday nights meant only a small crew was around. Everyone else was out on patrol.

Ben knocked on Captain Meyers's door. "Hey, Captain. I'm ready when you are."

"Thanks for getting here so quickly. Let's go have a chat with our suspect. His name's Elrod Harris. We picked him up out back of Willy's Seafood off King Street."

Stan and Ben entered the interrogation room. The room was cramped and like a sauna. No air stirred. The suspect was seated at the small table, forehead resting on his hand-cuffed hands. His dark brown hair was a stringy mop.

Both men sat opposite the bowed man. The captain flipped through the folder he had brought in under his arm and pointed to a handwritten note. Ben nodded.

"Okay, Mr. Harris, how about we talk about what you were doing with that young woman?" Stan said.

The man remained motionless.

"Elrod, are you there?" he asked.

Lifeless black eyes flashed, and an icy tingle went through Ben. The suspect raised his head slowly, and a crooked grin spread across his hollow face. Ben stared at the jagged scar that ran from just below his right ear to the tip of his chin.

The suspect licked his lips, then spat. "We were about to make love when your officers interrupted us."

"That's not the way the witnesses and our officers tell it," Stan said.

"They don't know shit. She's my girlfriend and she couldn't wait for it until we got home."

Stan closed the file and leaned back. "Okay, let's hear your version."

"We went out for a few drinks," Elrod said. "She wanted me, so we left and were about to get busy in my van when your fucking officers violated our rights."

Leaning forward, Stan asked. "You're telling us you two were together of your own free will and, because of your intense sexual magnetism, she had to have sex with you in the back of your filthy van?"

The suspect held up his hands. "Yep, that's what I'm saying."

Stan pointed at Elrod. "Here's my problem with your story. The young woman, Kerry Moss, says she doesn't know you. She says you took her against her will, slapped her around, and forced her into your van at knifepoint. You ripped off her clothes and were in the process of raping her when our officers stopped you. No date, no consent, and no way your story is true." Stan slapped his hand down on the table. "Conclusion, you're a lying piece of shit."

The suspect started laughing. "Guess my lawyer can sort this out—I ain't saying no more. Get me a damn lawyer."

Stan and Ben stood and left the room. As Ben closed the door behind them, he asked, "What do you think, Cap?"

"Our suspect, Elrod Harris, is going down for kidnapping, assault, and at least attempted rape. We have our victim and the witness who saw him drag her into his van. It should be open-and-shut. But is he the person who raped and killed our other victims? I can't tell."

Ben scanned the file.

Stan read his face. "You don't think it's him, do you?"

Ben exhaled. "I'm not sure, but it seems like a big break from the MO. So far, our unsub has been organized and careful—smart. It's stupid to drag a girl across a parking lot, beat the hell out of her, and then try to rape her in the back of a van."

"You may be right, Ben, but let's investigate the hell out of him. We know who he is and where he lives, so let's have the crime scene guys go check it out. The judge gave us the warrant to search his home and get his DNA. Let's send his DNA sample to Columbia and have them rush it so we can run it through the system. Check it against every assault and rape we've had."

Ben took the file and returned to his desk in the squad room. He was happy to be out of the sauna, but the quiet was replaced with his fellow officers' hubbub. It was amazing how such a small crew could make so much noise. He called the CSU and confirmed they had a team working the van and would meet him at the Harris home on Folly Beach.

As he drove to Folly Beach, Ben dialed CJ's number. "Hey, CJ. It's Ben. I'm so sorry to call you so late, but I wanted you to know we picked up a suspect. It's possible he's our guy, although I'm doubtful. I'm on my way to search his house now."

CJ sat up in bed. Her pulse quickened. "I'm up and can meet you in a few minutes."

"I'd hate for you to do that. It's after eleven, and he's only a suspect at this point. How about I see what we can find, and we can discuss it in the morning? A CSU team is joining me, along with two other officers. We can always go back and look again. I'm locking down the house."

CJ felt like she should go, but Ben was probably right. She wasn't even an official member of the Charleston PD yet, and wouldn't want some lawyer using her presence as a technicality during a trial. "Okay, but if you change your mind, call me, and I'll meet you."

"Will do." Ben hung up and saw the glow of the lights of Charleston in his rearview mirror. *Let's hope I'm wrong and this is our guy.*

SEVENTEEN

Sunday, April 18
Wando

CJ woke up a little after seven o'clock on Sunday morning and found Harry out on the back deck drinking coffee. "Good morning," she greeted him.

"Morning. How about a cup of coffee?"

"Coffee would be wonderful."

They sat drinking their coffee, looking out across the marsh. A large egret had replaced CJ's pelican and stood stoically on one leg by the water's edge as he fished for his breakfast. The sun peeked its face over the horizon and projected a yellowish-tan glow broken only by a few stray, floating clouds. Seagulls circled lazily and called to attract the attention of others, *ha-ha-ha-ha.*

CJ's cell phone disrupted the quiet of the morning. She looked at the number. "Hey, Ben. How was the search last night?"

"Our suspect, Elrod Harris, lives by himself in a real shithole. We scoured the house and a small shed out back for three hours. We recovered a large knife typically used to fillet fish and three pairs of women's underwear. They went to SLED, the State Law Enforcement Division, in Columbia, to see if we have any DNA. They'll run whatever DNA we get through CODIS."

The Combined DNA Index System or CODIS was a nationwide database that contained DNA profiles for a wide range of criminal offenders, evidence from crime scenes, and information about missing persons. CJ had used it many times.

"I sent the knife along, too, and asked them to process it and to see if they thought it might be the weapon used in our killings."

"Makes sense," CJ said. "What kind of underwear?"

"Panties."

"Where did you find them?"

"Wadded up and shoved in a drawer in a nightstand by the bed," Ben said. "I assume it's Elrod's bed. It's the only bed in the place."

"Could you tell what size the underwear was and if they were clean or dirty?"

Ben's face flushed. *Great, I'm discussing women's panties with my new female partner, who I've never met.* "The CSIs said all were smalls, and they guessed they had been worn. The place is damn filthy, so it was hard to tell."

CJ replied, "It is possible they would fit our victims, given their size. Absolutely worth having the lab test for DNA. Any signs of blood?"

"No. The CSIs used the UV lights and found no visible traces. The house hasn't been cleaned in years. It has old shag carpeting, so if there was blood, it would definitely show up."

"How about the shed?"

"Full of junk—old car parts, lawn mowers, and pipes. No way he had any of our vics in there."

"Anything in his van?"

"CSIs collected blood, which they expect to be from the victim he was with when we grabbed him, since it looked fresh. It's on its way to Columbia as well. We sent the carpet, too."

"Excellent," CJ said as she stood and walked over to the deck railing. "Anything else?"

"Nope. We didn't find any other women's clothes, jewelry, or belongings. We ran the cadaver dog around the yard and got nothing. Oh, we found a nice big stash of pot, so we'll add that to good ole' Elrod's sheet. He must be selling."

"Okay, thanks for calling. I'll see you bright and early tomorrow morning. Yell, if anything else comes up. Get some rest." CJ hung up and smiled. She liked Ben. He seemed on top of things and wasn't hesitating to keep her in the loop. *He may make a solid partner.*

An hour later, CJ and Harry rattled along Halfway Creek Road toward downtown Charleston in his jeep. The top was off, and CJ's reddish-brown hair waved in the wind. The rays of the sun brought out her red hues.

The shiny white pillars and cables of the Ravenel Bridge provided a stark contrast against the blue sky. The wind pushed against the Cooper River, kicking up small whitecaps as sailboats flew along the surface. Massive cargo ships dotted the shore at the Port of Charleston with the backdrop of the brightly colored homes of downtown.

After spending the morning driving around Charleston so CJ could get more familiar with the area, they stopped for lunch at Vickery's on Shem Creek. The deck overlooking the creek was a real treat. CJ tried the shrimp and grits, a Lowcountry favorite. The crab hush puppies with Cajun remoulade were even better—a touch of hot sauce, cayenne, and horseradish.

They talked about the case, what was known, and what next steps to take throughout the day. CJ was thankful Harry was on her side. He was an excellent sounding board and offered interesting perspectives on the unsub's motivations and reasons for his target group.

"Somewhere along the way, the perp believes someone did him wrong. He's picking victims who remind him of that someone—high school or college girlfriend, ex-wife, cheating wife, or mother," Harry surmised.

The two of them bounced up in front of his house again a little after five o'clock in the jeep. Dinner on the back deck included crab cakes and a spinach salad. Harry passed her a plate of golden-brown discs. "You'll like the crab cakes. I use Magnolia's Charleston Crab Cake recipe. The secret is fresh crabmeat and a touch of cayenne pepper. The recipe says to use one-eighth of a teaspoon, but I give it a pinch more."

CJ shoved a bite into her mouth. "Delicious. Who knew you'd turn into such a gourmet?" She sat back and looked around. It had only been her first full day in Charleston, but she could get used to moments like this.

PART TWO

ESCALATION

EIGHTEEN

Monday, April 19
Downtown Charleston

An adrenaline rush replaced the fluttery feeling in her stomach as CJ pulled off Lockwood Drive into the LEC at seven-fifteen a.m. Her first day in a new job in a new department. She parked in the front parking lot and briskly walked to the lobby.

A tall, well-built man who looked to be in his early thirties stood near the sign-in desk. He smiled. "CJ?"

"Yes."

"I'm Ben," he said as he stepped forward and offered her his hand. "Happy to meet you."

How does he know who I am?

He read her face. "I recognized you from the photo Harry showed me when I dropped off the files. I have to admit, the photo doesn't do you justice."

Her face flushed, and she took his hand. "Nice to meet you, too. I appreciate all your help so far."

Ben shook her hand. "I'm happy you're here. We've got our work cut out for us." He motioned toward the elevator. "How about we head upstairs? The chief's waiting for you."

CJ followed him. "That would be great."

They found Chief Williams standing in the hallway. "CJ O'Hara. I see you found us okay. And you've met Ben."

CJ smiled as she shook his hand. "Yes, sir. Ben and I have talked on the phone, and he's helped me get up to speed. I'm happy to put a face to the voice."

"Excellent. I'll take you to Stan and Paul, whom you met during your interview, and have Ben give you a tour. HR will handle the final paperwork. We can't waste any time chasing this monster. The mayor will swear you in at one this afternoon, and you'll be provided a badge, gun, and issued a vehicle."

"Perfect, sir. I'm anxious to go to work."

The chief escorted CJ and Ben into Stan's office. After a few pleasantries, he excused himself and closed the door. CJ felt a sudden surge of anxiety. She'd met Stan on her last trip, but only briefly. She didn't feel the same connection with him as the chief.

"Your trip from Boston go okay?" he asked.

"Long, but it went well."

"Excellent. Well, let's plow ahead."

CJ squeezed the case file she had in her lap. "Let's do it."

"Ben told me he'd briefed you on the case. I don't need to tell you that all hell is breaking loose, and the city is on red alert. The mayor's spitting fire and the press is working nonstop criticizing us. We must catch this crazy bastard, and I mean quick."

She nodded at him. "Yes, sir, I agree."

"You'll report directly to me on this case. Administratively, you'll be part of Lieutenant Grimes's CID unit. Ben is officially part of the Homicide Investigation Unit, but for this case, he'll report to you." He pointed at both of them. "I'm counting on you two to work your asses off and catch this guy. I'll make sure you have everything you need to do your job. Make no mistake, your job is to bring this guy down." He leaned forward. "Any questions?"

"No, sir," CJ and Ben replied in unison.

Stan leaned back in his chair, waved to the window, and smiled at CJ. "Welcome to Charleston."

The door opened, and Lieutenant Paul Grimes entered. CJ remembered the man from her previous visit—a thin, six-foot Black man of forty with receding black hair and a weathered face.

"CJ, I believe you know Paul?" Stan asked.

"I do," she said as she stood and offered Paul her hand. "Nice to see you again, Lieutenant."

Paul smiled warmly at her as the two shook hands. "We're glad you're here. I assume Stan has filled you in on the plan?"

"Yes, sir."

Stan spoke up. "CJ, I'm not sure how it worked in Boston, but here you can call me and Paul by our first names. The chief is fine with Walter, although we call him Chief Williams in public."

She smiled. "Thank you. Got it."

CJ and Ben left the captain's office and Ben gave CJ a tour of the station. The two of them would share a small second-floor office. He introduced her to numerous other officers and department staff. Most were friendly, although a couple teased her about her accent.

They spent the rest of the day going over the case and visiting the Forensic Services Division and Medical Examiner Whitehall. They had agreed to meet with the brass at nine o'clock the following morning to review the case and discuss the next steps.

As they stood in the LEC lobby, Ben checked his watch and smiled at CJ. "I think we've seen the most important things for day one. How about we go grab a drink?"

CJ smiled. "Sure. You'll have to pick a place since I'm new to town."

"I know just the spot to give you some local flavor."

He drove them across town and pulled up outside a two-story building, which had a purplish color in the fading sunlight. Red doors and red-trimmed windows accented the steel-gray paint of the walls. The exterior lights along the roof provided pale blue circles.

"Henry's is one of the oldest places in Charleston," Ben said. "Been on this corner since 1932."

A horseshoe-shaped bar stood in the center of a large room with whirling overhead fans casting a breeze from the white ceiling. The floor was small white tiles broken up by black flowers. The bar's dark wood was a nice contrast to the white above and below it.

"Let's go upstairs to the rooftop bar," Ben said. "We'll avoid the whiskey lounge."

They both laughed.

Ben pointed to a poster on the wall. "They have live music most nights. You can eat here, drink here, and dance the night away."

CJ swatted his arm. "Since we have to work tomorrow, I'll pass on the dancing. Oh, look, what a cute porch. It has a swing! I love the rocking chairs."

They found a table on the roof overlooking Market Street. The waitress came by and took their drink orders. They each ordered a Corona and agreed to try the gator bites.

CJ stretched her arms over her head. "This is so nice. Thanks for bringing me here. This place is wonderful."

The waitress dropped off their beers, and they clinked the bottles and said, "Cheers."

"It's been so crazy today we haven't got to know each other," CJ said. "How about you? Tell me a little about yourself."

Ben smiled. "Well, let's see. I was born here in Charleston and have spent all my life here except for the four years in the Marine Corps. After high school, I went to the Citadel. It's the military college here in Charleston. I enjoyed the military environment, the discipline, and the camaraderie. It was a big reason I joined the marines. After four years, I thought about re-upping but came back and went into law enforcement. It helped me get hired. I was local, went to the Citadel, had a college degree, and had four years in the service."

"When did you join the force?"

"About six years ago now," he said. "Until my recent move to investigations, I was an officer on patrol. When this case came up, I got promoted to an investigator."

CJ gave him a big smile. "Congratulations. What did you study at the Citadel?"

"I got my degree in criminal justice. My dad wanted me to get an engineering degree, but I always planned to go into law enforcement. How about you?"

"Sounds similar. Born and raised in Boston. Until moving here, that's where I spent my entire life. I went to Boston College and also got my degree in criminal justice. I started the application process for the Boston PD in my last semester at BC. Like you, the college degree made it easier to get hired. I spent my first seven years as a patrol officer. A little over three years ago, I made detective."

"Why did you decide to come to Charleston?" he asked.

"I wanted a change in scenery, and being in a smaller department made sense. Plus, I wanted to be here with Harry."

Ben offered her a gator bite. He thought about asking her about family, but decided against it. He really didn't want to talk about his, and maybe that was too personal so early on. Ben opted to stick with education. "How was Boston College? I've heard of it, but don't know much about it."

"It's a good school and has lots of degree options," she said. "I also got a scholarship offer to play lacrosse."

He laughed. "I knew it. You were a jock."

CJ flexed her arms. "Yep, that's me!"

"Did you wear those little skirts and goggles?" he asked.

"I did. Wasn't a big fan of the skirt. Did you play any sports?"

"I played baseball and football in high school and football in college."

CJ threw her mouth open and then laughed. "So, you were a jock, too!"

"Yep. I loved playing, and the teammates were the best part."

She nodded. "I agree. My two best friends were teammates."

"Yeah, I still see a few of the guys from the team."

CJ reached for another bite. "These are yummy. Never thought I'd eat an alligator. How do you like being a cop?"

"I like it," he said. "It's tough sometimes, but I like that I'm doing something where I can help people."

"What's the toughest thing you've had to deal with?" she asked.

Ben exhaled. "Oh wow. I've dealt with some nasty wrecks, a couple of overdoses, but the worst thing was a three-year-old girl whose stepfather sexually assaulted her."

CJ grimaced. "Aw shit. That had to be awful."

"Yeah. The baby's stepfather had gotten drunk and raped her. He sat there laughing when we arrested him. The baby nearly died, and it took all I had in me not to strangle him on the spot. It's hard to protect and serve sometimes—we're sworn to protect the good and bad, but . . ." Ben rubbed his face. He didn't want to relive the horrible moment. "How's being a cop worked out for you?"

"It's been mostly good. I love working with the public and, like you, find it rewarding when you help someone."

"Anything horrible?"

Deep breath and long exhale. "I had to kill a man."

"Jeez, I'm sorry."

"It happened a couple of weeks ago. My partner and I were on a burglary call, and the perp had a gun to my partner's head. I got a shot and took it—I had no choice but I regret it every second of every day. You hope you can go through your whole career and never fire your gun, but I'll deal with it. I had a round with the shrink before I left, and I'm supposed to have a couple more sessions here. Not fun, but it actually helps."

I wonder if that's the real reason CJ left Boston, Ben thought. After a pause in the conversation, Ben broke the silence and got them back on the sunny side of life. "I bet you looked cute in your skirt and goggles."

CJ cocked her head to the side and winked. "Oh yeah, I was a doll."

Ben stared at the reflection of the lights in CJ's emerald-green eyes. The tiny yellow flecks made her eyes sparkle. His pulse quickened.

They finished their beers and called it a night. Tomorrow was a big day.

CJ had to admit Ben was attractive. He was six-foot-four, had dark brown hair, light amber eyes, and an athletic body. He was tanned—no doubt he spent lots of his free time outdoors. *Tall, dark, and handsome.*

NINETEEN

Tuesday, April 20
Downtown Charleston

CJ's sleep was sporadic. Images of dead bodies filled her mind. The damage done to the beautiful young women was difficult to comprehend. How could anyone do such a heinous thing? She wasn't going to sleep, so she joined Harry on the deck at five in the morning.

Harry had volunteered to take her to the LEC and drive her Cherokee back since she'd have her police issued vehicle by the end of the day. He had also agreed to meet Walter for a cup of coffee. Harry explained he thought Walter wanted to get his thoughts on the offer to become a consultant.

"What do you think about taking on the role?" she asked.

Harry sighed. "To be honest, I'm still undecided. I miss the challenge of solving cases, but I don't miss seeing some things I've seen."

"I understand. You were a great detective because you gave it your all, but the downside is it can crush you."

"Yes, it's hard to do." He rubbed the top of his head. "Either way, I'll do my best to help you if you want."

CJ smiled. "You always do." She flinched when her phone rang. "Hello, this is CJ."

"This is Medical Examiner Whitehall—Thomas. I hate to call so early, but the parents will come in to identify our third victim this morning if you want to attend."

"What time are they coming in?" she asked.

"At ten."

She thought for a moment. She and Ben had their briefing at nine a.m., and she wasn't sure she could make it to the morgue in time for the viewing. "Tell you what, Thomas, I'll need to move an earlier meeting, but I will be there. I'll let Ben know so he can attend with me."

He thanked her. "These types of meetings are always tough. I think it'll give the parents peace of mind to meet the team who will get justice for their daughter."

CJ hung up and glanced at Harry. "You think I'm making the right decision? I hate to push back the meeting with the brass."

Harry nodded. "I believe you always make the right decision when you're present when someone loses a loved one."

At ten, CJ and Ben were waiting in the examination room of the morgue. She glanced at Ben, who had his head bowed. "This has to be the worst part of Thomas's job," she said.

Ben nodded slowly.

CJ knew how difficult this would be for them. She had only attended a body identification session a couple of times—all had been awful. She reminded herself how important it was to be strong, as others had been for her when she'd lost her family.

Thomas opened the door. Behind him was a couple in their early forties who were visibly upset and shaking. CJ knew they were holding out hope this wasn't their daughter.

Thomas gestured toward them. "Mr. and Mrs. Simmons, this is Detective O'Hara and Investigator Parrish of the Charleston Police Department. They're the team working to bring justice to the victims."

CJ and Ben said hello to them. Neither found it in themselves to include a "nice to meet you." The Simmonses didn't respond. They were struggling to maintain their composure. CJ and Ben stood silently. Thomas stepped to the table and gently pulled back the sheet to reveal the face of a beautiful young woman. He was careful not to expose the cut across her throat. He wanted to spare the parents as much of the gore as he could. CJ tried to prepare herself for the reaction of the parents. Her knees almost buckled with what came next.

Mrs. Simmons let out a wail and fell on her daughter. "My baby, my baby."

Mr. Simmons tried to comfort his wife, but he lost it and burst into uncontrollable sobs.

Both CJ and Ben had tears in their eyes.

Thomas had stood solemnly, his blue-gray eyes wet. "I cannot tell you how sorry I am. This shouldn't be anyone's daughter."

They stood for what felt like hours while the Simmonses expressed their grief. Then, finally, Thomas slowly covered the young woman's face and escorted them back out of the room.

Mrs. Simmons stopped abruptly and turned to CJ, tears rolling down her face. "Promise me you'll find who did this. Promise me!"

CJ steeled herself. "Mr. and Mrs. Simmons, you have my word we will find whoever did this. We will bring them to justice."

Mrs. Simmons suddenly grabbed CJ, hugged her, and cried on her shoulder. CJ could only hug her and whisper, "I'm so sorry for your loss."

After several painful minutes, CJ and Ben watched the group leave and silently went out the door to the car. Neither said anything on the drive back to the LEC until they reached the parking lot.

CJ's blood was boiling. "We're gonna get the son of a bitch who did this."

CHAPTER

TWENTY

Tuesday, April 20
College of Charleston campus, Charleston

He sat under a large magnolia tree laden with grayish-white Spanish moss, enjoying the briskness of the morning, the smell of the magnolia blossoms, and his hot coffee. He loved watching the young coeds hustle and bustle to and from the coffee shop before they headed to their first class of the day.

The warmth of the sun's rays stood in contrast to the damp and frigid conditions he had endured in Sitka. The long bright days were a polar opposite to the darkness of Alaska. But his abuse at the hands of his keeper was long over.

He hated the man who'd made him work seven days a week with long days at sea. Salt had stung the cuts on his hands from the ropes, and piercing fingers of cold had stabbed him all over his body. Drunken punches to his face had been the norm.

His father had banished him, but his mother had deserted him. She had sworn to protect him and help with his demons. She was a liar! At last, she had come to know how evil his demons were—she had deserved to know.

The College of Charleston had such a bounty of young women. He saw several natural beauties, but they'd have to wait before he could pick one out for himself. You'd think with the news in the papers, they'd be wary of strangers. *Nope!*

Several smiled sweetly at him as they passed, sitting there innocently under the canopy of the tree. He smiled and winked at a couple of them.

TWENTY-ONE

Tuesday, April 20
Downtown Charleston

A few minutes past one o'clock, Captain Meyers told CJ the floor was all hers. She had thought she'd be nervous on day two of a new job in a new department and new town, but seeing the Simmonses that morning had steeled her determination.

"Let me first say Ben and I had the terrible experience of watching two loving parents say goodbye to their twenty-three-year-old daughter this morning. It made our mission crystal clear. We cannot rest until whoever killed these young women is caught and behind bars.

"Second, Ben, Eddie, and Thomas have done exceptional work on this case so far." She motioned to the three men to her right. "I'll lead in presenting what we propose to do next, but this is a team effort. I'll ask them to help me cover key information and answer any questions. I know Ben has provided a summary once before for the first two victims. For completeness, I'll cover all three, so I apologize for any redundancies."

For the next hour, CJ went through the details of the three murders. She also provided a written summary she and Ben had prepared.

"Our three victims ranged from twenty-one to twenty-five in age and were five-six or five-seven. All had various shades of blond hair and blue eyes. All were fit and naturally attractive. Other than different locations where the bodies were found and tattoos on two victims, they appear similar."

CJ passed around photos of Mandy to the group.

"Victim number one was Amanda McCarthy, known as Mandy to her friends. She was found on Saturday, April 3, at seven-fifteen a.m. in the back storage area of the Low Tide Boat Shop here in downtown. She was a nurse at the MUSC and lived alone in an apartment on Calhoun Street, near the hospital. Her supervisor last saw her around eight p.m. on Thursday. She was due back at work by eight a.m. on Friday, but didn't show up."

CJ paused as the group reviewed the written summary—there were no questions.

"Victim number two, Laura Perkins, was found on Saturday, April 10, at six a.m. just off the dock next to the Sawgrass Marina in Mount Pleasant. Laura was a junior at North Carolina State University in Raleigh. She lived on campus in a sorority house. Her professor was the last person to see her around ten a.m. on Friday after her last exam.

"She was on her way to Kiawah Island for a bachelor-ette party. After stopping for gas, she called her girlfriends at 3:55 p.m. and said she expected to arrive in less than an hour. They called her parents in Charlotte when she hadn't arrived by six p.m. They drove along the route she was supposed to have used and found her car on Main Road on Johns Island near the Kiawah Island Bridge."

CJ passed photos of Laura around before continuing.

"Our third victim, Kelli Simmons, was found Saturday, April 17, at noon on the dock at the Town Creek Marina near the Ravenel Bridge. She worked as a veterinarian tech-nician in Mount Pleasant. She lived in a rental home on Sullivan's Island with a roommate. Her roommate last saw her at around nine on Friday morning before leaving for work. Kelli had the day off and said she was going to the beach. Her roommate got home around five p.m. Kelli's car was in the driveway, but she was not home. When her roommate couldn't reach her, she called her parents in Columbus, Ohio. Her parents told her to call the police if she wasn't home by ten p.m. She called us at ten-fifteen p.m. and came into the station on Saturday afternoon to file a report."

CJ passed photos of Kelli to the group. "I'll cover the headlines of the autopsies. Thomas, please contribute as appropriate."

Thomas nodded.

"For all three victims, Thomas performed autopsies and ruled the cause of death as a laceration of the throat. The cut was done from right to left, indicating a left-handed killer. Based on the body temp, blood pooling, and state of rigor mortis, our first victim was estimated to have been killed about twenty-four to thirty hours before being found. The second and third victims are estimated to have died approximately six to eight hours before being found.

"Secondary mutilation believed to have been done postmortem occurred to all three victims. This included a laceration from the sternum to the lower abdomen. All three victims had ligature marks on their ankles and wrists, indicating they were bound at some point. Tape residues were found on all three victims' mouths, wrists, and ankles. The perp used fishing line to crudely sew up the midsection back up."

CJ passed the gruesome crime scene photos of the victims to the group.

Walter exhaled slowly. "Oh my God."

CJ continued. "The victims were all raped multiple times. No semen was found in the autopsies, indicating the rapist wore a condom. No other residues were found for any of the three victims. Based on the lack of blood at each scene, the victims are believed to have been murdered elsewhere. They were all posed in the same manner and wrapped in a tarp. The CSU dusted for but found no fingerprints at any of the three locations. They also collected materials from the crime scene areas. Lab analysis were performed, but no forensic evidence was found. The tarps, which the victims were lying on, are generic and can be bought in numerous stores. The tarps appeared to be new in each case."

After she finished her summary, CJ asked for any more questions. Eddie answered a few questions about what materials were collected and analyzed. Ben answered some questions about those who had found the bodies. He described how they had been investigated and said all of them had been cleared as suspects.

Walter rubbed his chin. "What do you envision as the next steps?"

CJ paused. "We need to determine where these young women were when they were taken or lured away. This will require us to work from the point where they were last seen until we estimate they were taken or left on their own." She pointed at the board. "Our first victim left the hospital shortly after eight p.m. and, based on the appearance of her apartment, most likely didn't go straight home. We know our second stopped for gas before she stopped or was stopped on the side of the road. Our third victim was home at nine a.m., had planned to go to the beach, and was not home by five p.m. Our next step is filling in the gaps in these timelines and hopefully finding someone who witnessed something they didn't realize was important."

Stan asked, "What help do you need for the next step?"

"We could use a couple of patrol officers to help canvass stores, bars, restaurants, and so on," CJ said. "There's quite a bit of ground to cover. It would also be helpful to have our patrols make a point of checking marinas, docks, and marine-related businesses as part of their routine rounds."

Stan nodded. "I'll assign two officers to help you, and we'll alert the force."

Walter spoke up. "There are two other resources we can add. First, Harry and I had a good chat this morning, and if you ask him, I'm sure he'll agree to consult on this case." He smiled at her. "I'll leave the decision to you. Second, I can call the FBI and have them help us with a profile. I like the way you're thinking now, but a professional profiler could be helpful."

"I'll speak to Harry," CJ said. "I agree an FBI profiler could help us narrow down our search."

Walter nodded. "Anything else?"

"I'd ask you to run point on coordination between other law enforcement departments. So far, we have Charleston and Mount Pleasant involved, and we need a team effort."

Walter smiled. "Done."

CJ sighed. "I think we are all worried this is only the start of what this monster has planned. Since he's murdered his third victim, he's crossed from being a standard killer to a serial killer. Summer is coming. Not only do we have all our local young women to protect, but I understand Charleston will have lots of tourists coming into town."

TWENTY-TWO

Wednesday, April 21
Downtown Charleston

CJ met Ben at seven a.m. at the LEC, planning to fill gaps in the first victim's timeline. Stan was waiting with two patrol officers ready to assist. He told her she only needed to point them in the direction she wanted. They'd help cover the downtown area near the hospital where Mandy had last been seen.

CJ, Ben, and the two officers met in the conference room. CJ provided a list of the restaurants, bars, and shops to be covered. She had a picture of Mandy and a list of questions she wanted to use to collect information. Ben told her the two of them should go together, as she was still learning her way around. She knew he was right, but four could cover more ground than three.

CJ smiled at the two officers. "I appreciate your help with this. Here are my and Ben's cell phones if you find anything. Let's all get started and plan on meeting back here at four this afternoon to review what we got covered today."

The two officers nodded as they stood.

"We'll get to it and call if we find anything useful," the older of the two officers said.

Ben's cell phone buzzed. He answered it and jotted notes down.

CJ watched him as he listened intently, then she saw a smile cross his lips. "What?" she whispered.

Ben held up a finger, then hung up. "That was SLED. They got the DNA results on our buddy Elrod Harris. We got a hit in CODIS for a rape a year ago. It seems Elrod has a past, and it gets better. The lab found enough DNA on two pairs of panties to get results, and it matches two other rape victims. They had reported the rapes, but we had run into a dead end on suspects. Neither could describe their attacker as it was too dark, and their attacker wore a mask."

CJ smiled. "Sounds like we have two solid cases of rape and two more we can tie to him. Now the question is if Elrod Harris is also a murderer."

Ben watched her face closely. "Do you think he's our guy for the three other rapes and murders?" he asked.

She was staring at the list, nibbling at her bottom lip. "No. I think our guy is too smart to get caught dragging a girl across a parking lot. He's also more violent. That sounds silly since the Harris rapes have been rough, but our perp goes way beyond just raping his victims. He wants more than sex. He wants to torture his victims and—to see their blood."

"I agree," Ben said. "I wish it were Harris so we could solve the cases, but we have another guy out there who's far more dangerous."

"The good news is we will get justice for four rape victims," CJ said as she stood. "Let's talk to Cap, let him know what we have, and push ahead on our timelines. Maybe once we get more details, Elrod will be our guy." *We can hope.*

———

After meeting with Stan for a few minutes, CJ and Ben started at MUSC and spoke to Mandy's supervisor, Brenda Harrison. Ben had taken her statement earlier, but CJ wanted to find out whether she knew anything else that would be useful. Brenda, a short, stocky woman in her late thirties, led them to a quiet spot in the back of the break room to talk.

CJ flipped open her notepad. "You said Mandy changed into casual clothes and left a little after eight p.m., correct?"

"Yes. I wish now I had asked Mandy where she was going." She sighed. "We were so busy at the time."

CJ nodded. "That's understandable, and no one could foresee what would happen. Do you remember what Mandy was wearing when she left?"

"She wore jeans and a white shirt. Nothing fancy, just casual."

"Does she usually go home after work, or would she sometimes make stops?"

Brenda nibbled at the end of her thumb. "Mandy always walked to and from work. She loved walking around Charleston. I'm not sure about that night, but she left alone. She and a couple of nurses sometimes stop for a drink to unwind after a shift."

CJ was hopeful. "Are any of these nurses here?"

"Yes, Abby is here. She and Mandy often stopped for drinks together."

"Can we talk to her?" CJ asked.

Brenda nodded and stood. "Yes, of course. Let me page her."

Brenda left, and a few minutes later, the speakers called Abby to the nurses' station. Brenda returned with a young woman in her late twenties ten minutes later. Her straight brown hair was short, and she had close-set honey-brown eyes.

Abby sat down with tears in her eyes. "I'm not sure what I can do to help. I'll try. Mandy was my friend, and I miss her."

CJ smiled and patted the young nurse on her arm. "Thank you. I understand you and Mandy sometimes stopped off for a drink after work. Can you tell me where you would go, or if you had any favorite spots?"

Abby thought for a minute. "It would depend on what night. Some bars are busier than others on certain nights. Most of the time, we wanted somewhere less busy."

CJ showed her a list of bars. "How about any of these as possible Thursday night spots?"

CJ and Ben left the hospital with the names of four bars where Mandy may have gone, and started with the first on the list: the King Street Bar. It was closed, but the manager let them in the back door. It was a dive bar. College kids probably loved the décor with posters, beer lights, and deer heads with beer cans on their antlers. The musty atmosphere smelled of stale beer.

The manager said he worked on Thursdays until nine p.m. He took Mandy's photo and shook his head. "Pretty lady. I don't remember seeing her. I work downstairs, so I might not have seen her if she had gone up top. If you come back around three, the bartender who works upstairs on Thursdays can tell you if he remembers seeing her."

"Okay," CJ said. "We'll be back later. Thanks for your help."

CJ and Ben continued to the next three bars on the list Abby had provided. No luck. No one remembered seeing Mandy. They decided to continue down their list of bars and restaurants. They agreed shops would be the least likely places for Mandy to stop that time of night and gave them a low priority.

As they walked between locations, CJ called each of the two officers to check their status. She frowned when they indicated they were over halfway through their lists and so far, no one remembered seeing Mandy. One restaurant manager said he knew Mandy, but he hadn't seen her in a while.

CJ and Ben returned to the King Street Bar around three-fifteen p.m. The manager waved to them and said the bartender, Tim, was upstairs stocking for the night. CJ and

Ben went upstairs, where they found a young man putting Coronas in the refrigerator behind the bar.

"Hello, Tim, I'm Detective O'Hara, and this is Investigator Parrish. Can we bother you for a couple of minutes?"

Tim smiled. "Sure, let me put these last bottles in the fridge, and I'm all yours. By the way, your eyes are amazing. I've never seen eyes so bright green."

She smiled at the younger man. "Thank you."

Tim finished with the bottles and motioned them to the end of the bar. CJ showed him a photo of Mandy and asked if he remembered seeing her on the Thursday night in question.

Tim took the photo. "She's pretty, and I usually remember women like her. You said it was Thursday night after eight on the first?"

"Yes, she got off work at eight. She changed at the hospital and left on foot. It took us about twenty minutes to walk here, so she'd have gotten here around eight thirty or so."

Tim thought for a minute. "Yeah, I think I remember her. She came in around then. She ordered a drink and sat over at that table." He pointed to a small table in the corner. "She was about the first customer up here, and she ordered a margarita."

CJ's heart rate increased. "Was she alone or with someone?"

"She was alone. I think. Wait, she came in alone, but some guy sat and talked to her for a while. I remember he bought the two of them a drink, maybe more than one."

"Do you remember if it was a beer or a mixed drink?" CJ asked.

"I think it was a margarita, definitely mixed," he said.

It would be easier to slip something into a mixed drink. "Did you recognize him?"

"Not sure. I didn't pay much attention."

CJ nodded. "Can you remember anything about him?"

"Not much. The man was White, younger, I think. He was tall."

"What do you mean by younger?"

He shrugged. "Older than me. I'm twenty-five, so thirties."

CJ jotted down a note. "You said tall?"

"He was well over six feet, about your height," Tim said, looking at Ben. "I saw him coming out of the men's room there by the table."

"Anything else you can remember about him?"

"No. Sorry, I don't pay much attention to the guys, just the girls."

CJ smiled. "Did they leave together?"

"Oh gosh, hard to tell. We started getting slammed around ten, and I wasn't paying attention. I'm sure she left by ten-thirty, as a bunch of Citadel cadets came in and took her table. They were whooping it up and wearing me out at the bar, ordering shots. I had to go over and tell them to chill."

"Does anyone else work up here with you that may have seen anything?"

"Nah, just me. We have a few waitresses downstairs. Up here, folks just come up to the bar and grab their drinks. Don't have any video cameras for the area, either."

CJ thanked him, gave him a card, and asked him to call her anytime if he remembered anything else.

———

When CJ and Ben returned to the LEC, they met with the two officers who had completed visiting their list of bars and restaurants. Other than one restaurant owner, no one else remembered Mandy, and the owner hadn't seen her on the night in question. They agreed they would check the shops the next day, but they weren't optimistic since most closed no later than nine at night.

CJ called the Forensic Services Division before she left for the day. She asked if there was any video footage of the King Street Bar area. *Had they captured Mandy and the guy at the table leaving together?*

TWENTY-THREE

Wednesday, April 21
Wando

It had been a long day and, at just after six, CJ drove back to Harry's, ready for something to eat. For the second day in a row, she and Ben had skipped lunch. She also wanted to talk about the consulting role with her uncle. She hated to ask him, but she needed his help, and it would be better if it was official.

She walked through the front door, and Harry called to her. "Hey, how was your day?"

She smiled. "Okay, I guess. We found out a younger White male was seen with our first victim at the King Street Bar on the Thursday in question between eight-thirty and ten-thirty."

"Well, it's a start. Come on out here on the deck. How about grilled shrimp for dinner?" he asked.

"Sounds perfect. I missed lunch, so I'm starved."

Harry smiled. "Don't worry. I have enough to feed an army."

Harry cooked their grilled shrimp, dirty rice, and cole-slaw, and they sat on the back deck and ate. CJ was hungrier than she thought and ate at least a dozen shrimp. The meal was delicious.

After they finished dinner and cleaned up, she finally got up the nerve to ask Harry for his help. "Chief Williams wants you to work as a consultant on this case. Like you, I'm not sure it's the best idea, but—"

"I think I should do it," Harry said without hesitation.

Her eyes went wide. "You do?"

"I do. Chief Williams went through the details of this case, and I think I can help. I probably wouldn't help if you weren't involved, but it's a no-brainer for me now. These young women are only a little younger than you, and I cannot imagine their parents' grief. I have to help. Once a cop, always a cop."

"I worry about you getting into this nightmare with me, though."

"We'll stop the nightmare and catch the bastard, then I'll go back to fishing. I only agreed to help with this case, nothing more. I'll call the chief right now unless you don't want me around."

CJ leaned over and hugged him. "Thank you. I promised the mother of our third victim I would catch whoever did this. With your help, we can make it happen sooner."

Harry smiled. "So, as my boss, what's your policy on time off for fishing?"

CJ laughed. "You're the best."

Harry grimaced as he stood.

"You okay?" she asked, concerned.

"Oh yeah. I'm fine," he lied.

"You looked like you were in pain."

"Ah, probably tweaked something messin' with the boat today," he lied again.

TWENTY-FOUR

Wednesday, April 21
College of Charleston campus, Charleston

He knew it was too soon to take another one, but his urges had been surging all day. He couldn't wait any longer after seeing those natural beauties smiling at him this morning on the college campus. You had to love those college cuties.

He had a perfect plan. He grabbed his backpack of goodies and his little helpers, with a couple of notable additions for tonight. He'd satisfy his urges before midnight if all went as planned. At least, satisfy them for a while.

He arrived at the college campus and found a spot to park his truck. He sat there watching students pass by. It was early evening, so there were fewer students than this morning. He had planned it that way and, after all, he only needed the perfect one. Any others would just be in his way and cause him issues.

———

Kara Morgan walked toward the library. She had a major test in her business finance class, and she wanted to nail it. After almost three years, she had a GPA of nearly 4.0. She was well on her way to her hospitality and tourism management degree. She would finish the semester strong if she made at least a ninety on this test.

He watched her as she walked up the sidewalk across from where he was parked. Her sandy blond hair was up in a bun, and she wore a pair of cut-off jean shorts and a light blue top. She wasn't wearing make-up, and her body was incredibly toned. He waited until she passed, got out of his truck with his backpack over his shoulder, and followed her from a distance. He would have to take her when the time and the place were right.

Kara gave her mom a quick call before she got into the building. She paused at the bottom of the steps. "I'm great, Mom, thanks. I'm heading into the library now to study for my business finance test in the morning. I've got wonderful news. I made a ninety-five on my hotel management test and a ninety-three on my events management test."

Kara tap-danced away from a cockroach as it scurried past her feet. "Okay. I need to study." She laughed. "No, I won't stay all night, only until ten. I'll call you after my test in the morning and let you know how I did." Kara hung up, plodded up the steps, and through the library door.

His wait was about to be rewarded when she exited the library three hours later. She was more beautiful than he remembered. He was pleased there were so few people left in the area. The rain, which had been light and started to pick up, had helped clear things out. He snickered as she peered up at the drops and mumbled, "Poor thing is getting doused."

He slipped on his special tools for the night, a light jacket, and a hat. Kara left the library steps, trying to hold her backpack over her head to shield herself from the rain. He slowly walked on a path where they would meet. She was going back the same way she'd come. *Perfect!*

She smiled. "Hello, Officer. It's a wet night."

He smiled back. "Hello, miss. Yes, the rain is getting worse. You're getting drenched."

"Yeah, I forgot my umbrella."

He put on his best concerned face. "Can I escort you to where you're headed? I'll share my umbrella."

She hesitated. "I think I'll be fine," she said. "I'm heading back to my sorority house a couple of blocks away. No need to bother you."

"No bother. Hell, I'm a security guard, and keeping students safe is my job. Step under the umbrella, and I'll get you home. It'll be my good deed for the day."

Kara sensed something, but let it pass. "I guess it would be okay."

She stepped under the umbrella, and he caught the faint sweet smell of vanilla. He fought himself not to grab her. He had to wait, be patient, and let his plan work.

Kara's ocean-blue eyes stared up at him. "Are you sure you don't mind walking me?"

He was struggling to control his breathing as he gazed at her face, no more than two feet away. "Not at all." Even though he knew the answer, he asked, "Which way are we going?"

She pointed. "I need to go down Coming Street. By the way, I'm Kara."

"Pleased to meet you, Kara, I'm Jim," he lied.

They started back down the sidewalk in the direction where his truck was parked. Kara happily told him about her classes and that she was a cheerleader. Those two things kept her schedule full. He glanced to make sure no one else was around as they neared his truck. *What a lucky man I am!*

His hands were quick, and he had her in the back of his truck within seconds. Kara was strong and fought him, but the knife under her throat calmed her down—it always worked. She pleaded with him to let her go, but he only smiled at her. He left her whimpering in the back as he drove away.

When they arrived at his safe place thirty minutes later, he announced, "We're here, sweet Kara. I'll make you more comfortable, and we can begin our fun." *Fun for me, anyway.* He carried her over his shoulder to his metal table. He decided he'd take the tape off her mouth. Between the remoteness of his safe place and his music, he'd be the only one to hear her scream.

TWENTY-FIVE

Thursday, April 22
Folly Beach, South Carolina

CJ woke up to her cell phone ringing a little before six a.m. She rolled over, trying to focus as she grabbed her phone. "O'Hara."

"Hello, Detective. This is Grace from dispatch."

CJ bolted upright. "Yes, Grace."

"We have a fourth body. The Folly Beach PD received a call from the manager of the Sunrise Point Marina on Folly Beach. They called me and said it fit the descriptions of the other victims. I'll text the manager's name, cell, and address so you can plug it into your navigation."

"Thanks, Grace. Can you call the CSU and ME for me? I'll call Ben." CJ jumped out of bed and put on her clothes.

When Harry knocked and cracked the door open, she was struggling with her shoes. "I heard your phone ring. Everything okay?"

"No, not at all. We have a fourth body found at Folly Beach."

Harry exhaled. "Shit. I'm ready to go. I'll go grab us some coffee for the drive."

"I'll be ready in less than five minutes," she said. She grabbed her phone, called Ben, and told him, "We have a fourth body at the Sunrise Point Marina on Folly Beach."

Minutes later, CJ and Harry left for Folly Beach. She passed on using the siren since it was early and traffic was light.

She looked over at Harry. "I assume your call with Chief Williams went well last night."

"Yes, you might say he was happy. I told him I'd be in first thing this morning to do some paperwork, so I'm official, but that'll need to wait."

CJ sighed. "Tough to take the steps we need to complete for the first three victims with the bodies piling up. This bastard is escalating. His last kill happened less than a week ago."

Harry nodded. "Now that he's started, kills are only calming his urges for shorter and shorter periods. Sadly, this pace sometimes occurs with serial rapists. Serial killers usually don't kill this many in such a short period unless they're highly disorganized."

"You think our guy's unraveling?" she asked.

"He's organized, at least so far," Harry said. "He's planning his kills and not making any mistakes. He could be getting complacent or cocky."

CJ nodded. "Let's hope he made some mistakes this time."

———

Forty-five minutes later, CJ turned into the marina where three Folly Beach PD cruisers were waiting. She stopped, and a young officer told her they had been instructed to keep the entrance road blocked. No one other than law enforcement was to go in or out. They pointed her to the marina. CJ saw two men waiting near the marina's end. She parked, and she and Harry got out.

"I'll be observing this one," Harry said.

A man no more than five-foot-six with light brown hair stepped toward them. He was thin, and his jacket hung off him. "I'm Detective Hal Peters, Folly Beach PD. I told the guys to let you through. I'm trying to keep the damn press away."

CJ nodded. "How do you want to handle this?"

"We're on Folly Beach turf, but our chief told us to call you guys if we had a similar case," Hal said. "I do as I'm told. The young woman is dead, and her throat and stomach were sliced open."

She couldn't read in his deep-set eyes whether he was okay or pissed about her showing up. She didn't give a damn either way. "How about if the case is linked to our other cases, you and I work together? If not, you've got it."

He grunted. "Fine by me."

Another man stepped forward. "I'm Bob Spencer. I manage the marina. She's around the corner of the Sealand container number six. Around five-thirty a.m. I went to get some things out of the container and almost fell over her."

Bob stopped and let CJ and Hal turn the corner of the container. The top of a head was visible.

CJ yelled back to him, "Did you look under the tarp?"

Bob crept around the corner to answer. "Yes, when I tripped over it, I pulled the tarp back, but I didn't touch her."

CJ pulled on her booties and surgical gloves. She exhaled deeply and stared at the beautiful face of a young woman with tangled sandy blond hair and glassy blue eyes. She looked in her early twenties and had a gash across her throat. CJ carefully covered the body with the tarp.

As she turned, Ben walked up. "Same?" he asked.

"Yes, just like the first three." CJ leaned down and raised the tarp again to show him.

"Shit."

She nodded. "I had dispatch call the CSU and ME, so they should be here soon." She looked over at Ben. "I'll string some crime scene tape up. How about you look for folks on their boats and see if they saw anything? The manager says no cameras."

"Will do."

"I haven't taken the statement of the manager yet, but he said not to hurry. Let's let the forensics guys get going, and we'll talk to him together."

CJ, Ben, and Hal talked to the manager. He told them he was the only one there. His staff wouldn't arrive until eight a.m., and no one had overnighted on their boat.

The CSU and ME arrived and spent almost two hours processing the scene. Once the body was on the gurney, the lead CSI and ME provided their preliminary reports. Neither on the team that day had worked the last three scenes, but it was like they had read the prior information and simply changed locations—it was more of the same.

The ME estimated the time of death as only four to six hours ago. She had responded for the field exam, but Thomas would do the autopsy.

As the ME turned to walk away, she stopped. "Detective, there was one more thing I noted."

"That would be?" CJ asked.

"I found a small tattoo of a cougar on the back of her upper right shoulder blade."

Ben joined them. "What kind of cougar?" he asked.

"Not sure, but we got a photo, so I'll text it to you."

CJ thanked her and turned to Ben. "What's up?" she asked.

"The mascot for the College of Charleston is the cougar. Maybe she's a student."

CJ blew out a long breath. "Our unsub is hunting his victims in bars, on beaches, along the roadside, and now on a college campus."

Ben nodded. "Sounds like it, plus dropping bodies at marinas, docks, and marine-related businesses across the greater Charleston area."

Harry walked over to them. "It confirms he's a local and knows the ins and outs of Charleston. We need to focus on the rather narrow group he's targeting."

"How do we do that?" Ben asked.

"The best way is to make sure patrol is focusing on gathering spots for young women, and we need cameras up in key areas. As bad as it sounds, a county-wide alert is needed. The mayors may not be fans of this, but we can leave that to the chief to sort that out. The worst part is whoever is doing this doesn't look like or fit the mold of what people would expect of a serial killer."

CJ and Harry told Ben that they'd meet him back at the station. CJ said she'd alert the captain of the latest victim on the way back. She and Detective Peters agreed she had the lead.

As they headed to their vehicles, Harry gestured to Ben, and the two stopped.

Harry leaned closer to him. "You seem to be quite fond of my niece."

Ben squirmed a bit and attempted a smile. "I am. I'm just getting to know her, but I think she's great."

Harry's blood pressure increased. He knew CJ didn't need this right now. "Understood. She is great—the total package—but you need to back off and give her some space right now. Hell, she just got here and has lots on her mind."

Ben looked at the ground and pushed gravel with his shoe. He wasn't sure what to say. "Yes, sir."

CJ yelled to Harry from the Explorer, "Let's go! We don't have all damn day."

On their way back to Charleston, CJ dialed Captain Meyers and gave him a summary of the findings of the fourth victim. She let him know about the tattoo and the theory she was a student at the College of Charleston. Before she hung up, he told her a special agent from the FBI would arrive Friday evening to help with a profile. The FBI would also provide further assistance if needed.

Harry nodded when she passed this on to him. "It makes sense to involve them. The FBI can be helpful and a pain in the ass at the same time. It's all about who is assigned as the agent." He paused. "The most important thing is we stop this guy as soon as possible. I've learned to take the devil's help if it gets the job done."

As CJ parked at the precinct half an hour later, Ben called her on her cell.

"Helen got a call from a panicked mother reporting her daughter, Kara Morgan, missing."

"How long has she been missing?" CJ asked.

"She told Helen since last night. She understood a longer time is required to file a formal missing person report, but she's freaked out about the young women being abducted and killed in the city. She left her cell number. You think we should call her?"

CJ's stomach twisted, and she felt sick. Under normal circumstances, you'd tell an upset parent to sit tight if their child was missing for less than a day. Charleston wasn't normal right now. "Yeah, I'm coming into the LEC now, and I'll call her."

Harry held the door into the LEC for CJ. They went upstairs and got the mother's cell number from Helen. CJ dialed the number and heard sniffing on the other end of the line. She listened as the mother told her about her missing daughter.

CJ hung up and sat down across from Harry and Ben. "That was Krista Morgan, mother of Kara Morgan. Kara's a student at the College of Charleston. Her mother said she talked to Kara last night around seven. Kara was on her way to the College of Charleston library and planned to talk to her again at nine this morning after a test. She didn't hear from her."

Ben shook his head. "Jeez, that was a few hours ago. Maybe the girl overslept or something."

The horrible pit in CJ's stomach got worse. "Normally, I'd agree, but Ms. Morgan said she called her roommate, and she hadn't seen her since six last night. She spoke to her professor, and Kara didn't take her exam this morning. Her mom said she'd never miss an exam without letting some-one know. She's sending a photo now and driving over from Atlanta." She exhaled. "So, Kara went missing sometime after seven p.m. Let's shoot the photo to the morgue and determine if she matches the young woman we found this morning. The timing seems to fit since our young woman has been dead for less than six hours."

Harry rubbed at the knot in his neck. "Let's hope the mother finds her safe and sound once she gets here, and they have a nice laugh over dinner tonight."

Thirty minutes later, Thomas called and confirmed the photo matched the latest body. It was Kara Morgan.

CHAPTER

TWENTY-SIX

Thursday, April 22
Downtown Charleston

CJ's stomach had seized up during her early morning call from dispatch and had never released. She sat with the vision of the pale body of their fourth victim streaked with purples, yellows, and reds in her mind. The tangled sandy blond hair, cold ocean-blue eyes, and distant face flashed in her mind.

CJ, Ben, and Harry decided they needed to circle the wagons and go over where things stood. They settled in a small conference room near the bullpen a little after one o'clock in the afternoon.

CJ looked at the two men. "Let's review where we are with filling the gaps in the timelines for the first three victims. Ben, any word from the photography guys on possible video surveillance in the King Street Bar area?"

"Not yet, but they promised me something by early afternoon, so we should hear if they've found anything soon."

"Okay, Mandy was at the King Street Bar from around eight-thirty p.m. until no later than ten-thirty, based on the bartender's statement. The bartender said she was with a tall, younger White male—"

Ben's cell phone rang, and he looked down. "Forensics." He answered it and said, "Ben Parrish." When Ben hung up, he looked at CJ. "They found a video camera with footage from the side of the King Street Bar. They're sending a clip over, but they said at 9:58 p.m., a tall White male and a young woman are shown leaving the bar through the side door."

CJ's pulse rate increased. "Is the man's face visible?"

"No, only his back. There is no way to tell who he is."

She wanted to scream.

"We should be able to nail down his height and build from the video, and perhaps his hair color," said Harry.

Ben's phone pinged and he opened the message with the video clip attached. "Here we go."

The three of them watched as the young woman swayed as she walked, stumbling several times. Her legs were too weak to hold her weight. The tall male had his left arm wrapped around her, practically holding her body off the ground.

Ben pointed at the screen. "There he is. Jeez, the young woman can barely walk on her own. He's carrying her out."

CJ stared as they walked away from the camera. "She's either drunk or he drugged her. Faces aren't visible, but Harry's right. We can estimate their heights and builds. This will provide us some information on him and confirm if the woman is Mandy."

Ben grabbed his phone. "I'll call forensics now and get them working on it."

Captain Meyers stuck his head into the room. "Hey, guys. I've commandeered a conference room and think it's time we set up a war room. I also think we need to set up a task force and add resources as we need. We've got three jurisdictions involved, and things may turn messy. Grab your stuff and follow me."

CJ, Harry, and Ben followed Stan down the hallway into a large conference room with windows on one side overlooking the Ashley River. The Ashley River Memorial Bridge stood in the distance. The boat-shaped conference table sat twenty and had a speakerphone in the center. Black high-back mesh chairs contrasted with the honey-colored table. A chalkboard ran the entire length of one wall, with a pull-down screen in the center. There was also a blank portable evidence board.

Stan gestured for them to enter. "Here you go. You have a conference room table and will have three fully functional desks within an hour. If you need anything else, please yell. Until we catch this guy, this is your new home."

A young woman in her mid-twenties entered the room. She was petite, with golden-brown hair and sharp, pale blue eyes.

"Oh, one more thing," Stan said. "This is Samantha Ravenel. She's assigned to you full time for support. She's a whiz with the crime databases." Stan turned to Samantha. "Samantha, this is Detective CJ O'Hara, Investigator Ben Parrish, and retired detective Harry O'Hara, who is our case consultant. CJ is the lead on our new task force. Let's name the team the Lowcountry Task Force for now. We could use one of the suggested names for our perp from the press, but what they're coming up with doesn't sit well with me."

CJ nodded. *Yes, let's pass on the Marshland Murderer, South Carolina Slicer, or Blond Girl Butcher. Who comes up with these names?*

Samantha smiled. "Hello, everyone. Please call me Sam. I'll do whatever you need me to do to help catch this guy. I can provide whatever support you need, make coffee, compile information, and access federal and state databases. All you need to do is tell me what you need anytime, day or night, and it'll be done. I've ordered a late lunch for you. It will be here in ten minutes. I'll get this room all set up for you."

CJ smiled. "Thanks, Sam, and welcome."

Stan turned to Harry. "Chief said he'd like you to swing by and grab your badge and gun as soon as you can. You're a consultant and not a sworn officer. Still, you need credentials to show and the ability to use force if warranted."

Harry went to meet with the chief. CJ and Ben spent the rest of the day working on each of the victims' timelines. By day's end, they had established the timelines and filled the board with the noted evidence to support their conclusions.

- *Mandy McCarthy was abducted from the King Street Bar in downtown Charleston on Thursday, April 1.*
- *Laura Perkins was abducted on Main Road near Kiawah Island on Friday, April 9.*
- *Kelli Simmons was abducted from the beach at Sullivan's Island on Friday, April 16.*
- *Kara Morgan was abducted from the College of Charleston on Wednesday, April 21.*

CJ stared at the board. The unsub's hunting ground was wide. *What's the pattern?*

Ben needed a break from work and joined CJ at the board. "So, you're a big Red Sox fan?" he asked.

CJ smiled. "Yep. Love my Sox."

He chuckled. "Yeah, they do have loyal fans. I still love the Braves even after all the heartbreaks. I'm sure you can't stand the Yankees."

"Nope. They're a nemesis."

"Tell me about it. I remember in 1999 when the Braves had a great year winning more than a hundred games during the season. They went to the World Series and got swept by the Yankees. I was only nine and cried like a baby."

"I remember that year," CJ said. "The Yankees beat the Sox in the championship series. The only game the Sox won in the series was at Fenway. Thumped the Yankees thirteen to one."

"Wow, great memory."

She nodded. *It was the last game I saw with my parents.* "How about we call it a day?"

———

CJ sat alone at a table overlooking the sidewalk along East Bay Street as the early dinner crowds arrived. She mindlessly sipped her Blue Moon with its cloudy orange taste and citrus aroma. She couldn't seem to put the pieces of this puzzle together. Whoever was killing these young women was all over the place and showed no consistency other than his victim type. *What's the significance?* She stared at the label on her beer. Her head hurt from going through all the case details.

"Excuse me. Do you have change for a ten?"

Her breath caught as she looked up at a tall, gangly man with long blond hair who was talking to the waitress. His khakis had seen better days, and his red and black flannel shirt was too big. Tears filled her eyes. He looked like the man she had killed only a few weeks ago in Boston. She had been told he wasn't married—no wife or kids. Tears dripped on the table. *But he had a mother, and I took him from her.*

CHAPTER

TWENTY-SEVEN

Thursday, April 22
Downtown Charleston

Last night with the lovely Kara had quelled his urges, at least for a bit. She had been a treat. He'd had a wonderful time as her terror grew when she saw what was coming. She had struggled and screamed, but it had not saved her.

As he sat there finishing his dinner, he saw her and couldn't look away. She was the best of the natural beauties he had seen yet. She was tall and delicate, yet had an athletic body. She had long blond hair with piercing electric-blue eyes—intoxicating.

He watched her as she took the order for a family of four. She was genuinely friendly. She laughed sweetly at the little boy showing her a small truck. As she went from table to table, her demeanor never changed. She was warm and kind to everyone. He needed to take his mind off her. It was too soon to take another one.

"Sir, can I get you anything?"

He made eye contact with her. She smiled, and he smiled back. "No, thank you. Maybe I'll take something later." He felt a bead of sweat run down his face. It was too late. *I have to have her.*

CHAPTER

TWENTY-EIGHT

Friday, April 23
Downtown Charleston

Wendy Watts stared at herself in the mirror. Her hair, dyed platinum, would need a touch-up soon. Her eyes were blue but not a unique shade like aquamarine or electric. She hated them. *Maybe I need contacts to brighten these up a bit. A national news anchor's eyes need to pop.*

Her teeth dazzled and were oddly perfect. Hell, they should have been for what she had spent on them. Gone were the days of crooked teeth and that damn gap in the front. She cursed under her breath at the tiny scar on her chin from when her fucking brother had pushed her down. He had been pissed off because she'd kicked him out of the bathroom. Okay, she needed contacts and to take care of the scar—that should do it. *You've come a long way from the trailer park!*

The trailer park, officially called a mobile home park to make it sound fancy, had been home until she was eighteen. She'd shared the run-down double-wide with her drunken father, mousy mother, and three siblings—two little sisters and a snotty-nosed younger brother. *White trash!* Not her. She was going places.

The only thing they had that was close to nice was the forty-inch television her father had bought to watch his precious football games on. All day long on Saturdays and Sundays, his fat ass sat on their stained brown couch drinking beer and scratching himself—live games in the fall, reruns in the off-season. What did he used to say? "I need to rest after the stress of my job." Yeah, right. It was a tough job cleaning toilets, mopping floors, and scrubbing up puke from the kiddies.

Wendy ran her hands down her low-cut crystal-blue dress as she looked in the full-length mirror. It had to find every curve and hang perfectly to accent her tight, toned body. The work on her breasts and workouts with her trainer, Tony, were really paying off. She twisted her body and smiled. Her butt looked smaller, and her thighs and calves had the perfect hint of muscle—very sexy. *I may have to give Tony an extra ride.*

She checked the time—8:40 a.m. She didn't want to be late for her meeting. Success would mean she was one step closer to her goal. Failure wasn't an option, and, unlike many of her accomplishments, she wanted to earn this. Wendy laughed. She had always fudged, taken shortcuts, and, hell, downright cheated to get her way. She'd only screw the station manager as the last resort. The guy was fifty pounds overweight and smoked like a chimney, and the hairs on his head were abandoning him. Using sex as a tool wasn't an issue, but he was a fat pig.

The ringing startled her. She looked at her phone and smiled wryly. Speaking of screwing, the display indicated her latest ride, Congressman Randolph Lee Jr.

Wendy answered and cooed, "Hey, baby."

"Hi, sweetheart. I miss you."

"How's Washington?" she asked.

"Same old grind. Meetings and speeches."

"Poor baby. I wish you were here and I could relieve your stress."

"That would be wonderful," he said. "I plan on coming down the week after next, so let's get together then. My wife will be down at Hilton Head for part of the week, so we can have some quality time. Maybe we can try out that new bed I bought you."

Wendy rolled her eyes. *Great, he'll be here a whole damn week.* "I look forward to it, baby. I'll have a nice surprise for you. My only hint is Victoria's Secret." She got a soft groan from him and almost started laughing at the fool. Some men were so easy to control.

"How's the new Bimmer?" he asked.

"I love it, baby. It was so sweet of you to surprise me with it on my birthday."

"I'm glad you like it. You only turn twenty-five once. Sweetheart, I'd like to keep talking, but I have a committee meeting in a few. I'll let you know when I'm available."

"I can hardly wait."

She hung up and looked around at the townhome that she couldn't afford on her salary—three-bedroom, three-bath, with a view overlooking the Ashley River and Charleston Harbor. She had furnished it with new modern furniture featuring sleek, shiny, straight lines. The neutral-colored woods gave the place a warm feel. She loved the openness and uncluttered space after spending eighteen years crammed in an eighteen-by-seventy-foot box—it had been half the space and five more people. Lying on her back, letting him sweat all over her a night or two every couple of months wasn't too big a price to pay for it. She had her eyes on a bigger prize—his promise that he would help her with the ABC folks in New York.

Wendy got in her new candy-apple-red BMW and headed north to Highway 17. She crossed the Ravenel Bridge into Mount Pleasant and took a right on Allbritton Boulevard into the News 4 station parking lot. The station's white logo sat atop the reddish-brown building circled with windows. Sycamores in pine-straw beds, slightly taller than the one-story structure, broke up grass still struggling to turn green after the late winter. Wendy sighed. *It's not Manhattan, that's for sure.*

She parked and headed inside, dropping her briefcase in her office. She took a moment to appreciate her honors and awards on the wall and credenza—College of Charleston degree in communication with a minor in English, Rookie Reporter of the Year, and the station's top reporter for three years running. True, the latter was only for her station, and they were small, but she had beaten out several others. *I need a huge story that goes nationwide to get noticed in New York.*

Wendy walked down the hall and waited in the doorway for her station manager, Art Smith, to finish a call. She smiled sweetly at him. Her stomach turned as he shoved another bite of a greasy shrimp po'boy in his mouth. No wonder he was a fat pig. He hung up, sucked his fingers, and grinned at her—more of a leer than a grin. A cold chill went down her. The guy made her skin crawl. There was no way she wanted to use any special favors.

"So, Wendy, what can I do for you?" he asked.

"I wanted to follow up on our conversations about me hosting the weekend news or, better yet, having my own segment."

"Whoa there. We never talked about your own segment. What are you talking about?"

"I was thinking a thirty-minute slot where I'd cover hard-hitting stories. I could have guests and highlight big stories." She gave him a little wink.

He chuckled. "We're not some big city. We won't have enough interesting stuff for a show. There'd be lots of dead air."

Wendy frowned. "I disagree. Maybe we could try it?"

"Tell you what," he said. "I'll give it some thought, but let's not get our hopes up."

"Okay." She pouted. "How about hosting the news on the weekend? I've been on the air numerous times covering stories, and I'm good at it."

"Bit spots covering a story are different from hosting. What about Bob?" he asked.

"I would co-host with him. It would be great. He and I could provide our viewers with a young and old perspective. We have two hosts during the week."

"I'm not sure Bob would like being told he's old," he said. "Besides, he likes doing things his way."

Her frustration was rising, and Wendy worked hard to smile. "He's not old, but he's not twenty-five either. It would help with younger viewers."

Art laughed. "Our younger viewers are too busy partying to watch the news on Friday and Saturday nights."

Will I have to offer him something special? Art took off his glasses and rubbed his eyes. Wendy saw a grease stain on his cuff—his shirt was wrinkled, and images of her father flashed in her mind.

"Tell you what, Wendy, I'll make a deal with you. You land a massive story—I mean bigger than we've had in, say, the last five years—and I'll let you host with Bob on a trial basis."

She stood up, took a deep breath, and went around the desk and hugged him. She pressed her body against his and let the hug linger a bit as she tried not to vomit. "You have a deal. Thank you so much."

She backed away as he resumed leering at her. "I've only agreed to a trial provided you bring us a whopper of a story."

She winked. "I understand. I'm on it." *Now let me get the hell out of here.* She went back to her desk and doodled on a pad. She needed a story, the biggest Charleston had ever seen. The closest she had come was tormenting the Charleston PD about several unsolved murders in the area—a story she had made more significant with a few embellishments. Who was she kidding? She had added some of her own *facts*. The Charleston PD had been less than pleased with her, but it had gotten her the attention she needed. *A girl's gotta do what a girl's gotta do.*

Wendy picked up her phone. She didn't want to make this call. He was too rough with her, and she wondered if he was all there. But he had helped her with information before, and she needed inside information. If she got the story she needed, to hell with the Charleston PD.

When he answered, she purred, "Hey there. I was thinking about you and wanted to see if we could get together. I'll need a little favor, but it will be well worth it."

CHAPTER

TWENTY-NINE

Friday, April 23
Downtown Charleston

CJ and Ben left the morgue at eight-thirty a.m. after watching Kara Morgan's mother breakdown. Things kept fighting to gain the top spot on the list of the worst parts of her job—finding a dead young woman grotesquely mutilated, watching an autopsy, and seeing parents struggle to cope with the loss of their daughter.

CJ turned on her cell and received a voicemail message notification. She and Ben had their cell phones off during the viewing out of respect, so their phones did not ring or buzz during the worst moment of someone's life. She listened to the message. It was from Sam.

"Ben, we need to hustle back to the station. I think we have someone who may have escaped our perp."

———

CJ and Ben found Lillie Ferguson in a LEC interview room with Sam. CJ motioned for Sam to step out of the room before she and Ben entered. "Sam, before we go in, I need you to do something."

"Name it," Sam said.

"We left the morgue, and Ms. Morgan just told her only child goodbye. Her husband died two years ago, so she's all alone. Ms. Morgan drove here from Atlanta, and I understand she won't go home for a couple of days. I'm not sure how it works here, but can you make sure we arrange a counselor for her?"

Sam nodded. "Absolutely."

"I'm not sure where she's—"

Sam touched her arm. "I've got this. I'll find out where she's staying and make sure she has the help she needs. I'll double-check with the ME's office, and if they haven't arranged it, I'll have the grief counselors from the Medical University meet with her. Let me introduce you to Lillie, and I'll take care of Ms. Morgan."

CJ smiled at her. "Thanks, Sam."

Sam opened the door. "Lillie, this is Detective O'Hara and Investigator Parrish. They'll take your statement, and I'll go grab you some more coffee."

The young woman with electric-blue eyes, long blond hair, and delicate features stared up at CJ. "Would it be okay if I talked only to you?" She feebly smiled at Ben. "No offense. I had the worst thing happen to me last night, and I'd rather talk to a woman."

Ben smiled. "I'll go help Sam with your coffee."

CJ sat down beside Lillie. "Are you hurt?"

"No, not really. I was lucky and got away."

CJ nodded. "Can you tell me what happened?"

Lillie paused, trying to collect herself. CJ couldn't help but think of Krista Morgan; this was the second woman in the last hour she'd seen fighting to maintain control, most likely due to their unsub.

"I finished my shift last night at Sully's Restaurant, over on Calhoun Street. I got off at ten p.m. after I helped close up." She started to cry. "I should have listened when the cook told me to wait while he finished cleaning the stove area. He said he'd walk me to my car, but I was in a hurry to go home. So, I went out the back door to where I parked my car. I was about to unlock my car when this big guy grabbed me."

CJ listened closely. "By 'big,' do you mean tall?"

"Yes, he wasn't fat or anything. He was much taller than me, and I'm pretty tall for a girl."

"How tall are you?"

"Five-eight."

CJ smiled at her. "Hey, I'm five-eight too. How much taller would you guess he was than you?"

Lillie shook her head. "I'm not sure. I guess six or seven inches. When I was fighting with him, I think the back of my head hit him in the chin." She started to shake.

CJ slid her chair closer and put her arm around her. "Take your time. We have as long as you need."

Lillie took a deep breath. "He grabbed me around the throat and tried to grab me around my waist. He was trying to pin my arm down and pull my head back. I kicked him in his leg or knee. I'm not sure. He lost his grip on my neck. I twisted away and pushed him back and ran."

CJ softly asked, "Did he chase you?"

"He started to, but I ran out into the street, and a car almost hit me. I was screaming, and when the driver got out of his car, the man ran off the other way." Lillie pulled up her shirtsleeve and showed CJ an ugly bruise on her right arm. "He grabbed me hard."

CJ inspected her arm. "Was he wearing gloves?"

"Yeah, he had on gloves."

Damn it. No chance of fingerprints or DNA. "We should have a doctor look at your arm."

"I'm okay. It's just a bruise."

CJ rechecked the bruise, hoping for imprints of his fingers on her skin. Nothing. "Okay, your call, but if you change your mind, please let me know." She paused and then asked, "Did you see his face?"

"No. He was behind me. It's dark in the back, and I was scared and trying to get away."

Damn it!

Lillie teared up. "I should have tried to see his face so you could catch him. I'm sorry."

CJ shook her head. "No, no, you did the right thing. You got yourself to safety."

They sat quietly for a couple of minutes. Lillie stared blankly at the bruise on her arm.

"What happened after the man in the car stopped?" CJ asked.

"Tommy, the cook I was closing with, came outside and sat with me on the curb until my roommate came and got me. They wanted me to call the police, but I wanted to go home, so we did. My roommate slept on the floor at the side of my bed. This morning she dropped me off here."

CJ wanted to change the subject, as Lillie was getting upset again. "How long have you worked at Sully's?"

"For almost three years. I started not long after I graduated from high school."

"So, you're twenty-one?"

"No, I'm twenty, but I'll turn twenty-one next month."

CJ paused, then said, "Is there anything else you can remember?"

Lillie shook her head. "I don't think so . . . Wait, he was White and had dark hair."

"How could you tell?"

"His reflection in my window when he grabbed at me. I think that's why I got away. I guess I jumped as he lunged toward me."

CJ retook Lillie's hand. "I'm so glad you got away. You're safe now, and we'll find him, so he doesn't try this again with anyone."

Lillie nodded and tried to smile.

CJ squeezed her hand. There were other questions she'd have liked to ask, but she could tell Lillie was exhausted. "Okay, I'm going to have Sam bring you your coffee. I'll have her write down your address, phone number, and some other information."

"Okay, Sam's nice."

CJ got up.

"Can I stay here for a while?" Lillie asked.

"Absolutely. I'll make sure an officer takes you home when you're ready, unless your roommate is still here."

"Thank you. My roommate had to go to work, so I was gonna take a cab, but a ride would be better. My car's still at work. Can you make sure the officer is a woman?"

"I can."

"Can Sam go with me?"

"Sure."

CJ went out the door and found Sam waiting there with a coffee and muffin. She went in the room with Lillie and smiled sweetly.

"Lillie, I have your coffee. Two sugars and a little cream. I also have a blueberry muffin for you. I made it myself."

Ben came out of the viewing room. "Sound like our guy?"

CJ nodded. "I think so. She said he was tall, and she fits his type perfectly. She's twenty, fit, and gorgeous even after her ordeal and probably being up all night."

Ben exhaled. "Do you think he'll try to abduct another woman so soon, given he failed last night?"

"Part of me thinks there is no way he would try to abduct two women on back-to-back nights, but the other part is terrified that he did. It could mean he's escalating or losing control."

CJ had a female officer take Lillie home and asked Sam to ride along. Sam was proving to have many talents. She had done an excellent job with Lillie and CJ knew it had helped her open up.

CJ and Ben returned to the war room. Harry was eating a blueberry muffin from Sam's tin. He had notes written on sheets of paper he'd pulled off the flip chart and had taped the sheets to the wall.

Harry shoved a piece of muffin in his mouth. "Hey, guys."

"How's the muffin?" CJ asked.

"Wonderful! Even better if you dip it in your coffee."

CJ and Ben smiled.

"How was the interview with the young woman?" Harry asked.

CJ filled him in on her conversations with Lillie and her suspicions that she'd escaped their perp. She studied Harry's notes. "What are you doing?"

"Making some notes helps me think things through. I know Sam has our notes captured in the file."

Ben looked over the sheets. "Makes sense."

Harry leaned on the back of a chair. "Okay, guys, we have the FBI agent coming this evening. I thought we should go over the files and make sure we have our ducks in a row."

CJ rubbed her eyes. "Based on your experience, how will he want to start?"

"He'll expect us to brief him on what we have and what we know so far," Harry replied.

CJ nodded. "I sent over a copy of the briefing summary we did for the chief, captain, and lieutenant on Tuesday, but we've got more information now."

Harry was quiet as CJ and Ben talked about what was new since the last briefing session.

"What's on your mind, Harry?" CJ asked.

Harry exhaled. "I should probably tell you something. I guess it never came up, but during my time as a detective in Boston, I spent time at Quantico working with the Behavioral Analysis Unit. I learned how to profile, or at least the process profilers use. The Boston PD had visions of me becoming a profiler within our department." Harry frowned. "I gave it up after a terrible case where I had a different idea on a profile than the FBI agent in charge had."

"So, what happened?"

"My profile was right, and he was wrong. Two teenage girls lost their lives while we went down the wrong path."

Ben asked, "How was that your fault?"

"It wasn't, but I decided being a detective and taking action was better than coming up with hypotheticals, I guess. Look, I don't want to be negative about what the

FBI can do or how they can help. We need them, but let's also use what we can and not simply defer to them. The agent I worked with seemed to think more about his career and grandstanding than solving the case. Only his ideas mattered to him."

CJ smiled. "Other than studying profiling at the BAU, anything else you need to tell your favorite niece?"

Harry hesitated. *Like I have cancer?* "I need another muffin before Ben eats them all."

THIRTY

Friday, April 23
Downtown Charleston

Thomas was waiting for CJ and Ben in the exam room when they arrived at one p.m. His assistant escorted them into the room. He rolled over a chalkboard where he'd written down some information. "I have a written summary you can take with you, but I thought it best if I gave you a verbal presentation so you can ask questions. Also, I can show you the physical evidence by using photos of the victims."

CJ nodded. "Sounds great. Speaking for myself, I'm not as knowledgeable as I'd like to be on the forensic side of things, so now's a good time to learn."

Ben spoke up. "I'm in the same boat, so teach away."

Thomas smiled. "Okay, good. I thought it best to break my discussion into four parts: capture, rape, cause of death, and postmortem mutilation. Sound reasonable?"

CJ nodded. "Perfect."

Thomas cleared his throat. "The evidence shows our unsub got close to his victims. My guess is he befriended them and lured them to a place where he could capture them. As I examined the tape residues and ligature marks on the wrists and ankles, it appears these occur in two distinct steps.

"Whoever does this uses tape to subdue his victims when he first abducts them. This is quick and easy. Once he gets them to where he is holding them, he removes the tape and uses a rope to tie them down. This became apparent when I realized the tape residues were under the ligature marks, or, said another way, the rope was embedding the tape residues into the skin."

Thomas stepped back and examined the board. "One thing that threw me off was the ligature marks on the neck area. I'm not sure, but I think he's using the rope at the point of capture, maybe as a supplement to the tape. Maybe he tapes their wrists and ankles so they can't fight him and adds the rope to hold them down."

CJ nodded. "Is this consistent with all four victims?"

"Yes, clearer on some, but it appears on all."

CJ stood and walked to the board, staring at a photo. "So, he grabs them, tapes their wrists and ankles, adds a rope around the neck, and takes them to his killing location. Once they're safely stored away, he removes the tape and uses the ropes to tie them down to a bed, floor, or table."

"Correct," Thomas said. "I find it hard to say what he's tying them to, but we've not found any evidence of bedding materials. He's cleaning the bodies after he kills them and before he dumps them. He may be able to wash away any evidence of a sheet, blanket, or mattress."

She thought for a minute. "If I had to bet, he's using something hard, like a table. Why deal with the mess of blood on porous materials?"

"I think you're right," Thomas said. "I hadn't thought of that."

Thomas moved to the photos of the vaginal areas of the victims. CJ flushed. She was uncomfortable sitting there with Ben looking at these.

"The rapes of the victims were consistent. They were all aggressive and particularly violent. All four victims suffered bruising and tearing. I believe the evidence shows the unsub raped them more than once, and he intended to make it as horrific as possible. He wants to control and torture."

CJ wanted to move on. Ben looked down, rubbing at his hand. He clearly wanted to move on, too.

Thomas turned back to the board. "Now, about the primary cause of death, the laceration of the throat. The laceration always occurs from right to left. He's cutting deep enough to slice the carotid arteries, which causes massive bleeding. He starts the cut and doesn't hesitate or stop until he's all the way across. He's using an exceptionally sharp instrument, and he knows how to use it."

Ben leaned forward, looking at the photos of the cut. "Do you know what kind of cutting instrument it could be?"

"Hard to say, but it's very sharp and used for fine cutting."

CJ furrowed her brow. "What kind of instrument does fine cutting?"

"An instrument like a fillet knife that fishermen use to clean fish, or a boning knife chefs use to remove meat from the bone. It could also be a scalpel a medical professional might use. He needs to cut through tough tissue."

Ben nodded. "Could he be using a butcher's knife?"

"No, I don't think so. That's too big. This is a sharp cutting instrument with a smooth blade, and not too long." Thomas stared at his notes. "There is one small difference for our third victim, Kelli Simmons."

CJ's heart pitter-pattered. *Difference?*

"Here are the four photos of the victims' necks." Thomas pointed to a specific spot. "For Kelli, the cut starts more toward the center of her neck. This differs from the other three, where he began the cut further down the side."

CJ stood, examining the photo. "Hmm, different. Small but certainly different. What does this mean?"

Thomas exhaled. "I'm not sure. It may mean nothing other than the victim was struggling more, and he missed his normal starting point."

CJ made a note of this small but perhaps significant difference.

Thomas continued. "Let's talk about the secondary cause of death—the laceration of the midsection."

Ben rubbed his forehead. "Secondary cause of death, or do you mean postmortem? Sorry, I'm confused."

Thomas smiled. "Sorry. Once I examined more closely, it appears he may be making the laceration from the sternum to the lower abdomen before the victims were dead."

Ben's eyes went wide. "Jesus. You mean he cuts their throats, and while they're still alive and bleeding to death, he cuts them open?"

"I'm afraid so. There may be some time between the two, but it appears he's not waiting until they're dead before he cuts again."

Thomas pointed to the midsections of the victims. "He's consistent in starting his cut at the bottom of the sternum. I found small bruises on two of the victims. It appears the bruise occurred from a thumb." He pointed to the bruises. "I think he runs his thumb down their sternum until he finds the xiphoid process, the bottom portion of the sternum. This is still cartilage in someone in their early twenties, not yet bone. This is his marker to start his cut."

CJ used her forefinger to find the spot on her chest. She touched the end of the sternum as Ben stared at her.

Thomas went back to the photos. "Once he starts his cut, he continues it down through the three regions of the abdomen: the epigastric region, the umbilical region, and finally, the hypogastric region. In this case, about three inches below the victim's navel, or belly button."

CJ touched her abdomen under her belt line. A wave of nausea hit her. "How about internal damage?"

"Other than the cut into tissues, organs, etc., the unsub's not disturbing the victims internally. He's not reaching into them. Our second victim had some organ damage, but this was due to the seagulls."

CJ had witnessed the carnage firsthand, but seeing it this way sickened her more. "Why do you think he's mutilating the midsection if he's not interested in touching the organs?"

"No clue," Thomas replied. "He may just want to cause more pain—or draw more blood."

CJ nibbled at her thumb while looking at the board. "What about the tape on the mouth?"

"He could leave it on until he drops the bodies, which is why there's more tape residue, or he might have removed it earlier."

CJ nodded. "If he removed it, they would be able to yell or scream, but it wouldn't matter if he didn't care. He may want them to scream."

Ben looked at her, puzzled. "Why would he want them to scream?"

CJ growled, "Because screaming excites him. He loves the terror."

THIRTY-ONE

Friday, April 23
Downtown Charleston

CJ, Ben, and Harry had everything set up in the war room for the meeting with the FBI. It was four-thirty p.m., so they still had another thirty minutes before the attendees showed. Sam had made a complete copy of the case files. To no one's surprise, she had the information well organized.

CJ outlined her presentation on the chalkboard and pinned a set of photos on the corkboard. She'd prepared a written summary of her presentation, and Sam had copies ready for everyone. She planned to step through the case, hitting the headlines, and answering questions. Afterward, the FBI could take and review the complete file.

Sam had coffee and her homemade treats, so everything looked ready. All they needed was the attendees, and they could start the meeting.

CJ looked at Sam, who was making another pot of coffee. "Do you know where the FBI is staying?"

"Yes, at Martha's Bed and Breakfast, so they're within an easy walk to the station."

CJ nodded. "Sounds like a cozy place."

Sam smiled. "Yes. Very. By the way, I understand that two agents are coming. A senior and a junior agent."

Harry spoke up. "It's not unusual for two agents to come, sometimes more. The FBI likes to use real cases to train junior agents. So, if it goes like it normally does, the junior agent will sit silent, almost like an observer."

CJ nodded. "Okay, good to know. Holy smokes, Sam, what are these?"

Sam laughed. "Those are s'mores brownies. I got the idea from the Brown's Court bakery—graham cracker crust, fudge brownies, and toasted marshmallows."

Harry bent down and smelled the tray. "Oh, my! Perhaps I should taste one."

Sam swatted his hand. "No. Wait until our guests arrive."

Harry chuckled. "Yes, ma'am. Sam, whoever marries you will be lucky."

Ben rubbed his stomach. "And fat." He went to the side of the room and grabbed a cup of coffee.

Sam watched him and blew out a small breath. She struggled to get up her nerve. She had caught herself staring at Ben more than once. Embarrassing! She hoped her puppy-dog crush wasn't evident to everyone. *Oh well, might as well go for it.* She eased her way over to Ben.

"Ben, would you like to come over for dinner sometime?" Sam asked quietly.

Ben hoped his surprise didn't show on his face. Sam was great, but he wasn't sure if he was interested in her. She was so sweet. Maybe it was just a friendly gesture, not meant as anything more.

"Thanks, Sam. Yeah, I'd love that once we get a break from this case. I'm kinda frazzled now and wouldn't be good company."

Sam did her best to smile and not show disappointment. "Sure. Let's catch this guy, and we'll do it." Ben flashed her a smile, and she tried not to blush.

"Perfect," he said.

She wasn't sure what he meant, but she'd try to stay positive.

Their voices were low, but CJ had heard and her chest got tight. *A date?* She smiled at Ben as he sat down and hoped he couldn't see she was jealous.

At 4:50 p.m., the chief, captain, and lieutenant arrived, followed by Thomas and Eddie, whom CJ had invited earlier. Detectives Metcalf and Peters also came. The two FBI agents were downstairs in the lobby, and Sam went to bring them up. A couple of minutes later, the FBI agents entered the room. One was a man who looked to be in his mid-fifties, the other a young woman who looked about CJ's age.

The older agent was wearing a black suit with a maroon tie. Not a strand of his close-cropped black hair was out of place. He was graying around the temples and had a stoic face. His gun holster was visible, as was his badge, which he wore on a chain around his neck. This was one serious dude.

The younger agent had wavy brown hair and upturned chestnut-brown eyes. She wore a navy-blue business suit and a white blouse. She had on flat black shoes, a tasteful strand of pearls, and a pair of tiny pearl earrings. CJ sensed she was nervous and wondered how many times she'd done this.

Chief Williams stood. "Welcome, agents. Please come in and pick a spot. How about I introduce our team, and you can introduce yourselves?" He went around, introducing the attendees. As he got to Harry, he said, "Last but not least—"

The older FBI agent's onyx-brown eyes flashed. "Harry O'Hara. It's been a long time."

Harry glared. "Seven years." *Not long enough.*

Chief Williams smiled. "Well, I see you already know each other."

Harry nodded. "Yes, we know each other."

CJ could feel the tension between her uncle and the agent. It hit her. This was the agent with whom Harry had had an unpleasant experience.

The older agent spoke up. "I'm Special Agent Robert Patterson and this is Special Agent Christy Ellis. I'll be in charge, and Agent Ellis will be observing and supporting me."

CJ continued smiling, but the chief frowned, which she assumed was due to Patterson's "I'll be in charge" statement. She looked at Special Agent Patterson and smiled. "Should I call you Robert or Bob?"

He looked at her. "Special Agent Patterson."

She did her best not to frown. "Okay, Special Agent Patterson it is." CJ saw Harry squint and frown. Luckily, he was standing behind the group, getting more coffee. She thought, or at least hoped, no one had noticed this. She pointed to a plan she had written on the board. "Looks like we're ready to get started. There's a suggested agenda on the board. We can adjust as you desire, but I think this makes sense."

There was silence.

She continued. "I'll present a summary of the case so far, and we can answer questions. Written summaries are being passed around. For each of you, there is a copy of the complete file. This will let you go through all the information whenever you want."

Special Agent Patterson nodded. "This looks like a good agenda, and we appreciate the complete files and hard work in preparing for today."

CJ stood. "Okay, let's get started."

For the next two hours, CJ went through the case. She started with the first victim and continued through Lillie Ferguson, who had escaped an incident the night before. She was clear in pointing out they couldn't be sure if her case was tied to the other four victims. For each victim, she asked Ben to comment.

She covered the lab results from the crime scene team and discussed the autopsies. She called on Eddie and Thomas to add details. The group asked questions throughout, but she solicited questions when she had completed her summary. No one spoke.

CJ sat back down. "Okay, sounds like we covered everything. As I understand the profiling process, the first step is getting the input or organizing all the case information."

Special Agent Patterson nodded. "That's correct."

"I wish we had more, like an eyewitness, but we don't yet. Does what we went over and the file give you what you need to move forward?" CJ asked.

Special Agent Patterson sat quiet for a moment as he thumbed through the files. "The file appears to be well compiled and organized, so yes, this should let us move along and get to an initial profile. Special Agent Ellis and I need to plow through the detailed files to pull together a profile, but what do you think, Detective?"

Harry looked stunned he was asking CJ for an opinion.

CJ smiled. "You are asking me for our preliminary profile?"

For the first time, Special Agent Patterson smiled slightly. "Yes. So, spill it."

CJ stood and went to the board. Her pulse picked up, and she hoped she didn't appear as nervous as she felt. She took a deep breath and looked straight at Special Agent Patterson.

"First, this is one individual, and he's committing these murders as his primary objective. He gets his thrill from the capture, rape, torture, and ultimately the kill. Young Caucasian women in their early to mid-twenties who are incredibly attractive and have a natural look are the ones he's targeting. Light brown to blond hair and blue eyes is what he prefers. He's a local and familiar with the area, knowing not only where to find victims but where to dump the bodies. He's organized, planning his crimes, but verges on being disorganized."

Special Agent Patterson leaned back and folded his arms. "What else do your instincts tell you?"

I may as well go for it. "I believe he was the perp in the failed abduction of Lillie Ferguson. He acted outside his typical patient and planned MO. I think he's using his social skills, and probably his looks, to get close to these women. He's a White male from twenty-five to thirty-five years old. He's tall with dark hair and an athletic build. He's abducting the women and taking them to where he confines, terrorizes, rapes, tortures, and kills them. Something from his past has set him off."

Special Agent Patterson pointed at her. "Tell me his MO—clearly."

He was testing her. *Okay, let's do this.* "Our guy grabs them, tapes their wrists, ankles, and mouth, and takes them to where he kills them. He swaps the tape for rope and ties them down. He rapes them multiple times, cuts their throat from right to left and, finally, their midsection.

The last cut may be postmortem, or it may be the secondary cause of death.

"He's careful, cleaning up the bodies and wrapping them in a new tarp and dumping them in out-of-the-way locations. He wants them found, but makes sure not to be seen or captured on video surveillance. He poses them as a way to display them."

When she finished, she waited for Special Agent Patterson's reaction. She had talked fast, almost afraid he would stop her or, worse, laugh at her. She caught Harry smiling out of the corner of her eye. The chief was nodding.

Special Agent Patterson leaned back. "CJ, how long have you been a detective?"

"Three years total. All of it but one week I've worked in Boston. I started here in Charleston on Monday. I've been an officer for ten years and worked with some damn good detectives."

"How long have you been on this case?"

"Officially since Monday, but Ben and I started working together last week."

Special Agent Patterson looked her in the eye. "Do you think that makes you qualified to give me a profile?"

The chief opened his mouth to speak, and Harry stood up. She raised her hand. "Actually, yes, I do. It's not just my idea, but that of this team. Profiles evolve, and they're only a guide for us to catch this guy. What I gave you is a damn good start."

Special Agent Patterson's stoic face broke into a smile. "I agree with you. I do this for a living and what you did was pretty amazing after only working on the case for a week. Excellent job by you and your team."

She wasn't sure how to respond. Her blood pressure had gone up at being questioned, and now this was a shock. So, she simply smiled. "Thank you, Special Agent Patterson."

He smiled again. "Tell you what, maybe we need to go with Robert. I'm sure Special Agent Ellis would be okay with being called Christy."

Christy smiled and nodded.

Robert looked at the chief. "I expected the worst: chaos and no idea on how to move forward. I was wrong. There is lots to do to catch this guy, and we can refine the profile, but your team is better off than what we typically see. I apologize for my cranky start."

Walter smiled. "Thank you. Not only for your comments, but for your help. I'm proud of our team, and we are happy CJ is leading it."

Robert talked about the next steps of building or refining the profile in this case. He wanted the evening to carefully review the files and asked to reconvene the next day. He suggested he, Christy, CJ, Ben, and Harry meet at ten a.m. Everyone agreed this made sense.

Robert and Christy left to work through the files. CJ and Ben decided that since it was a Friday, walking around the bars and restaurants in the downtown area could be helpful. While they hoped the unsub would take the weekend off, they had a feeling this might not be the case. Harry was happy to go home and enjoy the sunset on his deck.

Sitting across from him in his office after the meeting, Walter smiled at Stan. "I think we made a great choice with CJ. She's tougher than what you see on the surface."

Stan was finishing an extra brownie from the meeting. "Yep. I enjoyed seeing she did not back down from the FBI. We had a little stare-down going there. Do you know why there's tension between Harry and Robert?"

Walter shook his head. "Nope. It was thick, though."

THIRTY-TWO

Friday, April 23
Downtown Charleston

CJ's adrenaline rush had slowed. The stress and anxiety of the meeting and the challenge from the FBI had faded. She should have been exhausted, but her energy levels were high. "Ben, how about we wander around downtown and see if we can get a better understanding of what we're up against?"

Ben nodded. "Sounds good to me. We can grab a drink and dinner later. After all, it's Friday night."

She laughed. "Oh yeah, party down."

They walked around the downtown area for a couple of hours, then decided to stop and grab a drink. Ben suggested the Market Street Tavern in the Business District.

They found a table under an umbrella out in front of the restaurant. It was the perfect locale for people watching.

The place was packed. The crowd filled the tables, and lots of people were leaning on the wrought-iron railing. Market lights hanging from the ceiling lit the area brightly. The brick on the facing and floor was worn and made CJ think about her visit to New Orleans.

A man sang blues on a corner stool. The tones of his guitar indicated he'd been playing for a while. Many people imitated Jimmy Buffett, but few pulled it off. The man on the stool wasn't Jimmy, but he wasn't bad. CJ's neck and shoulders relaxed.

The waitress dropped off their drinks; a Corona for CJ and a rum and Coke for Ben. CJ had opted to avoid hard liquor. *I need to keep control.*

"Is your family in Charleston?" she asked Ben.

He nodded. "Yeah, my dad and an older brother are here."

"How about your mother?"

Ben was quiet, then said, "I had a great mom until she left when I was ten. I had another brother who died in an accident, and my mom couldn't get over it. My mom always blamed my dad, I guess. It took a toll on the marriage. I haven't heard from my mom since she left." *Why am I telling her this?*

She saw the pain in his face. "You can tell me to shut up if you want, but what happened?"

Ben watched a young couple walk up the street. A little girl, maybe five, was between them. She held their hands and sang. "My dad and brother were out fishing, the weather kicked up, and my brother fell overboard and drowned."

"Ben, I'm so sorry."

"Yeah, me too. It was a bad scene." Ben then asked her about her family and Harry.

CJ felt a stab in her chest as she told Ben about how her parents were killed in an auto accident.

He put his hand on hers. "I guess we both lost a lot of our family."

She gave him a weak smile. "Yes. I am blessed Harry stepped up for me. When I lost my parents, Harry assumed responsibility for me with no hesitation. It's why we're so close."

Ben had been watching her as she talked. She was beautiful. "I do have to tell you, I agree with the bartender."

"What bartender?" she asked, puzzled.

"The bartender over at the King Street Bar. He said you had amazing eyes, and I have to agree." Ben felt foolish immediately. "I'm not trying to be forward, just commenting. Fact is, you're a beautiful woman."

CJ's face flushed.

Ben was happy that a couple interrupted to ask if they could steal a chair. He felt stupid. *She just got here, and you're chasing a serial killer—the perfect time to hit on her.*

They ordered some food and sat there, talking while they ate. CJ wanted to know what Ben enjoyed doing outside of work. He told her how he still loved to watch baseball and football, that he went to Atlanta to watch the Braves two or three times a year, and made three or four college football games each season.

"I enjoy going to the Citadel games, but watching the South Carolina Gamecocks is more fun. They're in the Southeastern Conference, so you get to see some of the best teams in the country come to Columbia. I also love to fish. My dad, brother, and I try to get to Alaska a couple of times a year. It's an absolutely beautiful place, and the fishing is great."

"I've never been to Alaska," CJ said. "I've always wanted to go. Where do you usually go?"

"Southeastern portion. Ketchikan and Sitka. How about you?"

"As you know, I love baseball. The Red Sox games are always fun. I'm not that big a fan of football. I enjoy hiking and love bike rides. Not the best, but I have a stationary bike I ride several days a week. I put on my earphones and get lost in the zone." CJ hadn't seen a wedding ring, but she asked, anyway. "Have you ever been married?"

He shook his head. "No, never really close. I dated some in college, but I guess I've never had that much time to get serious after that. You?"

Pain showed in her face. "No. I thought I had found my soul mate at Boston College in my junior year. A guy named Mark. He and I had a class together, and he began coming to all my lacrosse home games. Finally, he asked me out, and we immediately became joined at the hip. We were together for four years and moved in together after I started with the Boston PD. For the two years we lived together, life was great."

She exhaled. "I was excited when Mark asked me to meet him for dinner at one of the nicer restaurants one evening after my shift. After work, I rushed home, changed into a long green dress, and ensured my hair and makeup were exactly right. I thought it was the night he'd propose. Mark was nervous throughout dinner, and there was lots of small talk, which was unusual since we always talked effortlessly. Dessert came and went, no proposal.

"I was frustrated, and my world was turned upside down again when I finally had the nerve to ask him where he felt like we were going. I fully expected he would say he saw us being married soon, but instead, I got, 'We've had fun, but it's time we finally grow up.'"

Ben shook his head. "Ouch."

"I asked him what he meant by 'grow up'? He told me he had only ever seen me as someone to have fun with while we were young, nothing more. He moved out the next day, and I haven't heard from him again. A mutual acquaintance told me he moved to Southern California and later got married and had his second child on the way. I guess Mark grew up."

"Jeez, what a shitty comment," Ben said.

They finished their food and walked around for another hour before calling it a night. Seeing how many young women were out and about in downtown Charleston as it neared midnight was troubling. CJ looked over at Ben when a group of young college-age women walked by them. Two of them winked at Ben.

"There are so many targets out here," she said.

Ben nodded. "Let's hope they're being mindful of not being alone."

CJ asked, "How about we head back?"

CJ pointed to a two-story restaurant as they walked down Queen Street. The converted Victorian house was yellow with white trim with beautiful hanging baskets of multicolored flowers. A blue and black sign hung out front. "That's an interesting place."

Ben chuckled. "That's Poogan's Porch. Their chicken fried pork chop is one of the best things you'll ever eat."

"Who's Poogan?" she asked.

"The story goes that the people who owned the house before it was converted to a restaurant had a dog named Poogan. They left him when they moved in the mid-seventies, and he sat on the porch until he died in 1979. People loved him, and he was an institution, so the new owners named the restaurant after him."

"Really? Are you making this up?"

Ben held his hands up. "Honest to God. It's true."

"We'll need to go there sometime."

"We'll do that. You'll see a picture of Poogan inside, the porch dog."

They had just reached their car when the radio crackled. "Ten-twenty-six . . . abduction of a woman from the parking lot on the corner of State and Cumberland. All units in the vicinity respond!"

CJ turned the ignition, hit the gas, and raced toward the scene.

Ben shouted instructions to direct her. "Take a right, and stop up there on the left."

She braked hard and skidded to a stop behind two cruisers with flashing red lights.

THIRTY-THREE

Friday, April 23
Downtown Charleston

CJ and Ben jumped out of the truck and ran to the back of the parking lot. Three officers, guns drawn, used their Maglites to search under cars. Three more officers were searching the tall grass and weeds behind the lots. Beams of light went in all directions.

CJ scanned the dark area. "Guys, check the culvert."

Ben scaled the chain-link fence circling the lot and joined the search.

Her eyes kept scanning around her. She spotted movement behind a warehouse to her right, behind the fence. "Over there!" she shouted, and sprinted. She pushed her way through a hole in the fence. She saw him too late to avoid his fist as it smashed into her jaw—stars swirled. Reflexively, she landed a kick to his groin, and he went down. She was grasping at him as he struggled to run when Ben landed on him hard and pinned him to the ground. A knife flash missed Ben, and his wicked punch ended the threat.

"Damn it, CJ. You could have gotten yourself killed!" Ben berated her.

She sat struggling for breath. "He was getting away. I had no choice."

Ben cuffed the groggy man and motioned to two other officers. "Get him up. Take him back to the lot in the light. Bag his knife." He reached down, grabbed her hand, and pulled her up. "You scared the hell out of me." He wrapped his arms around her—his hand rubbing her back.

"Let me go. I'm okay." She pushed him away. "The asshole punched me, but we got him. We need to find the girl." *I'm no weak female. I can handle myself.*

They began another search. Whimpering. It was low, but CJ heard it. The young woman, maybe twenty, was hidden behind a battered sheet of plywood. CJ's light hit her eyes, and she flinched, using her hands to shield herself. "No!"

"It's okay," CJ said to her. "I'm Charleston PD. Easy."

The young woman had strawberry-blond hair and eyes the color of the clear blue sky. Her blouse was ripped nearly off, exposing her bra. Her pants were torn open at the waist. She was terrified but not seriously hurt.

Ben gently picked the young woman up and carried her to the light. She clung tightly to him. "You're safe now."

He carefully sat her down and covered her with a blanket, like he was handling a newborn baby.

She grabbed his hand. "Don't leave me."

"I won't. My partner and I will sit here with you until the paramedics arrive and check you out. What's your name?"

"Melissa Jones." Sobs shook her body, and she buried her face in Ben's chest.

He wrapped his strong arms around her and mouthed to CJ, "Statement later."

It was stupid, but CJ felt another tinge of jealousy. *Jesus, you're losing it.*

An hour later, CJ and Ben entered the cracker-box interrogation room at the LEC where Winston Jefferson sat hand-cuffed to the table. He was Black, six-two with short black hair, and his eyes were the color of almonds. His denim shirt was ripped at the collar, and his tan khakis had mud stains.

CJ cleared her throat. "All right, Mr. Jefferson, how about you tell us what you were doing in the back of the parking lot?"

"Nothing."

"Did you drag a young woman back there with you?"

Winston muttered. "Nope. I lost my dog and was looking for him. I didn't see a woman."

"How about the knife?" CJ asked.

"I didn't have a knife."

"You're just a poor innocent soul who decided to punch a police officer for no reason?"

"I thought you were a mugger," he said. "I was scared. You damn cops are always harassing innocent people."

"Wait. Just so, my notes are correct, which is it—I was a mugger or a cop?"

His lips slowly curled into a smile, revealing a chipped right front tooth. He shrugged.

Thirty minutes of questions yielded no real answers. Jefferson denied seeing the young woman or even knowing who Melissa Jones was when he was shown her photo—he claimed innocence and wanted the lawyer his rich father had hired.

After the interview, CJ and Ben headed to MUSC to check on their victim and see if she could provide her statement.

Ben looked at CJ as she drove. "How's the eye? It looks swollen. You'll probably have a nice shiner."

"It's fine. EMT checked it out. Told me to ice it."

He started laughing. "Yep. Ice for your eye and for frat boy Winston's balls. Nice kick, by the way." He could tell she was still pissed at him for yelling at her for chasing Winston down alone. *I was just worried about my partner. Yeah, right. I was protective of her.*

Melissa Jones was sitting up in bed when they arrived. The doctors had checked her out, and she was fine other than a few scrapes. They had interrupted the perp before he could complete whatever he was planning.

Melissa's eyes brightened at the sight of Ben. She was fixed on him, and not even aware CJ was present. He smiled at her as he sat down on the edge of the bed. She reached out and put her arms around his neck and kissed him on the cheek. "Thank you for saving me, Investigator Parrish."

"Call me Ben. You remember my partner, right?"

Melissa barely glanced CJ's way. She kept staring starry-eyed at Ben. "Yeah, sure."

Ben asked quietly, "Can you tell us what happened?"

Melissa sniffed and blew her nose. Her eyes got moist. "I met some girlfriends out for a drink and bite at Ricky's Crab Shack. I needed to get home 'cause I'm supposed to work tomorrow morning at seven. I had to park in the back of the lot on State and didn't see him. He grabbed me from behind. I screamed and tried to fight him, but he was too strong. Going there by myself was stupid, wasn't it?"

He smiled at her. "This wasn't your fault, but I'd prefer you have someone walk you to your car next time if you're alone. What happened after he grabbed you?"

Melissa rubbed her eyes. "He pulled out a big knife and told me to shut up or he'd cut me. I was scared, so I did. He pulled me through the hole in the fence and carried me over his shoulder to the back side of the warehouse where you found me."

She started to cry.

Ben took her hand. "It's okay. Take your time."

"He threw me down and ripped off my blouse, and then . . . he started ripping off my pants," Melissa said. "I tried to get away again, but he put the knife to my throat. I knew he was going to rape me. He only stopped 'cause you arrived and he got scared. When he ran off, I hid under that piece of wood." She started crying again. "I don't want to talk anymore. Okay, Ben?"

He patted her hand. "Okay. Just one more question." He showed her the photo of the suspect. "Is this the guy who took you?"

Slow nod. "Yes. That's him."

"Thanks, Melissa. The doctor said your mother was coming, and then you can go home."

"Will you call and check on me?" she asked.

Ben smiled and handed her his pad. "Sure. Write down your number for me."

CJ rolled her eyes. *Almost raped, and she's chasing after Ben.* She had to admit he was quite good with victims—being patient, tender, and handsome didn't hurt.

CJ and Ben left the hospital. The DNA sample would be analyzed and run through CODIS to see if Winston Jefferson had any priors. At a minimum, he'd be charged with kidnapping and attempted sexual assault. The witness who'd called 911, an elderly lady out walking her tan and black Airedale, and the victim herself would testify. It was lucky officers had been in the area.

———

He was disappointed in himself. His urges had almost caused him to make a mistake. A mistake would get him caught, and he wasn't going to get caught. Not now, not ever! He was too clever—way smarter than the cops.

She was such a natural beauty he had briefly lost control and tried to take her without his goodies to help him. Most importantly, he hadn't had his knife, which always calmed them down. If he had been patient and been as prepared as he was before, he would have had her easily. He wouldn't make that mistake again.

He smiled at how she had fought him. Like him, she didn't look the part. She appeared to be sweet and gentle. She had a kind and friendly name, Lillie, according to her name tag. Who knew she was such a fighter? He rubbed his knee where she'd kicked him.

He fantasized about her lying naked on the table, tied down, waiting for him. Oh, how she would squirm, trying to stop him. How she would scream as the blood flowed from her body.

THIRTY-FOUR

Friday, April 23
Downtown Charleston

Wendy knocked on the door. *Why can't this cheap bastard at least spring for a decent hotel?*

Officer Jared Parker swung the door open. "Hmm, you look good."

She gave him a sly smile. "Wait until you see what I have underneath. Make it worth my while, and I'll show you."

He grabbed her arm and pulled her inside—she lost her breath as his arms went tight around her. The small room had cheap furniture, and the bedspread was worn. The ceiling fan wobbled and only one lightbulb worked.

"Easy there, big guy. I'm fragile." *Don't rough me up like you did last time, you asshole.* Wendy hated resorting to this to get the information she needed. She had to have her big story, and this was the only way to get it and get it quick.

He kissed her and yanked her head back by her hair. His hand squeezed her breast hard.

"Damn it, not so rough."

"Come on, baby, you know you like a strong man who takes control."

She wanted to kick him square in the balls and leave, but she needed him. She'd have to put up with his aggressiveness until she got what she wanted. She purred, "Tell you what. You give me what you promised, and I'll give you what you want."

He kept pawing at her, trying to unbutton her blouse with one hand as his other hand went up under her skirt. She backed away. "Now, now. A deal's a deal."

"Shit! Okay." He grabbed a manila envelope off the fake wood desk and tossed it to her. She was trying to see what was in it as he started groping her again. She dropped the envelope when he picked her up and threw her onto the bed.

The next hour was painful—scary. He was worse than before, forcing her to do things she didn't want to do. Rough was one thing, but the flash of the knife terrified her. She lay there watching the overhead fan wobble as he got what he wanted. *No matter how badly I wanted the information, this isn't worth it.*

THIRTY-FIVE

Saturday, April 24
Downtown Charleston

He was fluffy and dingy white with black splotches. His hair was curly, and he needed a bath. He wasn't significant in size, but he had a huge personality. Everyone loved him, and he loved everyone. He was fond of back and belly rubs, and he always enjoyed treats. CJ stepped onto the porch and reached down to pet his head . . . frosted, glassy eyes stared blankly at her.

CJ jerked herself awake. Jesus! What a nightmare. She fought to calm herself and untangle her hair. She couldn't even think happy thoughts about a dog without death filling her mind.

Harry knocked. "Hey, you okay? I heard you whimper."

"I'm fine," she lied. *Just another shitty dream.*

———

CJ arrived at the LEC at nine-thirty a.m. She hoped to meet with the FBI at ten, obtain the profile, and use the afternoon to look at some apartments. Harry had told her she could stay with him if she wanted. He loved having her around. She appreciated this, but wanted her own place to feel more at home.

———

Special Agent Robert Patterson went to the chalkboard when the meeting started. "First, I think the initial profile you provided yesterday is accurate. Again, I compliment you on your analysis. A few minor refinements, and we'll have a profile we can use."

He wrote a few bullets on the board. "He's working alone, and I believe he's a thirty- to forty-five-year-old White male." Robert looked at CJ. "I think the age range is somewhat broader than what you were thinking."

Robert turned back to the board. "The unsub's about six-foot-three with dark hair. He's physically fit and not seen as a threat by his victims. He knows the area well and, most likely, spent most of his life here in Charleston. His sole purpose in taking these women is to rape and murder them ruthlessly. Both acts are where he gets his thrill. This man enjoys control, causing terror, and inflicting pain. Something personal to him has triggered his urges. Maybe he's had a failed relationship with a girlfriend or wife. He's skilled with a knife.

"He's targeting women from twenty- to twenty-five-years-old, who are naturally attractive. He targets only White females with blond or light-colored hair and blue eyes. My experience tells me he won't deviate. His victims are a surrogate for somebody who he feels has wronged him."

CJ nodded. "Do you think he's organized or unorganized?"

"He's an organized offender. He has tendencies to become unorganized when his urges overcome him. So far, his care means we haven't been able to find any evidence. Using an offsite remote location where he rapes and kills the victims allows him time to commit his crimes and clean up the bodies."

Robert sat next to CJ. "To catch him, we need officers to be on the lookout in bars, restaurants, and areas where lots of young women are present. I also believe we need to alert the community."

She made a note. "Is the best approach to ask the chief to alert the community through the news stations and papers?"

"Yes, and we need to alert the bars, restaurants, and college sororities through social media. We also need to make sure the security departments of colleges and hospitals are alerted. We can alert officers at their briefing at the beginning of each shift. I've also asked my researcher to run what we have so far and our profile through ViCAP. If we can match similar crimes to ours, it may give us a great start."

ViCAP was the Violent Criminal Apprehension Program database, which maintained the largest investigative repository of major violent crime cases in the US. It collected and analyzed homicides, sexual assaults, missing persons, and other violent crimes.

CJ jumped when her cell phone rang. She went to the corner of the room to answer. "Detective O'Hara."

"Hello, Detective, this is Officer James with the North Charleston PD."

"What can I do for you?"

"We were briefed on a case you've been working in Charleston related to murdered young women. We've found the body of a young woman, and our chief told us to call you if we found anything that might be connected."

CJ exhaled. "Can you give me any details?"

"The young woman was found wrapped in a tarp at a pier on Pierside Street here in North Charleston. She's nude, and someone cut her open. I'm here at the pier now and have roped off the scene. I've called our forensic unit and ME. One of our detectives is on the way."

Her heart sank. "Does the young woman also have a laceration to her throat?"

"No, just her midsection."

She dropped her head. "Text me the location. I'm on my way."

CJ hung up and turned to the group, looking at her. "There's a body in North Charleston. Let's go."

PART THREE

EVOLUTION

THIRTY-SIX

Saturday, April 24
North Charleston, South Carolina

Officer Johnny James of the North Charleston PD was waiting for CJ and the group on the Pierside Street sidewalk. He was a stocky officer in his mid-twenties with a neatly trimmed Afro. He introduced himself and took them to the body.

A lanky middle-aged detective was already on the scene. His bright green eyes met CJ's, and he introduced himself as Detective Ralph Simpson. "The forensic guys have just started to document everything and collect possible evidence. I assume you want to see her?" he asked.

CJ nodded. "Please."

One of the forensic techs gently raised the tarp.

"Looks like our guy," she said.

Thomas, who had arrived, spoke up. "Sorry, I'm a bit late. Since there's no laceration of her throat, it means we have a new primary cause of death. If it's the laceration to her midsection, she died an excruciating and slow death."

CJ looked at Ralph. "Will you share the forensics reports with us?"

He nodded and said he'd also let her know if anyone reported a missing person.

Thomas was inspecting the body and said, "There are no other wounds—no petechial hemorrhaging to indicate strangling."

"Any identifying marks on the body?" CJ asked.

One of the forensic techs spoke up. "She has a sun tattoo on the back of her right shoulder. It's about three inches in diameter and has a name inside: Toni."

Robert spoke for the first time. "Toni. That's a unisex name."

The forensic tech spoke up again. "She had breast implants."

Robert nodded. "Did any of the other victims have them?"

CJ shook her head. "No."

Officer James returned after canvassing the area for other witnesses. CJ looked at him. "Officer James, who found the body?"

"An elderly gentleman called 911, and I responded. He told me he was walking his dog. The dog had gone over to the tarp, so he looked underneath and saw the top of the woman's head. He said no one else was around and there're no video cameras anywhere close."

CJ's frustration escalated.

The group stood silent as they loaded the body into the coroner's van an hour later. CJ exchanged information with the North Charleston detective and officer and asked them to call her if anyone found anything else. Ralph said he'd be sure to send her all the reports and information. Once the body had left for the morgue, they headed back to the LEC.

CJ called the captain on the way. "Cap, I hate to spoil your day so early, but we have a fifth body found on a pier in North Charleston."

Once the group got back to the station, they agreed the FBI would visit the locations where the other women had been found. Ben volunteered to take them so CJ could make her scheduled times to look for possible places to live.

CJ's first stop was an apartment above Watkins Clothing Shop on State Street, west of East Bay Street. The location was excellent, close to the LEC, and close to bars, restaurants, and shops. In addition, the Cathedral of St. John the Baptist Catholic Church was within walking distance.

The apartment was beautiful, although there was only one bedroom. There was plenty of room for her, but not all her furniture. She'd need to sell her second bedroom set. It was not a deal-breaker, but she did like having the additional room. Besides lacking the extra bedroom, the apartment had everything she needed, even a new washer and dryer.

The owner, George Watkins, ran the shop. He was in his early sixties, plump and friendly. He liked the idea of having a cop as a renter. "This is a safe neighborhood, but you'll make it even safer." He told her the shop closed at six every day and was only open Monday through Friday. She wouldn't be bothered by any noise below.

George showed her a spot behind the building where she could park. She'd be near the steps, taking her up to the apartment. There was a small courtyard with magnificent yellows and purples of noisette roses and wisteria. A vibrant red Japanese maple centered a small sitting area. She told George she'd call him by the morning with her decision.

CJ floated across the Ravenel Bridge into Mount Pleasant. Her second stop was the Watch on Shem Creek, located on Johnnie Dodds Boulevard. The entranceway was a mix of colors. Pink and white pampas grass lined the road into the complex, and massive magnolias, complete with Spanish moss, highlighted immaculate landscaping.

The two-bedroom apartment backed into a marsh. The location was convenient for shopping, restaurants, and bars. The access to the highway leading over the bridge into Charleston was easy. CJ would have to do more driving to get around, unlike in the first apartment.

Her last stop was the Daniel Island Village. Red and white dogwoods underlain by flowers mixed with colors greeted her. The two-bedroom apartment was impressive, but the area was short on stores, restaurants, and bars. The drive to work would be longer.

CJ sat in her truck. Finding a place to live should have been exciting, but the killings hung over her. Her mind was mush. How could someone commit these acts of violence against innocent people? How could God allow it to happen? How could she stop it? *Okay, concentrate on one thing at a time!*

She drew a line through Daniel Island and decided she'd choose between the apartments in downtown Charleston and Mount Pleasant. She planned to only rent for a year before buying something. Either would work. *Which place felt like home?*

CJ smiled. She dialed the number for the owner of the downtown Charleston apartment. "Hello, Mr. Watkins, this is CJ O'Hara. I've decided I like your apartment best, and I'll take it."

"Great. Please call me George."

It was almost six when CJ arrived at Harry's, and he informed her he was taking her out to dinner at Coconut Joe's on the Isle of Palms. It wasn't too big, with a broad menu and an upstairs giving them a beautiful ocean view. He told her the coconut shrimp was to die for—the perfect appetizer—and it was spectacular. They followed their appetizer with lightly fried grouper as their entrées. The view from their second-floor table on the covered porch provided a sky of yellows and light pinks as the sun dropped out of sight, and a low growl and the salty scent of the waves crashing with high tide provided a soothing backdrop. Below them, a young man sat playing his guitar. CJ smiled at the young man's rendition of *Please Come to Boston*.

Harry seemed distracted and unusually quiet on the way home.

Is it the case? CJ wondered.

He parked and sat. He hated lying to CJ.

"What's up, Uncle Harry?"

"There's something I need to tell you."

Uh-oh. She hated that phrase and the tone. "What is it?"

He hit her with a bomb. "I have prostate cancer."

Her heart stopped as she stared in horror at Harry—eyes wide. She fought not to lose control, but moisture covered her cheeks. *All I do is lose people I love.* "What?"

He reached and took her hand—a little squeeze. "It's isolated, and the doc said it's very treatable. They can use a common procedure where they put radiation seeds in me. I don't need chemo or major surgery."

She struggled to breathe. *Cancer!* "When did you find this out?"

"Just recently. I was having some issues and went to get it checked out."

"What kind of issues?"

"I was having a little trouble peeing and then noticed a little blood."

Oh shit, oh shit. This was awful. CJ wasn't sure she'd survive another loss. *Not now, God, please.* "How long were you having these issues?"

Harry hesitated before answering. "A few months."

"A few months! And you didn't think I needed to know?"

"I, uh . . . I didn't know I had cancer, and I didn't want to worry you or make you feel you had to come to Charleston to take care of me."

"When I asked you a few days ago if you felt okay and you said yes, that was what?"

Harry stared at the floor. "A lie."

"Don't you ever lie to me again, ever!" She threw her arms around him and tears erupted.

———

CJ squirmed in bed and rolled over for the tenth time. She sat up, rubbed her eyes, and stretched, but sleep eluded her. She took in a deep breath and exhaled at length as she flipped off the blanket. It was just after one a.m. *May as well do something productive.*

She grabbed the case files and went through them. Was she missing something? She stared at her notes on the victims. There wasn't anything that jumped out to connect them to each other. Nurse, student, vet tech, student . . . *Hey, maybe . . . nope—bartender.* The only common denominator was gorgeous twenty-somethings with various shades of blond hair and eyes in different shades of blue.

She looked at the crime scene photos again. The MOs for vics one through four all mirrored each other. Grotesque purples, dark reds, and yellow splotches interrupted their unblemished pale skin. Glassy eyes, matted hair, and nasty gashes across the throat and down their midsections—tattoo, no tattoo. Other than the drop location and time of death, nothing was different.

Why had he deviated from his MO on the fifth victim and not slashed her throat? What was different about her? Same hair and eyes, beautiful—yellow sun tattoo, but that wasn't the first tattoo. Had she pissed him off somehow? She read through the report and closed her eyes. She had fake breasts. Did the unsub even notice that?

CJ peered at the gash and leaned back. Her fingers probed her left shoulder for her own scar from her recent perp. She unbuttoned her top and traced the still-bright red three-inch scar with her finger. Pulling her pants leg up, she traced the five-inch scar on her left calf, compliments of a drugged-out homeless man she had been trying to help not freeze to death. *I guess I should have kept walking and just left him alone in his alley.*

She traced the scar on her right side. Her first scar was from a perp who had grabbed a broken bottle and stabbed her when she was trying to arrest him. He'd beaten his wife nearly to death, and it had taken three officers to finally subdue him. She had been lucky the EMTs had arrived so quickly and stopped the bleeding.

CJ glanced at the growing pile of crime scene photos. She had been the same age as some of these girls when she got her scars. Unlike them, she'd only gotten scars. She wiped her eyes and turned off the lights—it was three a.m.

THIRTY-SEVEN

Monday, April 26
Downtown Charleston

On her way to the LEC to start her second week, CJ called Detective Ralph Simpson at North Charleston PD to see about any updates. Ralph let her know that no missing person reports had come in yet, but he'd let her know as soon as he got anything. He also let her know his captain had asked him to attend a Lowcountry Task Force meeting. She told him she would be happy with coordination across agencies.

CJ parked and headed upstairs. At Stan's office, she knocked on the door. "Good morning, Cap."

Stan looked up from a stack of files. "Good morning. Please come in."

She dropped into a chair. "For our task force meeting, do we have the other agencies on board?"

"Yes, the chief has worked it out. Every agency will send a representative. There was a little bitching and moaning, but the chief got his way—our lead." He chuckled. "You'll find he does that a lot."

She was glad it was sorted. "Great, thanks. I plan to briefly cover each victim and then have Robert give the profile. We can close with the actions for each group. Sound good to you?"

Stan nodded. "Yep, sounds fine."

CJ went back to the war room and joined Ben and the FBI agents. She gave them the plan. She had most of the critical points on the board, so her presentation was ready with only a bit of work. But first, she had to drop off her apartment contract, pay her deposit and rent, and get the keys to the new place. Since she was within a few blocks, she wouldn't be gone long.

CJ decided she would walk, since she was so close. As she walked down Spring Street, her cell phone rang. She recognized Ralph's number and picked up.

"Hey, CJ, we had a missing person report filed. It sounds like our victim. Her ex-husband filed the report and said the missing young woman had a sun tattoo on her shoulder with the word 'Toni' inside it."

She exhaled. "Do we have a name?"

"Kathy Meeks. She's twenty-four years old. 'Toni' is her two-year-old daughter."

CJ stopped in her tracks. Her heart ached. It was bad enough that a young woman was dead, but now they had a small child who had lost her mother.

"CJ, are you there?"

"Yes, I'm here just trying to wrap my head around a child losing their mother."

Ralph said he'd bring the missing person report with him to the task force meeting and email a copy to Medical Examiner Whitehall. The ex-husband would go to the morgue at two p.m. and identify the body, after taking the little girl to his parents in Beaufort.

CJ hung up and sat down on a bench. The pots with deep red, white, yellow, and purple flowers were beautiful, but her mind was filled with the image of a two-year-old girl crying for her mother. She took slow, pained breaths. *I need to get moving.* She gathered herself as she approached the men's clothing shop. She entered and saw her new landlord.

George looked up and smiled. "Hello, CJ."

"Hey, George. I had a few minutes before a meeting, and I wanted to get the paperwork and check to you."

"Thank you. I appreciate you coming in, but I hope it didn't mess up your day."

"Not at all. Here's the contract and my check for the deposit and first month's rent."

"Perfect. Here are two sets of keys each—one for the door handle and one for the dead bolt. When do you plan to move in?"

CJ was caught off guard by the question. She hadn't thought about the timing of her move. "You know, I haven't thought about it, but I guess after my furniture arrives."

He smiled. "When does it get here?"

"They called me and told me it should be here by ten tomorrow morning."

"Can I help you with it?" he asked.

"I'll do my best to be here unless something happens at work. I have a second bedroom set I will need to take to storage. I'll need my uncle's help."

"I have a storage area out back that has plenty of room. You can store it there if you want."

She smiled. "That would be great. I'm happy to pay you."

He shook his head and smiled. "No need. Happy to help you out, and the good news is the movers can put it right in with no trouble."

She thanked him and said she needed to get back for her meeting. She'd return tomorrow with the movers. He told her to call him if she needed him to help. CJ walked back to the LEC and joined the FBI agents and Ben in the war room.

The war room was packed for the eleven a.m. task force meeting. The chief opened the meeting and then motioned toward CJ. "Detective CJ O'Hara of our CID is the lead for this task force, and we have the FBI here to help us. CJ, the floor is yours."

CJ thanked the group for attending and asked everyone to introduce themselves. Then, she asked them to write down their name, cell phone number, and email on a sheet Sam would type up and make sure everyone had before leaving. "One of the main objectives for this task force is to work together and share information so we can catch this guy."

CJ approached the board. "I'll present a summary of the case to date, the FBI will present the profile, and we'll discuss actions. I'll ask Detective Ralph Simpson to help with a summary of the latest case and Medical Examiner Whitehall to answer questions on the autopsies."

After she completed the briefing, Robert delivered the profile using the summary he had written on the board.

- *White male*
- *30 to 45 years old*
- *6'3" to 6'4"*
- *210 to 225 pounds*
- *Dark hair*
- *Athletic build*
- *Local—knows the area*
- *Loner, likely lives alone—issues from his past*
- *Weapon—knife*

Sam handed out lunch to the group as they discussed what profession the unsub could occupy. Based on the type of cutting instrument and skill, Robert stated the perp could be in the medical field, the culinary profession, or the fishing industry. One officer asked if he thought the killer might be military, maybe at the Marine Corps Air Station in Beaufort.

"It's possible, but I give this a low probability, as the unsub seems to be too familiar with the area. Military personnel aren't normally in the area long enough," Robert answered.

Ralph asked, "Could he be part of the Citadel?"

Robert pondered this. "It's possible. An instructor or a student who grew up in the area is reasonable."

Stan spoke up. "This is a pretty long list of possible suspects. How do we focus our search?"

Robert summarized the best next steps he had covered earlier with CJ. "First, we need to get this profile out across all our law enforcement personnel and ask them to be watchful of areas where young women tend to gather. I'd ask each of you that represents an agency to do this ASAP." Robert looked directly at the chief. "Second, we need to alert the community and ask that young women be cautious and preferably not go out alone."

Walter nodded.

"Third, we need to notify bars, restaurants, college campuses, and hospitals to be wary of persons who may fit the profile. It's a tall order, but worth the effort."

Ben spoke up. "I can take the lead on that one. I can get some help from the comms folks, and we can use social media."

Robert turned to CJ. "I'll turn it back over to you for logistics."

She stood. "I'd ask each of you to be the focal point for your agency and route any leads or information through to me. Alternatively, if you cannot reach me, please contact Investigator Parrish. Call us anytime, day or night."

CJ and Ben made sure to arrive at the morgue before the ex-husband of the latest victim arrived at two p.m. Robert, Christy, and Harry had stayed in the war room, but the tension between the two men still clouded the air.

CJ had had about all she could take of it. *I'm going to have to straighten this out,* she reflected as they joined Ralph in the exam room and waited solemnly on the ex-husband. CJ hated the garb—gown, booties, gloves, and head cover. The smell of death permeated everything, but at least her clothes would be spared.

Ralph had his head down and whispered, "I hate this part of the job."

CJ and Ben only nodded.

Thomas brought the ex-husband into the room. His eyes were red, and he had a dazed look. They watched as he struggled to cope with seeing his daughter's mother laid out before him.

Thomas returned after escorting the ex-husband out of the room. "The guy is destroyed. He still loved her, and he's apprehensive about how this will impact their daughter."

Ralph spoke up. "Yeah, he had a difficult time giving his statement."

Thomas rubbed his forehead. "Well, let's go through the summary of the autopsy. I hate to say it, but like the prior victims, we have no forensic evidence. Based on my autopsy, the cause of death was the laceration of her midsection. The laceration pattern matches what I found on the prior victims. That, combined with the ligature marks and tape residues, tells me this is our guy."

Ralph stared at Kathy Meeks. "Why would he leave out a key part of his signature?"

Thomas shook his head. "I'm not sure why he changed the cause of death."

CJ couldn't come up with a link for the change in MO. "What else was different about this victim?"

Thomas touched his chin. "Well, let's see. The only difference is she had breast implants."

CJ thought of her late-night idea. "What if he decided that this was unnatural, and he punished her for it?"

Ben asked, "So the implants would make her seem unnatural to him?"

She nodded. "Yes, it's possible. Let's ask the FBI when we get back and see what they think. Behavior is their specialty."

They finished up with the autopsy summary. Thomas was correct. There wasn't anything to help them progress the case. As he had been doing, the unsub had been careful and done an excellent job cleaning the body of any clues.

CJ and Ben went back to the LEC. Robert and Christy were in the war room with Harry. They talked about Charleston areas they thought could be the most likely hunting grounds for the unsub. They were frustrated, as there was no clear area where he seemed to be hunting.

CJ walked up to the map of the area. "How's it going, guys?"

Harry frowned. "So far, this guy seems to be all over the Lowcountry. We've been trying to study the case file and find a pattern. No luck yet."

Robert added, "Couple that with his ability to blend in and his knowledge of the local area, and it makes it even tougher to determine how to find him. He won't stand out and be noticed."

CJ nodded. "About the only thing that is unusual is his height. Six-three to six-four is not a giant, but it's taller than most men. Robert, do you think the unsub might have considered our fifth victim's breast implants unnatural and decided to punish her?"

"That's interesting," he said. "I think you're onto something."

They spent another couple of hours discussing the unsub's possible patterns. They had no real luck seeing one.

Harry needed a break. "How about we go for a drink and an early dinner? I know a good place that's walkable. I'll even buy."

Robert laughed. "I can't pass up Harry O'Hara buying. Let's go."

Harry wasn't amused.

The group arrived at Slightly North of Broad and managed to get a round six-top in a corner away from prying ears. They planned to relax, but work always found a way into their discussions.

CJ went to the restroom before they sat down and realized she had to sit between Harry and Robert on her return. The hostess had removed a chair, so they had more room. Christy had grabbed the chair by Ben—*Jeez, girl, we can spread out, no need to sit in his lap.*

The group talked about non-work items throughout appetizers, dinner, and dessert. Robert talked about his career in the FBI and tried to get Harry to talk about his time with the BIS. Ben and CJ contributed to the conversation, mainly about Charleston and Boston. As usual, Christy said little. Over coffee, Robert asked Harry which was the worst case he'd worked on.

Harry flinched and mumbled, "You know which case was my worst."

Ben started to open his mouth, and CJ shook her head at him. *Let it alone.*

THIRTY-EIGHT

Tuesday, April 27
Downtown Charleston

CJ stood at the side of the room as the officers filed in for their morning briefing. Thirty-year-old Officer Jared Parker was sprawled out in a chair in the front row; he was six-foot-four and had dark brown wavy hair. He smirked at CJ.

"So, City Girl, you gonna tell us country boys how to catch a killer? You look more like a model than a cop."

Several officers laughed.

Ben, standing beside her, responded, "Parker, you're an ass."

CJ touched Ben on his arm. "Officer Parker, I'm sure you'll have him caught within the hour."

Parker grunted.

Ben was still pissed. "You don't have to take his shit."

She laughed. "No worries, I've dealt with lots of major-league assholes. You know us city girls."

Ben kept glaring at the officer. "I've never liked the guy. He played football at South Carolina and thinks he's hot shit."

Stan entered, kicked off the briefing, and turned it over to CJ. She spent about fifteen minutes with the headline version of the case. After she finished, she introduced Robert and asked him to give the group the profile.

In less than five minutes, Robert delivered the profile. CJ had to admit she was growing fond of him. She was impressed with his direct, effective delivery—no hesitation, extreme confidence, and commitment. She knew he wouldn't take shit from anyone in pursuing a case.

Wendy Watts looked at the caller ID on the phone in her apartment. *Shit!* "Hey, Jared."

"Hey, baby. I called to tell you I really enjoyed our night together. I have something else for you that will get me another roll in the hay."

"I'm not sure about that," she said. "It'll have to be *real* good."

"How about the details for the Lowcountry Killer?"

"What do you mean 'details'?"

"Copies of the case files plus crime scene photos. Not the released stuff, the raw info, and proof O'Hara has no clue about catching the Lowcountry Killer."

This could be huge for my story, but can I stand another night with this bastard? "Well, if you're telling the truth, I might be willing to meet again."

Jared laughed. "I thought you'd say that. Tomorrow night at ten. Same place. I'll text you the room number. Wear something red."

Wendy listened to the dial tone.

———

CJ walked to Stan's office to let him know where the group was headed. As she approached his door, she heard loud voices arguing. She wasn't sure who was in with the captain, but they weren't happy. The door flew open and slammed against the wall. A well-built man of about forty stalked out of the office. He was red-faced and agitated. He glared at CJ.

"I have years of experience on you, and this case should be mine. The only fucking reason you have this case, sweetheart, is cause you're . . ." He stormed off.

CJ knew he'd stopped himself from saying all he wanted to say. She was happy he had.

Stan came out of his office and shook his head. "Meet Detective Vincent Jackson. One of my biggest crosses to bear."

She wasn't sure how to respond. "Seems like a lovely fellow. Good luck with that."

Stan burst out laughing. "Did you need to see me?"

"I wanted to let you know Robert, Christy, Ben, and I are going to revisit the locations where we believe the unsub abducted the victims."

"Okay. Keep me posted."

As she walked back to the conference room, CJ called her landlord. "George, this is CJ. I hate to ask you, but I'm tied up on a case. I wanted to see if you were serious about your offer to help with the movers."

"I'd be happy to help," he said.

"Thank you so much. The movers should arrive in about an hour. If you'd let them in and have them put the furniture in the apartment, I'd be forever grateful."

"I will do that, and I'll be sure they put your stuff in the right place. I'll put the second bedroom set in the storage room. Is it marked so I know which one?"

"Yes. It should be marked as 'spare.' Thank you. You're the best."

He laughed. "When you meet my wife, please tell her."

Robert, Christy, Ben, and CJ visited each of the scenes where victims had been abducted. They looked at what video surveillance was present and where additional coverage could be provided for each location. Robert got permission to install the new equipment the FBI would cover.

Ben took them to a local spot on Sullivan's Island—Dunleavy's Pub at lunch. The Irish pub reminded CJ of places she had gone to in Boston, and the food was simple, but excellent. CJ ordered the grilled mahi-mahi sandwich. Fresh fish was always tasty, and she was becoming addicted to hush puppies. There was something about golf-ball-sized fried cornmeal batter she couldn't resist.

———

After a long day, the team reassembled in the war room late in the afternoon and discussed the six sites they'd visited. Robert called the crew that would install the cameras he'd agreed to supply.

He hung up and turned to CJ. "The cameras will be installed and up and running by tomorrow. The more I think about how the Sully's Restaurant's owner has placed his cameras to cover key areas, the more I think we should encourage his approach at other bars and restaurants. Part of the charm of Charleston is the nooks and crannies of the city, but it sure opens us up to bad actors."

She nodded. "I agree. Perhaps we can talk to the restaurant association about some recommended guidelines. Ben, do we have a restaurant association?"

"Yes, I'm sure we do."

Sam had entered the room and spoke up. "We do. I know a person who is part of the leadership. I'll call her if you like and set up a time to talk."

CJ smiled. "Thanks, Sam. That would be great."

THIRTY-NINE

Tuesday, April 27
Downtown Charleston

CJ swung by her new apartment to see how the moving had gone after the group broke for the day. She suddenly felt guilty she hadn't been there. Her new landlord was happy to help her, but she should have handled it.

She pulled around the back and parked. She decided to go through the front door. It wasn't quite six p.m., so the shop should still be open, and she could thank George for his help. He looked up from the counter when she walked through the door.

"Hello, CJ. How was your day?"

CJ smiled. "Hello, George, it was fine. How was yours?"

He walked toward her with a big smile. "It was terrific. Today, I had several big sales, and the movers dropped off your furniture. I checked the furniture to ensure it wasn't damaged and had the movers set things up. I hope I put things where you wanted, but if not, I'll help you move it around."

She hugged him. "I cannot thank you enough. I feel bad I asked you to do that for me."

He laughed. "Remember, you didn't ask, I offered. It was no problem at all. Let's go up and see how I did."

They went out the front door and around to the steps leading up to her new apartment. CJ unlocked the door and stepped into the den area. "Oh wow, it looks like I've lived here for a while. This is perfect."

George beamed. "I thought your couch on this wall would give a spectacular view out of the picture window. You can see Fort Sumter."

They went into the kitchen, and CJ's boxes of kitchen stuff were organized on the counter. Her bedroom was like the den area. It looked like she already lived there.

"This is great. I can't believe you went to all this trouble."

He smiled proudly. "My wife stopped by and made the bed for you. She put your extra linen and towels in the linen closet as you go into the bathroom."

Their gestures touched her. "George, I appreciate this so much, and it confirms why I felt this was the place for me."

"Well, welcome home. I'm going to get back downstairs and close for the day. Oh, I almost forgot. My wife put some dinner in the refrigerator for you. She said all you need to do is zap it in the microwave. If you're not up for it tonight, it'll keep for at least three or four days. It's one of her casseroles, and I'm biased, but it's excellent."

"Please thank her for me."

He left and headed downstairs. CJ hadn't planned to stay at her apartment tonight since she'd thought the place would be a wreck. She decided she'd put away her bathroom stuff and kitchenware. She didn't have much left to do but hang a few pictures and bring over her clothes from Harry's.

She finished in the bathroom in a few minutes. When she went to the kitchen, she noticed new shelf paper had been placed on all the shelves. All she had to do was open the boxes and put her dishes away. In about an hour, she had the kitchen all set up. She called Harry and let him know she was on her way. She told him how her new landlord and his wife had moved in her things and even set them up.

Harry chuckled. "This is Charleston, where you find Southern charm and hospitality. Did his wife leave you dinner?"

She laughed. "Yes! How did you know?"

"Well, I'm not surprised. It's a Southern thing, I guess."

They both laughed and hung up. CJ walked around her apartment one last time. She had a few small items to buy and a couple of things left to do, but the place looked like home already. She locked her door and headed to Harry's.

As they sat on the back deck having a late dinner, CJ reflected on her day visiting the locations where the young women had been taken. She couldn't help but think about how careful the unsub had been to pick the perfect spots to abduct his victims. If cameras were present, he'd managed to stay out of sight. The unsub had been seen at only the first location, and only from the back.

"Uncle Harry, why do you think the perp allowed himself to be captured on the cameras when he took the first girl?"

"I'm not sure. Maybe he wasn't aware of the camera across the street, or since it was his first abduction, he wasn't as careful. If you think about it, that's the only thing close to a mistake this guy has made so far." Harry snapped his fingers. "I almost forgot. The chief gave an alert on the six o'clock news. I taped it for you if you want to see it."

"Yes, I'd love to. I understand all the other police departments held their briefings today, so we should have more eyes out looking for the perp. Most importantly, young women might start being more careful."

Harry found the recording and started it. CJ watched as the chief talked about the case, the unsub's profile, and the type of young women he was targeting. He warned the public about being alone in vulnerable spots. He asked everyone to keep their eyes peeled for anyone suspicious.

"Let's hope people heard and listened to his request," she said when the report finished.

Harry nodded. "Yeah, it's a start, but the target group probably doesn't view the news much. Hopefully, their parents saw it and tell them. Social media is the best approach for the younger crowd. As I understand it, the communications team made progress on the social media campaign today."

"Yes, I think so. Sam has proved to be a real asset, and is all over them to get it done. She takes the initiative, jumps right in, and pushes things along."

Harry laughed and nodded. "Yes, I agree. She's a little firecracker. She's so sweet most folks jump on what she asks them to do. I have no doubt you wouldn't want to cross her."

They sat silently and watched the last light of the day fade away. She looked at him. "What's the deal with you and Robert?"

"I told you about the case we worked on and how it went south. Not much else to say."

"The tension between you two is getting old." She stood and went to bed.

She had seemed like a natural beauty, but he had been wrong. She wasn't natural at all. He was so disappointed and angry at her for fooling him. He had shown her what happened when you cheated him with a false promise.

He was still angry, and it was hard to focus on what was before him. He stood there pretending to stretch as runners went by and began to feel better. There were several natural beauties here, he was sure of it.

He was starting to lose his anger and replace it with another feeling as he gazed at them doing their nightly exercise on the pathway along the river. It was such an excellent path, with lots of bushes and little light.

FORTY

Wednesday, April 28
Downtown Charleston

After breakfast, Harry helped CJ load her clothes back into her truck. She planned to drop them off at her apartment on her way to work. Hands-on hips, Harry asked her if she needed help to get her clothes up the stairs and into her apartment.

"I'm fine and can handle it," she said.

He wasn't persuaded. "Okay, let me try this again. I'm going to follow you to your apartment, and while I'm there, I'm going to carry your clothes into your place. I thought I'd go into the station for a while, anyway." Before she could respond, he added, "Besides, I want to see your new place."

"Okay, okay, you win."

Harry laughed and punched the air. "Yes!"

She could only laugh at him. "I love you, but you're a stubborn ass."

As Harry went to get his keys, he yelled back over his shoulder, "Takes one to know one."

CJ and Harry got to her apartment just after seven a.m. It took them about thirty minutes to get her clothes unloaded and in the apartment. Harry was impressed, especially with the view out her picture window. "This is a great view. Not quite the view from my back deck, but it'll do," he said with a grin. "Hey, I can see Fort Sumter. It's pretty far away, but I can see it." CJ came over, and he pointed. "See, it's small, but it's there."

"Fort Sumter. Wasn't it built to protect Charleston and where the Civil War started?"

"That's right," he said. "The first shots of the Civil War happened there. This city has lots of history. When you get time, we'll take a tour."

She nodded. "I'd like that. Let's catch this guy, and I'll take a couple of days off, and we'll tour away."

Harry put his arm around her. "Deal."

She gave him a quick hug. "Okay, let's get to work."

When CJ and Harry arrived in the war room, Sam was already there. She had coffee made and hustled over and got them both a cup. "Good morning, guys. Here's some coffee, and I've got some fresh cinnamon rolls if you want one."

Harry thanked her. "Well, I had breakfast, but I can't pass on a cinnamon roll."

CJ chuckled. "Yeah, me too, please."

Sam smiled. "Don't go getting my files all sticky now."

CJ and Harry wanted to review the medical examiner's reports again. They knew what the files appeared to show, but they needed to compare each case for deviations. After working so much over the last four weeks, Ben had taken the day off. The FBI agents would spend the morning on the phone trying to run down anyone who might fit the unsub's profile in the FBI's database.

CJ spread the five medical examiner reports out on the table. "How about we start with the neck ligatures and work our way down?"

They spent some time looking over the notes and photos of each victim's neck. The rope patterns looked identical and suggested the same rope or type was used each time. The only difference was some ligature marks were more pronounced than others. They concluded this was due to the amount each victim struggled.

Next, they looked at the lacerations to the victims' throats. CJ pointed to a note on one of the files. "Oh jeez, look at this. Thomas added a note that the scalp of victims three and five appeared to be stretched near their foreheads. Does that mean what I think it does?"

Harry slowly nodded. "This indicates the unsub is pulling on their hair. I'd guess he grabbed their hair and held their head down when he cut their throat. Based on what I see here, he grabs their hair with his right hand, pinning their head down, and then cuts their throat with his left hand."

CJ replied, "Well, we know the rope isn't in place then, as he couldn't cut their throat. It further confirms the theory that the rope was only used to stabilize and transport them." She looked at files again and the photos of the victims' midsections. "These look the same to me. They start at the bottom of the sternum and run to the lower abdomen. The cuts appear to be the same type. It's hard to tell how deep they are from the photos, though."

Harry looked at the file. "It says depths ranged from two to three inches. That's pretty deep and the cuts are through tissues and into organs."

"I can't imagine the pain of that. Hopefully, the victims were already dead when he made this cut." She looked down and softly said, "Except for the last victim. She felt this cut without anything to numb her." She sat down. "Do you see anything that would lead us to believe there is anyone else involved other than our one unsub?"

Harry shook his head. "No, I think this is one guy. He gets his jollies from the capture, rape, and execution. He loves to hunt, dominate his victims, and have total control. He wouldn't want to share."

CJ stood and got more coffee. She sat back down, and they started looking at the photos of the tape residues on wrists and ankles. They both agreed these occurred at the point of abduction. The unsub used this to gain quick control of his victims.

"If it's one unsub, how do you think he can hold the victim down and tape their wrists and ankles?" she asked.

Harry looked puzzled. "Well, he's probably using a weapon, most likely a knife, to scare the victims into cooperating. He's taller than his victims, so he has leverage, and my guess is he's strong."

Harry asked her to stand up and turn around. "Let's say the unsub grabs you from behind and grabs one wrist and pins it on your stomach. He can easily force your other wrist over and hold them both with one hand and tape them."

He put his hand to CJ's throat. "If this doesn't work, he can put a knife to your throat and force cooperation. Most victims would freeze at this point. Once your wrists are taped, he could force the victims to the ground and tape their ankles, and then he has them."

They sat back down.

CJ looked at Harry. "It explains how the waitress got away from him. She said he grabbed her and tried what you just showed me, but she fought him and twisted out of his grasp. She was able to get away."

He nodded. "She was lucky, or our guy screwed up. It could mean he wasn't prepared."

"How so?"

"Maybe he didn't have his knife ready or with him. If so, it means his urges caused him to lose control. Or she could have just been damn lucky." Harry exhaled. "Good news for her, maybe bad news for us. He likely won't make the same mistake again."

She leaned back in her chair. "Yes, and we need a mistake so we can find him."

"Excuse me."

CJ turned around and saw Sam standing behind them. "Yes, Sam."

"I wanted you to know the alerts have gone out on social media, and universities have sent alerts to all students. I also got Special Agent Patterson connected with the restaurant association. They'll have alerts out to their members by day's end. The good news is that almost all our bars are on their list as well."

"Thanks, great work."

CJ and Harry decided to take a break and grab an early lunch. CJ called Robert, and he agreed to meet them. He told her the FBI database didn't show anyone who fit the profile of committing rape and murder anywhere near the Lowcountry.

Over lunch under an awning at Wally's Deli, the group discussed what CJ and Harry had gone over that morning. They all agreed they were clear about how the unsub was doing what he did, but still had no clues about who he was or how to find him. Robert told them he thought they might need to bring in some more FBI support to help, which they all agreed was a good idea.

Robert stood and said he would go outside and make a quick call. "If we can get eight to ten agents down here, we'll position them in spots we think are the most vulnerable to supplement local law enforcement."

CJ was so glad to have him here. Even Harry had seemed glad they had him and had said on their way to lunch, "He's damn smart and has access to lots of resources. Now that he seems not to be solely focused on his career, he's focused on just solving his cases." She'd wondered if Harry was softening his stance on the man.

They finished lunch and went back to the LEC. Thanks to Robert's call, they had ten new FBI agents headed their way. They needed to plan how best to use them.

As they walked into the war room, CJ called Ben to let him know of the new FBI resources, and to ask him about where best to deploy them. He knew Charleston best since he had spent most of his life here. She called his cell, but he didn't answer, so she left a message.

After they finished the day, CJ and Harry went back to her apartment. CJ heated the casserole, they ate an early dinner, and Harry left so she could spend her first night in her new home.

FORTY-ONE

Wednesday, April 28
Downtown Charleston

He'd enjoyed last evening. He'd seen several natural beauties, and some had even smiled at him as they ran by. Thankfully, he had been able to control himself until he was well prepared. Now he was ready to pick one out for himself. It was a perfect time, early evening, when fewer people were around, and sunset was beginning. There wouldn't be as many young women jogging, but he only needed the perfect one.

He watched as young women ran by. He was close enough to the path to observe them, but far enough away not to be that recognizable. It amazed him that so many young women ran alone. *I guess they don't watch the news.*

It surprised him how few men were out tonight. Families were never around. It was another reason he loved this running path. As he had done the evening before, he pretended to be stretching. *I'm simply a guy out for a run.*

She came down the path straight to him. Her sandy blond hair was up in a ponytail, and he loved the shorts and shirt she wore. They fit nicely. She had the type of body he loved—lean and athletic. He loved fit young women. And she was all by her lonesome. *Perfect!*

He eased closer to the path and pretended to be tying his shoe. He glanced up as she was within a few feet of him and smiled. She smiled back. "Hi." She continued down the path, but she had confirmed it. She was a natural beauty. He'd have to get acquainted with her.

One of the other reasons he loved this path was it circled runners back around to a small parking area. She'd come back to him, and his truck would be handy. His urges surged.

She came down the path thirty minutes later. She was running a little slower now. Perhaps she was tiring. Tired was good, as she'd have less energy to resist. As she neared, he pretended he had finished his run and was getting water out of the truck. He had a plan.

She slowed to a stop and bent over, hands on her knees. When she looked up, their eyes met. She smiled. "Hello again."

He smiled. "How was your run?"

She stuck out her tongue and laughed. "It was tough today. How about yours?"

"Me too, tougher today. Maybe because it's mid-week."

She walked over to him and offered her hand. "I'm Beth."

This was too easy, he thought. "I'm Jim. I'm pleased to meet you. Do you run here often?"

"Couple times a week and usually once on the weekend."

He smiled. "I try to run four or five times a week, but I don't come here often." He didn't mind the chit-chat, but he wanted to move things along before someone else came by and stopped. He had seen another runner go past. Luckily, they were too far away to see much.

He smiled at her again. "How about we grab some water? I've got some bottles in my truck."

"Sure, that would be great."

He pointed to his truck, positioned at the end of the parking area, partially hidden by some overhanging trees. "After you." She walked toward his truck, and he followed closely beside her. He glanced around to be sure no one else was near.

As they got to his truck, he opened the back and took the top off the cooler. "Help yourself, Beth. I have a couple of types to choose from."

She smiled and reached for the cooler. He quickly grabbed her from behind, one hand over her mouth, the other gripping her wrist and pinning it to her stomach.

She squirmed, but he was too strong. He forced her face down on the back floorboard. "You make a sound and I'll use this." He flashed the knife. She cried, but didn't scream. He taped her mouth, wrists, and ankles. He put her in the truck, tied the rope around her neck, and secured her to the floor. With a flip of the tarp, he jumped in the truck and drove away.

She lay in the back of the truck in the dark. He'd appeared to be a great guy, and he was nice-looking. It was almost dark, and she was alone. She hoped someone had seen them, but she didn't remember seeing anyone else. She didn't know where he was taking her, but she knew it wasn't good. *Why was I so stupid?*

When he pulled into his safe place, he stopped the truck and opened the back. He pulled off the tarp. "Hello, Beth. Was the ride okay?" He laughed when she tried to kick him. "Now, now, don't be a naughty girl."

CHAPTER

FORTY-TWO

Thursday, April 29
Isle of Palms, South Carolina

CJ woke up after her first night in her new apartment. She rolled over, facing the clock—5:50 a.m. Perfect timing. She started the coffeemaker. In a few minutes, she'd have a hot cup ready. She had picked up coffee the evening before, but she still needed to stock her shelves. While she waited for her coffee to brew, she made a grocery list. She didn't want to eat out all the time. *Maybe I'll grab some frozen dinners.*

She surveyed the city from her picture window as she sipped coffee. The morning was clear, and the sun sent a white line across the glistening waters of the Charleston harbor. Fort Sumter was visible in the distance through a thin fog. Harry was right. It was a great view.

The city was waking up. A few people meandered on the sidewalk below, and only a few cars passed. She watched a young man of about fifteen delivering papers. He worked his way down the street, dropping papers by the front door or into wire baskets. He saw her watching and waved. She smiled and waved back.

She got dressed and decided to grab something to eat at a small coffee shop on the corner of Chalmers and Church— Sal's Coffee. The shop front of a pale robin egg blue with a bright butterscotch sign was hard to miss. It reminded CJ of Easter. She pushed the door open, and it chimed.

The barista gave her a big smile. "Good morning, young lady."

She smiled. "Hi there."

"I have some cinnamon muffins today. Fresh out of the oven!"

"They sound delicious. Give me one of those and a coffee, please."

"Anything for you, darling. By the way, I'm Sal."

He got her muffin and a large cup of black coffee. She paid him and found a spot at a small table on the street under an awning. CJ watched a horse-drawn carriage as it came down Chalmers Street. Chalmers was one of the few cobblestone streets left in Charleston and quite beautiful, with its gray, white, pink, and brown stones. The horse's hooves clickety-clacked as he neared. The horse was a beautiful gray color with a flowing black mane. The beefy-faced driver waved to her as he got close.

As he drew beside her, the driver stopped the horse and made a kissing sound. The horse stood and bobbed his head up and down. The driver smiled at her. "He's dancing for you."

CJ walked over to the horse. "What's his name?"

"General Lee."

She laughed. "What a perfect Southern name. He's a big boy."

"Yep. He's almost eighteen hands."

She wasn't sure what he meant. "Hands?"

"Hands are how horses are measured. You measure from the ground to the top of the back. Each hand is approximately four inches. At eighteen hands, General Lee is six feet tall."

She reached up. "Hello, General Lee."

The horse dropped his head and started nudging her ear. It tickled.

"He likes you!" the driver said.

CJ thanked him and kissed General Lee on his nose, and the horse and driver continued down the street. Clickety-clack.

She was finishing her muffin when her cell phone rang. *Back to reality.*

"Detective CJ O'Hara . . . Where was the body found? Okay, I'm on my way." She hung up and exhaled. "Well, that's one way to ruin a morning." She jogged to her truck.

The diamond-shaped towers of the Ravenel Bridge sparkled in the morning sun. Cables rising more than five hundred feet gave the bridge a spiderweb appearance. CJ turned onto Highway 517 and crossed the Isle of Palms Connector. The Intracoastal Waterway provided a blue divider between Mount Pleasant and the barrier island.

With little traffic, CJ arrived at the scene within twenty minutes. The Isle of Palms officer stood near the walkway of the End of the Island Marina. She recognized the slim woman with curly brown hair from the task force meeting.

"Officer Angie Fisk?"

"Yes. Hello, Detective O'Hara."

"CJ."

Angie nodded. She was clearly shaken up. "She's over this way. A dockhand was cleaning the area when he found her and called us. I told him to wait in the office."

CJ followed her down the walkway to a row of storage containers. The place was beautiful in the morning sun. Too bad it was all about to change.

"She's in between those two containers. Do you need me to do anything?" Angie's eyes were downcast.

"Here's some crime scene tape, and it would be a big help if you could rope off the entrance to the marina. Please keep the press away. I'll check out what we have."

Angie nodded and turned back to the marina entrance.

CJ sighed and approached the body, careful not to disturb the area any more than she needed. The tarp was open on one end. The face of a young woman with glassy eyes was visible.

She lifted the edge of the tarp so she could examine the neck and torso. There were lacerations to the throat and down the midsection. She eased the tarp back down and stood. "It's our guy." She retraced her steps back out to the walkway. A few minutes later, the CSU and ME arrived. She recognized Eddie and was happy to see Thomas. "I'd like to say good morning, but I honestly can't. Thanks for getting here so quickly, guys."

Eddie pulled on his surgical gloves. "Same guy?"

"Afraid so."

He shook his head and exhaled loudly.

Thomas stood by CJ. "The area is tight. I'll let these guys do their thing first."

CJ nodded. "There are cuts to the throat and down the midsection. She fits his type. Let's hope he left something we can use to find him."

Ben walked up. "Hey, sorry I missed you yesterday. I didn't listen to your message until late. I have some ideas for the deployment of the FBI agents once we finish here."

"No problem," CJ said. "Can you interview the dock-hand and get his statement? He's in the office."

"Sure." He turned and headed to the office.

Robert and Christy appeared as CJ watched the techs process the scene.

CJ looked up. "Hey, guys. Another day in paradise."

Robert rubbed his chin. "What time was she found?"

CJ pointed to the office. "I'm not sure. Ben is interviewing the dockhand who found her."

Robert motioned to Christy. "How about you go help him?"

"Sure. Happy to."

About an hour later, the body was loaded for transport to the morgue. Eddie and Thomas walked over to where the group was waiting.

CJ looked at Eddie. "What did you find?"

He shook his head. "Well, I've worked four of the other scenes, and this is almost identical. We found some small materials, which we collected and will analyze. Like the other victims, the tarp was new and the kind that is available everywhere."

"What kind of small materials?"

"A couple of small pieces of twine, gum wrappers, and small pieces of paper. Things like that. They weren't on the body or in the tarp, but we want to be as thorough as we can and test anything near the body."

CJ nodded. "Thomas?"

"Well, my initial report is like those for the last scenes. I noticed a new bruise on her lower back—no tattoos or other markings. I'll be able to examine her more closely at the morgue. It's our guy."

"Can you estimate the time of death?"

"My best estimate now is he killed her late last night. What time was she found?"

Ben had returned and answered. "The dockhand said he got here at six a.m. when he started his shift. He found her around six-thirty and called for help. He said he didn't touch her, but he did pull the tarp back. He said she wasn't here when he left at six p.m. yesterday. He's really shaken up. I got his cell number if we need to reach him."

CJ said she'd call Sam to have her check for any missing persons' reports. All jurisdictions were sending her notifications for missing persons, assaults, and rapes, so she had a central file. CJ thought a minute. "I'll have Sam also check for any reports of abandoned vehicles since our second victim was taken on the roadside."

Robert nodded. "Makes sense."

CJ, Ben, and the FBI agents returned to the LEC. As CJ drove, she called Sam. Sam said she didn't have any missing person reports or reports of assaults or rapes. She said she'd check if there were any reports of abandoned vehicles and let her know. CJ thanked her, hung up, and called Harry. "We have a sixth victim."

FORTY-THREE

Thursday, April 29
Downtown Charleston

CJ, Ben, and the FBI agents returned to the LEC a few minutes past ten and met in the war room. When she entered, Sam told CJ that she'd had no luck finding any reports of abandoned cars yet. However, she said she had asked all the agencies to let her know ASAP if anything popped up.

For the next two hours, the group planned the deployment of the FBI agents arriving the following day. They decided it was best to use the agents near areas with concentrated bars and restaurants, the College of Charleston, the Citadel, and the beaches at the Isle of Palms and Sullivan's

Island. As the group was finishing the assignments, Sam received a call.

"Yes, thank you. Please email me a copy of the report . . . Yes, even if it's preliminary for now." Sam hung up. "CJ, an abandoned car was reported at a parking area at the Ashley River trail near Brittlebank Park. It's a place lots of people go running and walking. I've been there. It's a beautiful place, but it's pretty secluded."

Ben added, "Yeah, I run there three or four times a week, and it's out of the way."

CJ pointed toward the window. "Isn't that across the street?" *Is this car our victim's? Is he toying with us now?*

Sam's eyes teared up. "Yes, pretty much."

"Do they know who the car belongs to?" CJ asked her.

"They're emailing me the information they have so far, and it includes the name on the vehicle registration."

CJ nodded. "Okay, good. As soon as it comes over, let's look. And Sam, please call and ask them if the car is still there."

Within five minutes, Sam had the information printed and handed it to CJ. "CJ, the officer who found the car, said it's still there. He's waiting on the tow truck."

"Please call them and make sure the car doesn't get moved yet."

Sam nodded.

CJ looked at the information Sam had handed her. "The car is registered to Elizabeth Atkins. The address shows she lives in downtown Charleston. Unfortunately, there is no photo yet, but it says she's twenty-one with blond hair and blue eyes."

Robert spoke up. "Let's split up. We need to see where the car was found and where she lived." He looked at Sam. "Sam, can you find out where she worked or went to school?"

Sam nodded and headed to her desk in the corner. "Yes, sir."

CJ looked at Ben. "Ben, can you take the agents to her home, and if we find out where she works or goes to school, see if she's there? Harry and I will take a look at the car."

Ben stood up. "Yep, can do," he said, leaving with the FBI agents.

CJ and Harry prepared to leave for Brittlebank Park, but CJ stopped and looked at Sam. "Can you ask the CSU to meet Harry and me across the road? It might be a long shot, but I have a hunch this is our victim's car, and I'd like to scour the area for any clues."

Sam nodded as she picked up the phone. "Got it."

When CJ and Harry got to the park, they found Sam was right. The abandoned car was within a few hundred yards of the LEC.

"Ballsy bastard," CJ mumbled. *Is he taunting us?*

The officer standing with the car waved her over.

CJ saw him. "Oh, great."

Harry looked at her. "What's up?"

"Nothing. The officer is my old buddy, Parker. He calls me City Girl. He told me I look more like a model than a cop. He did compliment me on how my jeans fit, though."

Harry laughed. "There's always that special one."

CJ and Harry got out of the truck. CJ looked at Officer Parker. "This the car?"

He looked at her and smiled. "Yep, City Girl. I must say, you look especially nice today."

She glared at him. This case had worn her down, and she was in no mood for his crap.

He grunted at her. "The car was locked when I got here, so I opened it and found a copy of the registration in the glove box. I also found a small wallet under the driver's seat. No license. Not much else."

CJ asked, "Who called the car in as abandoned?"

"A lady who lives near here had walked her dog late yesterday and again this morning. She called to complain that the car was parked here in a 'no overnight parking' area. I waited here for over an hour to make sure someone wasn't on the trail and coming back, then called it in as abandoned." He looked toward the road. "Damn, that tow truck is taking forever. It's a nice day, though, so it's all good."

Ben's right. This guy is an ass. "How about we take it from here? We have the CSU on the way and they can wait on the tow truck."

He shrugged and headed toward his cruiser. "Suit yourself."

CJ looked at Harry. "If this is our victim's car, then we can probably assume this is where he grabbed her. The area is isolated. There probably weren't that many people around."

Harry looked into the car's side window. "Yeah, I think that's a good assumption. Guess our alerts aren't working too well."

She shook her head and exhaled. "Guess not. How many vehicles do you think could park here at one time?"

"I'd guess maybe ten at the most," Harry said.

CJ stepped off the parking area to estimate how wide it was. "That seems about right. Hopefully, we can find some tire tracks or something useful."

The CSU pulled up, and the driver looked at CJ. "Detective O'Hara?"

CJ had hoped for Eddie. "Yes. Thanks for getting here so quickly. We're not sure yet, but we think this may be the car of the young woman who was found dead this morning."

The CSI opened the back door to his van. "Tell you what, we'll process the car for fingerprints and so on, and the area for possible clues."

"Perfect. If you start with the car, Detective O'Hara and I will walk the area and see if we see anything."

The CSI was puzzled.

CJ smiled at his confusion. "There are two Detective O'Haras. He's my uncle."

The CSI laughed and went to work. "Hey, if you find anything, there are some numbered flags in the van. You can mark it, and we'll collect it for processing."

"Will do. The ground's pretty dry, but if we find tire tracks, let's mold them."

He nodded. "No problem."

CJ and Harry got the flags out of the van and walked around the area. Every time they found a can, a piece of paper, or anything dropped, they marked it. The soil was dry, so tire tracks weren't present. At least not enough to make a mold.

CJ saw something unusual. "Uncle Harry, look at this."

He walked over. "What is it?"

CJ leaned down. "I'm not sure. Maybe just a piece of plastic." With her gloved hand, she picked the piece up. "It's the top of a cooler. Igloo." She placed it back where she had found it and flagged it. CJ walked over to the abandoned car. "How's it going, guys?"

The CSI looked up. "We're about finished here. We collected a few fingerprints on the two door handles and inside the car. We also found a coffee cup in the cupholder— we may have some DNA, but my guess is it's the owner's."

"Thanks," CJ replied. "We found some items we'd like to process for fingerprints."

He looked where she pointed. "Sure, no problem. We'll collect everything and take it back. It's easier to look for prints in the lab. We'll also look for DNA on the cans and bottles."

The tow truck arrived, so CJ thanked the CSI. "We're going to head out. Here's my card if you need to reach me."

He took the card. "Will do."

CJ walked over to the tow truck driver. "It's all yours as soon as they're done, which I expect will be any minute."

He nodded. "No problem. I'll hook it up and take it back to the impound lot. The owner can come to pay the fee and pick it up. Here's a card with the number you can give them so they can call first to be sure we're open."

CJ thanked him and took the card with the information on it as a sudden wave of sadness hit her. The owner of this car might never claim it. Her cell rang—Sam.

"Hey, Sam, what's up?"

"It looks like the car was the young woman's. I pulled her driver's license and got her photo. I sent it to the morgue, and it matches the victim."

"So, it is Elizabeth Atkins."

Sam continued. "Ben went to her house and met her roommate, who said she didn't come home last night. The roommate thought she spent the night somewhere else. She told Ben Elizabeth worked at Madeline's Bridal Shop. It's a high-end shop on Queen Street. Ben went there, and she didn't show up for work today. The shop owner said she has never missed work in the two years she worked there, and she would call if she couldn't make it."

CJ hung up and said to Harry, "Well, it looks like we have more parents that will be devastated."

Harry stared out the window. "I cannot imagine losing you."

He'd had a wonderful time last night, and the monster within him wanted more. He had to calm himself as he made sure his goodie bag was ready for the next time. Going through the back of his truck, he came across the cooler he'd used it to lure her close enough to grab her. He looked at it and then under the tarp and truck. It wasn't there. "Where in the hell is the top of my cooler?!"

A brief moment of panic hit him until he calmed himself. He was sure he had left no evidence behind. Besides, they wouldn't find it. He was too smart. *Hell, I snatched a woman right under their damn noses.* He smiled.

FORTY-FOUR

Friday, April 30
Downtown Charleston

CJ and the FBI agents had broken the area of Charleston, where most of the bars and restaurants were located, into four zones. They planned to have two FBI agents work together undercover and patrol each zone. They'd assign one agent to work with campus security for the college campuses. Since they only had ten new agents coming and eleven slots to fill, Christy would cover the College of Charleston. Since it was a lower priority, Harry would coordinate the patrols of the bars and restaurants on the Isle of Palms and Sullivan's Island with their local police departments. Robert, CJ, and Ben would split up and patrol marinas and dock areas in Charleston. They were in vehicles instead of walking, so it should work fine.

CJ was unhappy the mayor hadn't agreed to the midnight closures of the bars and restaurants. "We don't want to upset the tourists," she'd said. This meant ten-hour shifts from five p.m. to three a.m. *Politicians!*

There was something else CJ needed to deal with, and there was no time like the present. "Ben, can you and Christy give me a few minutes with Harry and Robert?"

"Sure," he said as he stood. "Christy, how about we go get some air?"

Christy gave him a big smile. "I'd love that."

CJ watched them leave. *Interesting.* "Okay, you two, sit there." She pointed to two chairs, side by side, directly across from her, and unloaded on them. "I've had it with you two! This tension between you has to stop. I won't tolerate it any further. This case is taking its toll on all of us, and your bullshit has to end."

Harry tried to interrupt. "CJ, I'm not—"

"Hold on! I'm not finished. I need both of you to help me, and that doesn't include acting like asses toward each other. Do whatever you need to do to solve this problem. Yell, punch, whatever, but get it behind you now!" CJ stormed out of the room.

Harry and Robert looked at each other, eyes wide.

Robert took a deep breath. "I'm not sure how best to do this, so I'll just do it. I owe you an apology. My arrogance and selfishness caused me to only focus on my ideas.

It could have cost two young girls their lives. I should have listened to you."

Harry was stunned. "Apology accepted. Unfortunately, even if we had used some of my ideas, we probably wouldn't have saved those girls."

Robert stuck out his hand. "New start?"

Harry took his hand, and they shook. "New start."

"Your niece is something," Robert said. "I haven't had my ass chewed like that in a long time."

The FBI agents began entering the briefing room a few minutes before ten a.m. There were eight men and two women.

Once everyone was seated, Robert looked over the room. "Welcome to Charleston. Our case is one of the most complex I've worked on in my career. Our unsub is extremely aggressive and brutal. He will not stop until we catch him, so I need everything you have so we can prevent more deaths."

He covered the profile in a straightforward and concise manner, leaving no doubt about what he expected to be accomplished. After he'd finished the profile, he covered the strategy for their deployment to priority areas. He then turned to CJ. "Detective O'Hara, your close."

CJ addressed the last questions and adjourned the briefing. "Thank you all again. We'll let everyone go to check into the hotel. Good luck, and good evening."

The agents all left the room. Robert and Christy moved from their bed-and-breakfast to the Regency Charleston Waterfront to stay with the other agents. Harry and Ben headed home to take a break until the evening.

CJ went back to the war room. "Sam, I'm going to take a little break. I need to go to the grocery store and stock my shelves, then try to get a little nap."

Sam smiled at her. "Good deal. Oh, hang on. Let me write down the address of the Piggly Wiggly. It'll have everything you need."

CJ took the paper with the address from Sam. "So, the Piggly Wiggly." She laughed, thanked Sam, and headed to the store. She laughed again when she pulled up in front of the store thirty minutes later. The sign on the front had a smiling pig wearing a butcher's hat. She wasn't sure why, but the butcher's hat made her blood run cold. This case was everywhere and in everything she saw.

Everyone was in their assigned areas by five o'clock. Even with the alerts on the news stations, in the newspapers, and across social media, young women were still out on a Friday night. As CJ drove down East Bay Street toward the Charleston port, she was shocked at just how many people were walking around downtown. *Jeez, I guess everyone thinks it couldn't happen to them.*

CJ listened to the chatter on the scanner. So far, there was nothing unusual for a Friday night. As she drove through the Port of Charleston and by the area where the first victim had been found, her cell phone rang. She recognized the CSU's number.

"Detective O'Hara," she answered.

"Hello, Detective, this is Barry over at the Latent Print Unit."

"Yes, Barry, what can I do for you?"

"We finished processing the fingerprints we found on the car. They all belonged to the victim or matched her girlfriends'. We also found a fingerprint on the cooler top. The print is only a partial, and it's not clear."

CJ's heart jumped. "Can you identify who it belongs to?"

He sighed. "Not yet. We are rerunning the print, but we don't have anything definitive yet due to its lack of clarity. We're going to keep at it, though."

"Okay, thanks. Please let me know if you find anything."

"Absolutely."

They ended the call, and CJ dialed Robert. She told him about the conversation with the lab about the latent print.

"How familiar are you with AFIS?" Robert asked.

CJ wasn't sure what Robert was asking her. *I know what AFIS is.* "I know AFIS is the Automated Fingerprint Identification System, where a fingerprint can be matched to a print in the system. Not sure what you mean."

Robert chuckled. "Correct. The key is it's not automatic. Lots can depend on how well the forensic tech can identify the minutiae to focus the search on. Reading the ridge forks and diverging points takes experience for partials.

Matching a latent is successful less than fifty percent of the time."

"Okay, that makes sense," she said. "I guess I never really watched a tech perform the analysis."

Robert laughed. "It always works like a charm on TV. Tell you what, let's have the sample sent to our guys as well. Hell, we may fly them down to check it out."

"It couldn't hurt. I'll call the lab and have them share the print."

As she continued her patrol, her emotions were all over the place. They had no clues, and a fingerprint would be huge. If they matched the print to its owner, its owner could be the unsub. On the other hand, they might not be able to find a match.

Throughout the night, agents kept checking in. So far, no one had seen anything suspicious. Just lots of young men and women out partying, and couples and families having dinner.

———

At two-thirty a.m., CJ and Robert met at the lobby of the Regency and waited for the agents to return. The desk agent had made a pot of fresh coffee for them.

CJ sat down on the couch across from Robert. "I guess it's good news, bad news. No one has seen anything useful, so hopefully, no young women have been abducted. Let's hope we won't wake up tomorrow with another body like on our past four Saturdays."

"Yes, let's hope so." He smiled at her. "So, how do you like being a lead detective so far?"

She shook her head. "To be honest, it's surreal. It seems like I've been on the case forever, but it's only been two weeks."

Robert nodded. "Definitely trial by fire, that's for sure."

"How long until you retire and get away from all this?" she asked.

Robert thought for a minute. "Well, I'm fifty-five now, so I have two more years before mandatory retirement age. I have eighteen months left."

"How do you feel about that?" she asked.

"I'm ready. It's getting harder and harder with the travel and extended time away from home. I'm a grandpa, and I'd like to get to know my grandson before he graduates from college."

"Good for you. That's got to be exciting."

He nodded. "Very much so. I plan to take some time off after retiring and spend time with my family. If I start missing the chase, I can always consult like Harry."

CJ looked at him thoughtfully. "Can I ask your opinion on something?"

"Sure."

"Do you think it's good for Harry to be back in the mix again? I asked him to help, but I feel a bit guilty about it."

He smiled. "Knowing what I do about Harry, I think it's fine. Harry wouldn't do it if he didn't want to, even if you asked. He did tell me he missed solving the puzzles. That's really what these cases are. To be honest, I imagine after a break, retirement may get old for me. It's hard to not want to help when you know you can be of use."

They sat silently for several minutes. CJ was lost in thoughts about the case and catching whoever was committing these crimes.

Robert read her face. He got up and went for another cup of coffee. As he passed her, he patted her on the arm. "We'll solve this case. This guy will not get away with this. He will pay." He winked at her. "I'm happy you straightened Harry and me out."

FORTY-FIVE

Friday, April 30
Beaufort, South Carolina

He sat drinking his beer, watching the Charleston police chief on the local news talking about him. Well, he was talking about the unsub. He didn't know it was him. He saw the FBI special agent standing there beside the chief, looking smug. He had to smile. All this effort, and they weren't even close to finding him.

He had started his rampage. His mother should have protected him, and he'd made sure she knew that now. He had to admit that he enjoyed not only getting revenge but the game of cat and mouse with these fools here in Charleston and at the FBI.

His eyes went back to the girl across the bar. She was a natural beauty, perfect for him. He wanted to go over and introduce himself, but she was sitting with a friend. He couldn't risk being seen with them. For a moment, he thought about taking them both, but that was too risky. He wasn't sure he could control two women. Besides, her friend wasn't his type. She had on a ton of makeup.

A young man came in and joined the two women. He kissed the other woman, which disgusted him. Why would anyone want her with all that makeup? He watched as they did a round of shots, then another. It was almost closing time when the young man and his girlfriend stood up. *Hmm, what's this?*

The bar was closing and emptying. He'd need to leave soon. He watched the three of them talking, and then the two young women hugged each other. The couple turned to go while his natural beauty headed toward the ladies' room. Did he have a chance?

He left the bar and went out into the parking lot, where there were only a few cars left. The parking lot was out of sight and not well lit. She came out of the side door— alone. He stood near his truck as she stumbled to her car. It was meant to be. She was parked almost right beside him.

As she neared, she looked up and smiled. "Hello."

He smiled. "Hello."

She stood at her car, digging in her purse for her keys. He could tell she'd had too much to drink.

"Listen, it's none of my business, but are you okay to drive?" he asked.

She looked up at him and laughed. "I'm not sure. Guess I'll find out."

"Can I give you a hand finding your keys?"

She pulled her keys out of her purse. "I've got them, thanks." She struggled to get her car door unlocked.

He gently placed his hand on her shoulder. "Hey, how about you leave your car here, and I'll take you home? I only had a couple of beers, so I'm fine to drive."

She looked at him, considering his offer. "I'm okay. I'd hate to put you out." She opened her car door, got in, and started her car.

He walked over to the passenger side and tapped on the window. She rolled the window down. He tried to look concerned. "I'm sure you'll be okay, but I'm worried about you driving." He lied. "I had a sister that was killed in a wreck on her way home from a bar, and it still haunts me. I won't sleep tonight wondering if you made it home safe."

She looked at him sadly. "I'm sorry about your sister."

"Thank you."

She smiled. "It's adorable that you're worried about me."

He was about to respond when he saw another patron coming to their car not far away. He squatted down so he could still look into her window, but be hard to see. There were no lights on inside her car with her car door closed. He was safe.

He tried to look concerned. "Please, let me give you a ride home. Do you want me to sleep tonight?"

She bit on her bottom lip. "Well, I guess it's the right thing to do. Are you sure you don't mind?"

He smiled. "I don't mind at all. I'm Jim, by the way."

She smiled. "I'm Maggie." She turned off her car and started to get out.

The other car had pulled away, but there were still three cars left in the lot. He wanted her to hurry before someone else came out. She was drunk and taking forever, so he went around to her side of the car. "Here, let me help you."

She reached up and took his hand. "Thanks. I think you're right. I shouldn't drive."

He put his arm around her and steered her out of the car and around the back of his truck. "I'll get you settled in, and you can tell me where you live. Wait here for a minute so I can take the junk out of your seat and put it in the back."

He reached down and opened the back of his truck. She stood there obediently with her hand around his arm. Within seconds, he had her tucked away.

CHAPTER

FORTY-SIX

Saturday, May 1
Beaufort

"We found another body."

CJ's heart sank as she listened to Helen from dispatch at just before eight o'clock on Saturday morning. She struggled to understand how this had happened with so many law enforcement personnel across the Lowcountry. She took down the address and headed for her truck and the Coosaw River Marina, northeast of downtown Beaufort. The sixty-mile drive took CJ almost an hour-and-a-half. When she arrived, two police officers walked towards her.

"Detective O'Hara?" one asked.

"Yes. Hey, guys."

"I'm Officer Wilkins, and this is Investigator Pell. We're from the Beaufort PD. Our chief told us to call you if we found anything similar to the case you're working on."

A third man walked over and introduced himself. He was the medical examiner for Beaufort County. "I'll do the autopsy unless Medical Examiner Whitehall wants to do it," he said. "We help each other out when it makes sense. I called him, and he's on the way."

CJ nodded to the three men. "Thanks for calling me. Let me look, and I can tell you quickly if this is the guy we've been chasing."

She walked over to the edge of the marsh. The young woman was lying on her back, partially wrapped in a tarp. CJ didn't need to closely examine the victim to confirm this was their guy. She stood shaking her head as the CSU team waited on her go ahead to proceed. Eddie wasn't on duty today, and she didn't recognize this team.

"Go ahead, guys. We have victim number seven," said CJ. "Let's be sure we cover every inch of the area."

Thomas arrived and squatted near the body, careful to not get too close while the techs scoured the areas for any fibers. "I'm going to give these guys some room, and then I'll do my field examination."

CJ nodded without speaking while she tried not to scream. She was beyond frustrated and wanted this perp so badly she couldn't focus on anything else. She was in a new city, and a new place to live, but consumed with wanting to stop this monster. The pace of death was almost unbearable, and she fought feelings of helplessness. She mumbled under her breath, "Focus, CJ, focus."

While the crime scene was being processed, CJ went to the marina office. The man who found the body sat alone at a small table. Billy Marr had an untouched cup of coffee sitting in front of him. As she approached, he looked up. His eyes were red and dazed.

Billy explained he had found the girl at six-thirty a.m. near the end of the marsh. He had seen seagulls and thought it was trash. The gate was locked, so someone had to have carried her there. He said he didn't know anyone who would do such a thing.

"Anything else you can remember?" CJ asked.

Billy sat for a moment. "I saw a truck leaving when I arrived."

"A truck?"

"Yeah. A black truck. I think it was a Ford Bronco."

"Did you see who was driving?"

"A White man with dark hair," he said. "I've never seen him, but I just figured he was turning around since the gate was locked—it happens a lot."

Sounds like our guy.

CJ was back at the scene when Robert, Christy, and Ben arrived, and the forensics team finished an hour later. The lead CSI walked over to them. Thomas was on one knee, still completing his field exam.

"There's not much left by whoever did this—no unusual materials except from the seagulls, which made one hell of a mess. Not much for the lab to do on this one. Sorry," the CSI said.

She shook her head. "That's exactly what we've found everywhere else—a whole lot of nothing."

While waiting for Thomas to finish, the group talked about the upcoming night's planned actions. Beaufort was over an hour away from Charleston, so they hadn't planned coverage. They agreed they'd need to rely on the Beaufort PD until they had revisited everything.

CJ noticed how Robert seemed to be watching Ben. He'd positioned himself off Ben's shoulder, slightly behind him, as Ben stared at the body. She thought Robert's actions were odd. Maybe it was her imagination.

Thomas stood, stretched, and joined the group. "I think I've got all I can get here in the field. She's been dead less than twelve hours. I'll start the autopsy as soon as I get her back, and I'll let you know if I find anything."

CJ thanked him, and everyone headed back to Charleston. They agreed to meet at the LEC at three o'clock before starting the evening surveillance shift.

As she drove, CJ called Harry and agreed to a late lunch.

FORTY-SEVEN

Saturday, May 1
Downtown Charleston

Lillie stepped out of the dressing room. She wasn't sure about her dress.

Sam clapped her hands. "That looks great on you!"

"I'm not sure. I love the floral print, and it feels really comfortable, perfect for our hot Charleston summers. Is it too short, though?"

"No. You should definitely buy it. Add a pair of flats, and you're in business."

Lillie stared at herself in the mirror. The dress was pretty, and she loved the way it fit, but it was still a bit short for her.

Sam stood and walked up behind her. "You're still worried it's too short, aren't you?"

"Yes. I only wear dresses to church, and I'd never wear this."

Sam laughed. "This isn't a church dress, silly. It's a night-on-the-town dress."

Lillie shook her head. "I don't know. What if the wind blew my dress up?"

"That won't happen, Lillie, it's not that short."

Lillie's face flushed. "I guess. I don't go out that much, and when I do, I just wear jeans or maybe a pair of shorts—no short ones."

"You do have dates, right?"

"Sometimes. I wear jeans and a nice blouse, though."

Sam watched Lillie check the price tag . . . again. *Maybe she doesn't want to spend the money.*

"I tell you what," Sam said. "You have your twenty-first birthday coming up in a couple of weeks. How about you let me get this dress for you, and if you don't have a date, I'll take you to dinner. We can go to Magnolias."

"Sam, that's really nice, but it's kinda expensive."

"Nonsense! Not for my friend. Pleeeease."

Lillie stared in the mirror. It was beautiful, and she did look good in it. "Okay, but under one condition—I take you to lunch."

"Deal! I get to pick the place, though. I want to go to Sully's."

Lillie smiled at her. "Okay." She knew Sam probably wanted to go to Sully's, so she wouldn't spend that much. She really liked her new friend.

Fifteen minutes later, Lillie and Sam got a table by the front window. Lillie's co-workers at the restaurant all stopped by to meet Sam. The owner came by and dropped off hot bread. He told them lunch was on him and recommended the new daily special of lasagna.

As they ate, they talked about how Sam liked being in law enforcement and how Lillie liked working at Sully's. They both loved what they were doing. Lillie planned to take some classes at the College of Charleston, but she would keep her job.

Finally, Sam got up the nerve to ask her something more personal. "So, how are you doing after the incident?"

"I'm fine. I try not to think about it." Lillie fidgeted with her napkin.

"Do you think it would help if you saw a professional? I know a—"

Lillie cut her off harshly. "No. I'm fine, so let's not talk about it anymore."

Sam fought tears and replied softly, "Okay. I'm always here if you want to talk."

They ate in silence until the owner returned with two slices of apple pie for dessert.

Sam reached out and put her hand on Lillie's—a little squeeze. "Only happy talk for the rest of the day."

CJ pulled into a parking spot in front of a weathered white building with a red door. Boat oars crisscrossed an American flag on the wall. *Jeez, this place is tucked away.*

"Welcome to The Wreck of the Richard and Charlene," said the hostess with a huge smile and a ponytail on her head.

Before the bubbly young woman at the desk could ask if she was meeting anyone, Harry waved to her from the ground-level back deck.

CJ smiled. "Thanks, I see my party."

"Enjoy your lunch."

Harry met CJ as she came through the door to the deck and gave her a big hug. He escorted her across the boiled-peanut-shell-laden floor. He told her he'd ordered some lightly battered fried grouper fingers as an appetizer.

"Thanks, Uncle Harry. I need a beer. I actually need a case of beer, but one will have to do since I'm working the night shift."

Harry pointed to a tub near the front door. "Here, it's help yourself—honor system. Grab what you want and tell the waitress."

CJ grabbed a Corona and sat down heavily in the wooden chair painted with bright colors.

Harry frowned. "Sorry, sweetheart. You're up for a challenge, but this case is a ridiculous way to start a new job. Even the most experienced detectives are struggling with this one."

She nodded. She felt defeated, but somehow Harry's determined face helped her.

"Listen, Cassie, I think you should assign me a zone tonight. I'm only a consultant, but I need to be out in the field."

CJ smiled. "You haven't called me Cassie since I was in high school."

Harry laughed. "Well, I was going to use Cassandra Jane, but that seemed too formal. Besides, I save that name for when you're in trouble."

She appreciated how hard Harry was working to cheer her up. "Don't use Cassie around the station. I'm already known as City Girl to most of them, and I'd hate to cause confusion."

"Okay, I'll stick to CJ. Unless I should also call you City Girl," he said, chuckling.

"No way, unless you want me to call you Harrison."

They both laughed and dug into the grouper fingers the server sat on the table.

"Oh, wow, these are delicious."

"Yeah, grouper is one of my favorites," he said. "Not too fishy, and cooked this way is perfect. We'll go catch us some when we have a chance. I'll make us a special lure." Harry pointed at the returning server. "Ah, here's your real favorite."

The server dropped off a large bowl of hush puppies.

CJ immediately reached for one. "Yes, these are my new favorites." She smiled at Harry. "Thank you. I needed this."

Harry was concerned by the angst on her face. "You have to compartmentalize cases every so often. Give your brain a break."

She nodded. "Yeah, I understand. It's difficult since this guy is killing a new victim every few days. Have you ever seen anyone kill at this pace?"

"To be honest, no. Not like this guy. I've had several multiple murderers and a couple of serial killers, but none like this one." Harry changed the subject. "Let's talk about fishing!"

CJ and Harry sat eating and talking about everything but the case for the next hour. They enjoyed the grouper and hush puppies so much they ordered another round. They swapped their beer for sweet tea, another Southern favorite. CJ needed the caffeine and sugar for the night.

CJ asked Harry about her other uncle. "Uncle Harry, you've not mentioned Uncle Craig. When will I meet him? It's hard to believe he lives here and I've never met him."

Harry rubbed his chin. "I've asked him, and I think he'll come around. Hopefully soon."

"Why won't you tell me more than just he and Dad had a falling out?"

"Jeez, CJ, it's complicated. Maybe not complicated, but hard."

She leaned over close. "I'm thirty-two-years-old and have been through about everything, including killing someone. I can handle it."

Harry stared at a boat slowly making its way down the tidal creek. He kept his eyes fixed on it. "The falling-out was over your mom. She originally started dating Craig, but he was too much of a free spirit and not interested in settling down. He was always fishing, out with the guys, or doing something without your mom. I don't think they meant for it to happen, but your dad and mom fell in love. Craig couldn't handle it. He felt like your dad stabbed him in the back, so he left for Charleston, and they never spoke again." Harry wiped his eyes. "I worked my ass off trying to mend fences, but Craig is the most stubborn person on the planet. Then your father died, and I lost any chance of reconnecting them."

CJ had tears in her eyes. "I'm not sure what to say. You two are the only family I have left, and I'd give anything to have my other uncle in my life."

"I'll keep at it. He's stubborn, but I think I'm wearing him down after almost twenty years." They got up to leave, and Harry touched her arm. "So, you ignored my request to be on the streets tonight?"

"How about you ride with me tonight? she asked. "I could use your company as I cover the marinas and docks."

"Deal! It's the perfect place for me. I'll meet you at the station."

FORTY-EIGHT

Saturday, May 1
Downtown Charleston

CJ and Harry started their rounds of the marinas, dock areas, and marine businesses at five o'clock. They listened to the agents and field teams checking in as they rode along—nothing unusual. The evening had the usual early drunks and a few minor skirmishes in a couple of the rowdy bars in the downtown area. The drunks and raucous crowd would pick up as the night wore on.

CJ's cell phone rang, and she hit the speakerphone button. "What's up, Thomas?"

She heard Thomas reply excitedly, "We may have a break!"

CJ's heart skipped a beat as she pulled to the side of the road, and Harry, who was listening, snapped to attention.

"I finished my autopsy on the young woman we found this morning. I don't think I've ever taken so long during an external exam. There was nothing of note." Thomas was almost hyperventilating.

"I decided to look at her body again from head to toe. I started my internal and removed the fishing line the unsub used to hold the midsection together. That's when I found a small hair. I'm not an expert in hair analysis, but it looks like human hair. It's not from an animal. I've triple-checked, and it can't be hers. I believe the hair is from someone's head. She's a natural blond, but the hair is dark brown."

Harry squeezed CJ's arm.

Thomas continued. "We may be able to get DNA of whoever's hair it is."

CJ's excitement went through the roof. "Holy shit! This may be the break we need."

"I know," Thomas said. "There can't be any way a hair from someone's head got inside her body cavity unless it's our guy. The forensics crew wore head covers, and even if they didn't, they couldn't get a hair inside her body."

"When will we hear about the DNA?" she asked.

"I've sent a tech with the sample to Columbia. The SLED guys have the best hair analyst. They're making it their top priority. I expect to have something in the next few days. I can't tell if we got much of the follicle, which is where we'd find DNA. Hair strands won't help us."

CJ tried to calm herself. "Thanks, Thomas. This is great news. I'll let the FBI know and let's keep this quiet for now."

"Got it. No problem. Let's not get our hopes up until we have a result."

"Too late," she said. "My hopes are sky high."

CJ turned to Harry when she finished the call, who pumped his fist. "This is what we've needed," she said. "We have the partial print, which isn't helpful by itself, but coupled with DNA, we're hot on the unsub's tail."

CJ hit the speed dial for Robert. She told him about the hair that had been found. Like her, he was excited this could be their break. He asked her to keep the information between them for now, but she could tell the captain. *Okay . . .*

"Should we at least tell Ben since he's been with me on this case from day one?"

"No, no one else but the captain for now."

They hung up. CJ looked over at Harry, who was staring out the window.

"Uncle Harry, I agree with Robert. We need to keep this tight for now, but I sense I'm missing something."

Harry nodded. "There's more to the story. Your senses are right. Robert knows something or has a hunch he's not shared." He saw her bristle. "Don't take it personally. Robert is damn good at what he does, and he has a reason for being tight-lipped. In the past, I'd think he wanted to be the one to solve the case for his glory, but he's moved on. I think he has a hunch, and he's not sure it's real yet."

CJ nodded slowly. "Okay, I'll try not to let it bug me. We may have great news, and we just need this guy off the streets and locked away somewhere."

"That's the number one thing," Harry said. "Get this asshole, and quick. Everyone in the Lowcountry can celebrate it as a huge win."

She smiled at him. "When we solve this one, I'm buying."

"I'll put that in my notes," he said, chuckling.

The night shift ended and, like the night before, there was nothing to report and no new leads.

CJ and Harry met Robert in the Regency lobby for a quick recap a little after two o'clock in the morning. It had been a long forty-eight hours, and all three were ready for a night's sleep. They had agreed to take Sunday off and reconvene early Monday unless the killer had other plans.

CJ had just walked into her apartment when her cell phone rang. "Hey, Ben."

"You weren't asleep, were you?" he asked.

"No, not yet, but I hope to be soon. I'm beat."

"Yeah, me too. I wanted to invite you to go out on the boat with me and my dad tomorrow, since we're taking the day off."

CJ was undressing as she talked to Ben. "Yeah, that would be fun. I was hoping to make the nine o'clock Mass."

"No worries. I wasn't planning to go early. How about we go to my dad's place around noon? We can eat lunch and then ride around in the boat for a bit."

"Okay, sounds good. How about I call you after I get out of Mass?"

"Perfect. Sleep well."

CJ was in bed within minutes. For the first time since she had arrived in Charleston, she fell asleep without lying there for hours, thinking about the case.

FORTY-NINE

Sunday, May 2
Johns Island, South Carolina

CJ woke up, not feeling like death warmed over. She'd gotten up once to pee, but managed to get a decent night's sleep. She felt like they were closing in on the unsub. She showered, dressed, and planned to grab breakfast before going to Mass. She peered out the window. It was going to be a beautiful day, so she'd walk to breakfast and church.

Usually, Harry would meet her for Mass, but he had decided to go fishing since working on the case had taken so much of his time. CJ smiled as she thought about Harry's comment, "I'll be sure I pray while I'm out on the boat."

After she got home from Mass, she called Ben. "I'm back home. Do you want me to meet you somewhere?"

"I'll pick you up in front of your apartment in about fifteen minutes, if that works?" Ben said.

"Okay. Just call me when you're downstairs, and I'll come down."

She hung up and went to change. The day would be warm, so she put on a pair of shorts, a T-shirt, and tennis shoes. She grabbed a light jacket just in case.

Ben arrived and picked her up. He introduced her to Jake, who immediately licked her face. "He likes you," he said.

CJ scratched Jake behind the ears. "You're a handsome boy."

Ben's father lived on Johns Island, about thirty minutes away. They agreed on the way over there would be no talk about the case today. They both needed to clear their heads.

Ben took the bridge over the Ashley River as they left downtown Charleston. It was beautiful. CJ loved the boats, and she had her window down, so the breeze hit her face, and she smelled the salty air.

"This is the first time I feel like I'm seeing the Charleston area."

Ben chuckled. "Yeah, when your eyes aren't peeled for serial killers, it's a different view."

CJ sat quietly, staring at the seagulls that circled overhead. In the distance, she saw the marshes and tidal creeks. The Atlantic Ocean sparkled. In some ways, the surroundings reminded her of Boston, with lots of boats and water. She loved how much natural beauty there was so close to the city. She remembered she'd promised to take a tour of Charleston with Harry.

"Ben, is that another river?" she asked, pointing out what she'd seen.

"The Stono River. We have lots of rivers here. Let's see, we have the Ashley, Stono, Wando, Cooper, Wadmalaw, Edisto, North Edisto, Kiawah, Folly, and Dawhoo." Ben laughed. "To name a few."

Ben's father's house was on the Wadmalaw River. The home and setting reminded her of Harry's place, with the same beachy appearance and no doubt a big deck on the back. She could see a large boat docked behind the house.

"Wow, Ben, that's a big boat. Much larger than Harry's."

"Yeah, my dad loves that boat. Although I keep telling him he can't go offshore, he goes too far out. I worry about a storm kicking up and him getting caught in it. He has a larger boat that he keeps at Shem Creek. He should only go offshore in it rather than the smaller one, but he's stubborn sometimes."

CJ got out of the car. "Does your dad still work?"

"He does. He's a commercial fisherman and has been all his life."

CJ smiled as an older version of Ben came around the side of the house. Like Ben, he was six-four with dark brown hair starting to gray. "Hey, guys."

"Hey, Dad. This is CJ." He pointed to his dad. "My dad, Bill."

Bill hugged his son and looked at CJ. "Son, this day will be a whole lot better with this beautiful lady on board." He clapped his hands. "Let's eat!" He held out his arm, and CJ took it. "I'll escort you around back. The grill is ready, so I hope you're hungry."

"I'm starved."

They sat on the deck having a beer while Bill finished grilling burgers. The smell of the burgers and salty air was a nice blend, especially with the breeze coming off the water. CJ had to admit the burger tasted great. Bill had fried potatoes and coleslaw as sides, and she laughed when he came back from the kitchen with a massive bowl of hush puppies.

"CJ, try one of these. I make the best damn hush puppies in the Lowcountry. The secret is just the right amount of powdered sugar and a touch of cinnamon. Since they're sweet, they're good before and after a meal."

Ben listened as his dad and CJ talked about everything from fishing to what CJ did in Boston as they ate. He didn't think he'd seen his dad light up like this since his mom had been around. He could barely remember her since he had been so small when she left them. It made him happy that his dad was enjoying this, and it was good for CJ, too.

His dad was right. CJ was beautiful. Her autumn hair and emerald-green eyes complemented her face, and he had to admit she had a perfect figure. She wore almost no makeup and didn't need it. She was a natural beauty.

After they had finished lunch, they got ready for the boat. Bill looked at CJ. "You want to fish or just ride around?"

She smiled. "I'm game either way."

Ben suggested they ride first so CJ could see Charleston from the water. Bill agreed, and Ben knew he would enjoy telling CJ about the history of Charleston.

Bill extended his hand. "Let's go for a ride."

Bill backed the boat out and turned into the middle of the Wadmalaw River. He pushed the throttle forward, and CJ felt the boat surge. She sat on a bench along the railing. The spray of the water felt great on her face.

Bill yelled, "You're not getting too wet, are you?"

CJ put her hands up. "No, it feels invigorating."

They continued down the Wadmalaw River to the North Edisto River before entering the Atlantic Ocean. The sun was warm on CJ's face, and the mixture of water spray and the breeze made it perfect.

Bill told her to come stand beside him at the bridge. She staggered back as the boat rocked from the waves, and she laughed loudly. "I guess my sea legs haven't kicked in yet."

CJ stood alongside Bill, and he told her what they passed on their left. "That is Seabrook Island, and coming up is Kiawah Island. They play lots of professional golf tournaments there. Be sure to go there when you can. Both are really nice."

They passed Folly Beach, and soon they were at the mouth of where the combined Ashley and Wando rivers made up the Charleston harbor and exited to the ocean. Bill told CJ they'd keep going and come back so he could show her Sullivan's Island and the Isle of Palms.

CJ was impressed with the beaches on both barrier islands. Worry crept in when she saw several young women lounging in the sun alone. Her anxiety eased when she saw an officer driving along the beach on his four-wheeler. *At least we're watching.*

As they came back down the shore, Bill swung into Shem Creek, where numerous restaurants lined the shore. CJ found her mind going to the bodies found at Shem Creek and Sullivan's Island. She did her best to put those thoughts out of her mind. *Only happy thoughts today. Only happy thoughts.*

Bill turned the boat into the Charleston harbor and toward Fort Sumter. Ben was right. Seeing Charleston from the water was vastly different from seeing it from the land. They passed Patriots Point Naval Museum, and Bill pointed out the USS *Yorktown*, which was docked at the museum. Bill told CJ this ship had been used in World War II and it had recovered the Apollo 8 space capsule after its orbit of the moon. Ben smiled as his dad went on and on about the history of Charleston.

Finally, Bill looked down at CJ. "Okay, time for you to drive."

"Are you sure?"

"Yep. You ever driven a boat?"

"Only a little. My uncle will take me out more, but we haven't had a chance yet."

Bill showed her the controls and stepped back. She steered the boat past Drum Island to where the Cooper River and Wando River first came together and back along Charleston's shore. As they exited the harbor, Bill took back the controls. He sped the boat up, and CJ was flying. With every wave they hit, she giggled and laughed. Ben and Bill enjoyed watching her have so much fun. Bill eased the boat into the dock. Ben jumped off, rope in hand, and tied up the boat.

Bill smiled. "Did you have fun, CJ?"

"I had the best time. Thank you so much for taking me."

"You're welcome."

It was late afternoon, so they sat on the deck and watched the sun start to set. Bill brought out some chips, dip, snacks, and more hush puppies. Ben focused on the chips and French onion dip, Bill ate pretzels, and CJ went for the hush puppies. Bill was happy to provide her with more history of Charleston.

CJ listened to Bill tell her that Charleston had been founded in 1670 and originally called Charles Towne. The city had grown and, for a brief period in the American Revolution, had been held by the British. The city later survived eighteen months of siege during the Civil War. Since its founding, the city had stood through wars, hurricanes, and earthquakes.

"The old lady has been through a lot, but she still stands as strong as ever," he said.

CJ smiled. *Sounds like my life—battered and bruised, but still standing.* "Bill, how was Ben growing up?"

He smiled. "He was a good kid. Always loved to go on the boat with me."

Bill continued talking about Ben's childhood and how proud he was that he had graduated from the Citadel and served his country. Ben tried to intervene when he talked about Ben's forays with his girlfriends. CJ laughed at them as they went back and forth. Bill spilled the secrets, and Ben tried to stop him.

"Am I missing the party?" asked a voice.

Everyone turned to see Ben's older brother, Will, coming up on the deck. He was a mirror image of Bill. He had to be six-foot-three, with dark brown hair, and the same facial features. Ben had the same height and hair color, but his face was somewhat softer. CJ thought maybe the time on the water gave Bill and Will their more rugged look. However, she had to admit that all three men were attractive. Even Bill didn't look like he was in his late fifties.

Will asked Ben for help to unload a boat motor from his truck. The two men got up and headed to the front yard. Bill brought CJ another beer and sat beside her.

"Bill, thank you again for today. I needed it."

"I enjoyed it," he said. "How is it working with Ben?"

"It's good. He's a good officer, and we're all working our tails off."

"Yeah, this is a mess with all these murdered young women. I've never seen anything like this here in Charleston."

CJ nodded, and her throat tightened. "Yes, it's terrible."

Bill patted her on her shoulder. "Let's change the subject."

"Works for me."

Bill and CJ continued to talk while Ben and Will moved the motor. They struggled to push the cart with the motor across the yard to the boathouse. Both swore as they went.

CJ laughed and yelled, "Be careful, boys."

CJ wasn't sure how they'd gotten on the subject, but her family's loss came up. Bill listened to her quietly as she told him how she had lost her parents and sister when she was eleven.

Bill rubbed her arm. "I'm so sorry—it's tough to lose loved ones. I guess sometimes God calls his angels early." He stared at his shoes. "I'm sure Ben told you we lost his brother, and my wife left us. It was too hard for her. I guess she blamed me."

"He did tell me," CJ said, nodding. "I'm sorry for you and him."

They sat there until Bill decided it was time for key lime pie. "Enough sadness. It's pie time."

CJ smiled and stood. "You need me to help you?"

"No. I'll grab the pie, plates, and forks and be right back."

As he cut the pie, Ben and Will returned. Ben had grease all over his hands.

CJ watched Will clean some fish he had caught earlier. He was quick with the knife and very skilled. Blood covered his hands and forearms.

Pointing to the house, she said, "You boys got dirty. Go wash your hands."

They both laughed. "Yes, ma'am."

They went inside to wash up. Returning, the four sat and ate the pie Bill had plated.

CJ licked her lips. "Ben, I may have another new favorite. This pie is delicious."

Bill winked at her. "The secret is to use fresh limes. The tarter, the better."

They had a cup of coffee with their pie and watched the sun as it slowly dropped below the horizon. The last light had a reddish-yellow color as the seagulls dotted the dim sky. CJ and Ben agreed it was time to head back. Tomorrow would be a busy day. Bill walked them out to Ben's truck and hugged CJ.

"It was so nice to meet you. You come back anytime, with or without Ben."

"Thanks. I will, and when you get into downtown, please let me know."

Bill winked at her. "It's a date."

Ben and CJ talked about their day as they drove back to Charleston. They agreed it was a welcome break from the work grind. CJ told Ben she was impressed with Bill's knowledge of Charleston.

"Yeah, my dad has been all over the area. He knows every nook and cranny. Part of it is from his time on the boat. The other part is he loves to wander."

"Have you talked to your dad about the case much?" she asked.

"No. Like most people, he gets his information from the local news channels and the *Post and Courier*." Ben looked over at her. "Why do you ask?"

"Just wondered. It came up in our conversation, but we didn't talk about it." She stared out at the moon's reflection on the water. "Will seems nice."

"Yeah, I'm happy he works with my dad. I worry about Dad being out on the water by himself. He's been stranded at sea more than once. Once, about five years ago, during a bad storm, his boat capsized, and he nearly drowned. Having Will around makes me feel better. He keeps him from going out alone anymore. Besides, Will is around the house every day, so my dad's not alone."

"Does Will live with your dad?"

"No. He has a small place a few miles away. He's never been married—a lifelong bachelor."

CJ looked out the window at the lights of Charleston. "I hate to end such a nice day with the case, but tomorrow should be another busy day. Robert has two people for us to interview."

"Suspects?" Ben asked.

"I'm not sure, but his researcher has been pouring through locals who fit the profile in general. I'm not sure what to think, but maybe we'll get lucky."

Ben shook his head. "Not sure we can find our guy using a computer."

"We can only hope, I guess."

As Ben got into the downtown area, he asked her if she wanted to stop for a drink or a late dinner.

"I appreciate the offer, but I'm tired after the day on the boat. I'd like to get to bed early."

"No worries. We need to get some rest for the week."

Ben pulled up in front of CJ's apartment. "I'm glad you went today. I think my dad enjoyed it more than we did, and he has a crush on you." There was a pause before he spoke again. "If I'm honest, I do, too."

She ignored his last remark. "Thanks again. See you tomorrow."

Ben watched as she headed up the stairs. *Damn it, I keep screwing up. The last thing she probably wants is some guy chasing her.*

CHAPTER

FIFTY

Sunday, May 2
Downtown Charleston

He'd enjoyed his Friday night treat. Who knew he'd find such natural beauty in a no-name bar in Beaufort? He had only stopped for a drink when he saw her. When opportunity knocks, you answer.

She may have been his favorite so far. The carpet didn't match the drapes most times, but she was a natural blond. Even after all she'd had to drink, she had put up a good fight. She had an incredible scream. He replayed the night's events in his mind.

He watched the delicate young woman as she busily brought food out. She had a warm smile for everyone, and he could tell it was genuine. Her electric-blue eyes sparkled, and her long golden hair flew as she hurried around.

He wished he were in her section, but he had to be cautious. He wasn't sure if she'd gotten a good look at him. *Stupid, stupid, stupid.*

It would be a disaster if she recognized him, but he had to know if he was safe. He knew she had gone to the police station and reported him. The only way to tell if he was safe was to let her see him.

He waited while she made her rounds. She went to each table, checked on her guests, and topped off their coffees. When she got close enough, he raised his hand to get her attention. He barely breathed as she approached.

Lillie smiled at him. "Yes, sir, can I help you?"

He smiled. "Ah, yes. I'd love a little more coffee. The young lady helping me is so busy I thought I'd see if you could help."

"Absolutely, no problem." She poured coffee into his cup. "Can I do anything else for you?"

He could think of several things she could do for him, but that would come later. "No, thank you. I'm good for now."

She smiled. "If you change your mind, please let me know."

As she walked away, he suddenly breathed easily.

Soon, my dear Lillie, I will let you help me. Soon.

PART FOUR

ENDGAME

FIFTY-ONE

Monday, May 3
Downtown Charleston

CJ met Robert for breakfast at the Regency at seven at his request. He wanted to meet before going into the station. Robert was standing in the lobby waiting for her when she arrived. They found a table in the far back of the restaurant.

CJ stared at Robert. "I need to ask you something."

He was expressionless. "Ask away."

"There's something you're not telling me."

"Really?" he asked.

She looked him straight in the eyes. "Really."

He smiled at her. "I like you. You're damn smart and even more perceptive. I like your direct approach."

He was stalling and CJ's internal temperature went up, so she leaned into him. "So, spill."

"Okay. Here's the deal. I've had a researcher comb through everyone in Charleston who fits the profile. It's an academic exercise, but I've used it many times to narrow the field of possible suspects. I have a list I want us to work through."

She nodded. "You told me you had a couple of possibilities for us to talk about today. What are you not telling me?"

"There are a couple on the list I haven't told you about."

"Who?"

"Two cops. One is your buddy, Officer Parker. When he was in college, he was accused of two date rapes. The school handled it internally and couldn't or wouldn't prove he was guilty."

She shook her head. "It's maddening when schools don't get law enforcement involved. Do we know anything about the two cases?"

Robert flipped open a file. "The first was at a fraternity party. The girl said he forced her into a bedroom and raped her. Problem is she was drunk, and it was a classic, 'he said, she said.' Parker said it was consensual, and there were no witnesses. In the second case, the victim said she was drugged. She said she only had one drink at a party before feeling dizzy. Her friends put her in a bedroom. Parker allegedly came in and threatened her with a knife. No one saw anything. Again, it was a 'he said, she said.'"

CJ's pulse rate picked up. "A knife?"

"That's what the file says."

"And the second cop?"

Robert shifted in his chair. "Ben."

Ben? What the hell! CJ shook her head. "How could it be Ben? What's in his past to make you include him?"

"He fits the profile, he matches the researcher's screening criteria, and his prints match the pattern. Plus, he has two incidents in his past."

Her heart skipped, and her hand went to her mouth. "What?"

"At the Citadel, a young woman accused him of rape at a party and, in the marines, he was accused of attempted rape at knifepoint. We don't have the details about how either of these allegations were resolved yet, but they're in the record."

She struggled to breathe. *No, no, no.* It couldn't be Ben. He had been on the case before she was. He couldn't have committed these horrific murders. She rubbed her face. "Now I understand why you didn't want me to tell Ben about finding the hair with our last victim."

"Correct," he said.

"And it's why you've been watching him so closely?"

"You noticed?"

She smirked. "Yep."

He nodded. "Harry's right. You're going to be a top-notch detective. Nothing gets past you."

A young woman with red curly hair came to take their order. They gave her what they wanted and waited until she had left.

CJ was still irritated. "How does your researcher do what they do?"

"She's a bulldog. You give her a profile and an area, and she will find anyone who matches and provide a list. She will then preliminarily research where those people were on dates matching the crimes. It's not exact, but it gives you a solid list to run down possible suspects."

"You've done this before?" she asked.

"Many times, and before you ask, her lists have helped me solve multiple cases in the past."

CJ nodded. "Well, it's worth a shot. I'm hopeful we'll get DNA from the hair, and we have a partial fingerprint."

He nodded. "We can hope. My concern with the hair is it's only trace evidence. We have hair, but only part of the follicle. It makes getting DNA tough, and it won't be as certain."

There was a long pause in their conversation.

Finally, Robert said, "Look, trust me on this. You're concerned about Ben being on the list, but I'll handle that. Let's let it play out."

"Wait! If Ben is on your radar, why wouldn't his dad and brother also be potential suspects based on physical and fingerprint similarities?" The sight of Will cleaning the fish flashed into her mind.

"They meet most of the criteria, but Bill is too old to be our guy. Will appears to have been out of town fishing during the period two of our victims were abducted based on airline info my researcher uncovered. We'll confirm it, of course."

CJ was numb. "Who knows about this?"

"You, me, and my researcher."

Their food arrived, and Robert ate while CJ stared at her plate. Robert headed back to his room when they finished, and CJ headed to the LEC, still unable to wrap her head around their conversation. *It can't be Ben.*

She told herself she had to let it play out, as she'd agreed, to prove the FBI wrong. She wanted to call Harry, but knew she had best keep it to herself. At least for now. She also could not let Ben know he was on some list the FBI had pulled together.

Ben was a good cop, and she was getting closer to him. *Closer to him.* She had ignored his "crush" comment last night, but she was afraid she felt the same way about him. She had made the mistake of getting too close to a coworker before. *That was a royal cluster!*

———

Robert, Christy, CJ, Ben, and Harry met in the war room at eight a.m. They had two main objectives. First, review the weekend's activities and adjust the FBI agents' coverage for the week. Second, review the list of profile matches the FBI researcher in Quantico had provided. CJ was interested in how Robert would spin the list since two Charleston PD officers were on it.

As usual, Sam was busy getting coffees for everyone, and she brought a buttermilk breakfast cake for them. She had already been there long enough to have the case file updated and copied.

CJ noticed a new addition to the war room. "Sam, we have a new evidence board."

Sam smiled. "Yes. I hope it's okay with you. I had another board brought in, so I could spread out the information on the victims." She sniffed. "There are too many victims for one board."

"This makes it easier to see our info, and you've rearranged everything well," CJ said. "Let's hope we won't need any more space."

They all stood looking at a map of the zones they had covered over the weekend. Sam had color-coded the chart on the wall, so the FBI agents' zones were blue. The zones local law enforcement covered were green. CJ noticed something else new.

"Sam, what do the red and orange flag pins with numbers mean?"

"I added those to show where each victim was abducted and found. The red flag pins are where we believe they were abducted. The orange flag pins are where the bodies were found. The numbers on each are the victim numbers."

Robert smiled at Sam. "I love that you took the initiative on this. I may steal you away and take you back to Quantico with me."

Sam beamed. "Thanks, but I'll have to pass. I'm a Lowcountry girl."

They spent the next hour discussing the locations young women had been taken and where they had been found. Could they find a pattern? It was hard to tell since the area was so large, and there didn't appear to be logic to the locations. The real prize would be narrowing down where the unsub took the young women to kill them. Sadly, it wasn't clear.

Harry stared at the map. "This perp has us strung out from Beaufort to North Charleston. His capture spots have been a college campus, bars, restaurants, jogging trails, and the side of the damn road. Our only consistency is he drops bodies near marinas, docks, and marine businesses. He does like marshes on the edge of drop areas."

Robert nodded. "It's not a short list either. At this point, all we can do is keep focusing on areas with higher concentrations of young women and the typical drop areas."

"So, other than adding the Beaufort PD to cover us to the south, we keep the plan the same?" CJ asked.

Robert sighed and nodded. "Yes, that's our best approach."

They took a short break while Sam got their assigned point persons on a conference call for each department. She did a roll call and gave CJ a thumbs-up to indicate everyone was present. CJ went over the latest on the case, and everyone returned to work.

Everyone dug into the cake Sam had brought. As they ate, they talked more about the evidence board. The group discussed interviews with those on the list of individuals who met the profile. Robert explained how the list had been developed and those on the list so far. Finally, he went to the whiteboard, where he had written down some bullet points.

"My researcher in Quantico takes the profile and then combs through records to find persons who match. She alyzes which may have been in the area at the time of the murders. The last step is determining if there are alibis, but we'll cover that as part of the interviews.

"The downside is my researcher can only cover people who reside here—transients or visitors are not captured. Remember, though, our profile points to a local and someone who knows the area."

Ben asked, "So a local would be who?"

"Someone who has lived here for at least a year. The list includes how long the person has lived here."

Harry nodded. "Casting a wide net and narrowing the field makes sense. I've used this approach before."

Robert said he had four names on the initial list, and he started writing on the board. CJ's heart pounded. *Is he going to list Officer Parker and Ben?*

Robert wrote down the first name. "The first person is Peter Martz. He's a doctor at the Medical University." He continued. "The second person is Richard Johns. He's a chef at the culinary academy. The third person is Aaron Ward. He's a psychology professor at the College of Charleston." He added the fourth name. "The last person on the list so far is Ricky Floyd. He's a supervisor at Crocker's Fish and Shrimp. They're a fish and seafood processor."

He sat back down at the table. "There are a couple more people, but we need a little more vetting before we interview them. I'd like CJ and I to take the first two. Harry, you and Ben take the third and fourth. It's Monday, and these individuals should be at their places of employment. Let's hit them right after lunch.

"As part of our interview, let's ask them to volunteer to have their fingerprints and a DNA sample collected. We'll take a tech with us. The key to our initial interview is to determine if they have an alibi for the dates of our murders. We also want to read how they respond."

CJ heard her phone chime with a text. It was Thomas, telling her the seventh victim's parents were coming in later in the day to identify the body. CJ exhaled. That relaxed feeling from yesterday's boat ride with Ben was long gone.

"Come in, guys."

CJ and Ben dropped down into chairs across from Stan. She handed him a sheet of paper. "Cap, we wanted to brief you on where we stand with Elrod Harris. The district attorney is moving ahead with charges for all four victims. The woman who he was caught with, a second rape his DNA connected him to, and two more rapes based on the DNA found on the underwear he had in his house."

Stan looked at the paper. "What's the DA thinking?"

CJ replied. "Four counts of sexual assault and battery."

"Is the DA happy with the evidence we provided?"

"Yes," she said. "The first case is rock-solid. Elrod was caught in the act, and the victim and the witness who called it in will testify. The second case is good since his DNA was found on the victim. He wore a mask, so she'll testify to recognizing his voice and appearance."

"How about the last two?"

"He wore a mask, so the victims didn't see his face, but they will testify it was the underwear they were wearing when they were raped," CJ said. "They will also attest to recognizing his voice. The DA said the statute calls for up to twenty years as a felony and he'll go for four consecutive twenty-year sentences, classifying him as a serial rapist. If convicted, it's basically a life sentence."

Stan nodded slowly. "Are our witnesses solid to testify? As you know, rape victims often decline."

CJ nodded. "They are. The DA, Ben, and I have spoken to all of them. They're pissed and ready to go to court. We'll keep a close eye on them to make sure they show."

"Have we ruled him out as the Lowcountry Killer?" Stan asked.

CJ sighed. "Yes. He was in a cell for the last four murders."

Stan turned to Ben. "Any updates on Jefferson?"

"He's been off our list," Ben said. "He's the wrong race and has been in jail for the last three murders. He'll go down for kidnapping and attempted rape. His father's a doctor and hired a good lawyer, but it looks like he'll take a plea."

"Okay, good work, you two. At least we've got these scumbags off the street."

FIFTY-TWO

Monday, May 3
Downtown Charleston

After lunch, CJ and Robert went to the Medical University and waited for Dr. Martz in a small meeting room. The nurse indicated he would be available within ten to fifteen minutes when he finished his rounds. She said she'd bring them a cup of coffee while they waited.

A few minutes later, a tall man with dark brown hair walked into the room. His cheekbones were high, and he had a Roman nose. "I'm Dr. Peter Martz. How can I help you?"

CJ and Robert introduced themselves, and the three of them sat down at a small table.

Robert cleared his throat. "Detective O'Hara and I are working on the case of the seven murdered young women here in Charleston. We're talking to several people to see if they can help us."

Dr. Martz raised his eyebrows. "Not sure how I can help. Why me?"

"You fit the general profile."

"What profile?"

Robert rattled off the profile. "Thirty- to forty-five-year-old White male, dark hair, six-foot-three to six-foot-four inches tall, two hundred ten to two hundred twenty pounds, athletic build, local to the area, and skilled with a knife."

Dr. Martz leaned back in his chair. "Wow! Quite a list."

Robert kept his eyes locked on him.

Dr. Martz squirmed and shook his head. "I may be those things, but I'm no killer. I'm a healer."

Robert slid a list across the table. "Can you tell me where you were on these dates?"

Dr. Martz picked up the list. "I can check my day planner for more accurate details, but I was in town for all these dates except for April 16 and 17. I was at a medical conference in Columbia from the evening of the fifteenth until I returned on the eighteenth. I led panels on Friday and Saturday."

Robert wrote down the dates. "Is there someone who can confirm your attendance at the conference?"

"Sure. I can give you the contact details of the conference chairperson and a copy of the travel expense report with the receipts. Let's go to my office, and I'll get you what you need."

Robert stood. "Sounds fair. Then we can go, and you can return to your patients."

The three of them went to his office. He wrote down the names and numbers of people who could verify he had been at the conference. He pulled the expense reports and called his assistant to copy them.

Robert stared at the frames behind his desk. "What type of doctor are you?"

"I'm a gastrointestinal surgeon. I focus on the digestive system. I removed a gall bladder earlier today."

His assistant brought the copies back to him, and he handed them over. Robert thanked him and said, "One last item would be helpful. Would you be willing to give us your fingerprints and a DNA sample, so we don't bother you again?"

Dr. Martz exhaled. "Yes. If you send someone over, I'm happy to. I have nothing to hide."

"I'll have a tech come in shortly," Robert said.

The doctor was stunned. "No time like the present, I guess."

CJ and Robert left the hospital. They agreed the doctor wasn't their guy, but they'd verify his time out of town. It was better to be safe than sorry.

As CJ drove to their next suspect, she thought about how Robert had conducted the interview. Direct and to the point. He had almost challenged the doctor. "I assume your direct technique was to provoke a response?" she asked.

Robert smiled. "Yes. I can read a person when they're under stress. He wasn't concerned, which tells me he's not our guy. If he misleads me, he'll run, and we'll hunt him down. I have alerts with the airlines in case he tries to leave the country."

"Makes sense."

When they arrived at the Culinary Institute of Charleston, they asked the receptionist to call Richard Johns for them.

The woman looked concerned as she picked up the phone. "He's in class, but his assistant will get him." She pointed to a door down the hall. "If you want to wait in the conference room over there, I'm sure it won't take long."

They were soon joined by another six-foot-four man with raven-black hair in chef attire minus the hat. As with their last interviewee, it appeared Chef Johns wasn't their guy. He had been on a weekend sailing trip from April 23 to April 25. The chef gave them names and numbers to verify this. He also agreed to be fingerprinted and provide a DNA sample.

It was after six when CJ and Robert joined Harry and Ben in the war room and went through what they had found in the four interviews. Out of the four persons interviewed that day, only Ricky Floyd was a possibility. He matched the profile and, unlike the other three, had been in town on the critical dates. Ricky had provided alibis, but they needed to check them out. He'd declined being fingerprinted or giving them a DNA sample.

Harry picked up an evidence bag containing a soda can. "On the forensic samples, Mr. Floyd forgot his can, so I collected it. I'll head over and drop it with one of our techs. It should solve our fingerprint and DNA issue."

Sam interrupted them. "CJ, Lillie called and asked if she could talk to you."

CJ's breath caught. "Is she okay?"

"She said she was fine, but remembered something else she wanted to tell you. She's at work at Sully's until eight this evening, and you could come by anytime."

"Okay, thanks. I'll swing by on my way home."

The door opened, and Stan appeared. He pointed at CJ. "In my office now."

She got up immediately and followed him out of the door to his office.

"Sit!" Stan leaned forward and looked at her. "Someone has leaked case information to the press."

CJ's mouth dropped open. "What?"

"I'm not sure who, but the chief wants to talk." Stan hit the button on the speakerphone.

"Stan, who in the hell leaked this information?" Chief Williams spat over the phone.

"We're not sure—"

"You damn well better find out who, and I mean quick. I wanna know who did it, and there'll be hell to pay! I'm sick of this department getting raked over the coals by the press. Find out who gave Wendy Watts details that will jeopardize us doing our jobs."

"Yes, sir."

Stan hit the end button on the speakerphone and glared at CJ. "The chief is as mad as I've ever seen him. Who has access to the war room?"

"The two FBI agents, Ben, Harry, Sam, myself, and you. No one else has been given the access code, and the door locks automatically. We don't even allow the room to be cleaned by the janitor."

"Well, I know I sure as hell didn't give that witch Watts our files," Stan said.

CJ's face flushed. "Stan, there's no way any of the five who have access gave out the information. We're all working our asses off to catch this guy, and no way would jeopardize that. We've had briefings. Some of the information could have come from someone else outside our core team, but some information wasn't covered in our briefings."

The media was camped in the LEC's parking lot, all clamoring for a statement. Wendy Watts's opening statement on the six o'clock news had stirred up a hornet's nest: "Charleston has a ruthless rapist and murderer running loose. Charleston PD and their new female detective are totally clueless."

Her story covered confidential information of each case—complete with all the gory details. Thankfully, the crime scene photos were too grotesque to show, but the deceased's parents were furious. The Charleston PD and CJ looked like fools, and giving out specific details made it harder to solve the case.

Stan sat with his face in his hands. "Jesus Christ. This is a fucking disaster. You lead the task force, so find out who did this. I wanna know sooner than later."

CJ stood and mumbled, "Yes, sir."

CJ got to Sully's Restaurant around seven-thirty p.m. and watched Lillie take orders from a table of six women in their late fifties. *Girls' night out, perhaps.*

Lillie smiled when she walked past CJ on her way to the kitchen. "I'm slammed, but if you can wait about thirty minutes, I'll take a quick break. I may be here a little late."

CJ smiled. "No problem. Tell you what, I'll grab a table and order some dinner."

Lillie waved to the hostess and asked her to seat CJ in her section. The hostess said she'd have a table in a few minutes. She pointed to one where a man was finishing up at a two-top near the back.

Lillie hustled to the kitchen to drop off her latest orders. CJ watched her as she went from table to table. She had a pleasant disposition and a sweet smile, which only added to her natural beauty. Her shoulder-length blond hair and piercing blue eyes made her stand out. Sadly, it also made her a target of sickos, like their perp.

CJ had settled at her table when Lillie took her order. She agreed to try the special, the bourbon maple glazed salmon. She also ordered a side of hush puppies, her latest new addiction. She wondered if they used powdered sugar and a touch of cinnamon, like Ben's father.

When Lillie brought CJ's dinner, she told her she could take her break and sit with her while she ate if that was okay.

"That would be wonderful, Lillie. As long as you don't mind if I eat in front of you."

Lillie laughed. "I'm used to it. Everyone eats in front of me."

Lillie sat down and they talked about how she was doing since her near escape. Lillie told CJ she remembered more about her foiled abduction.

"He had dark brown hair. I'm certain of it. I think I said dark hair before, but it was dark brown. Does that help?"

"Absolutely! The more details we have, the faster we catch him." CJ could tell she was trying to smile, but tears were forming.

"His hair was also wavy."

CJ was puzzled. "Wavy. You mean curly?"

Lillie shook her head. "Not curly, but it wasn't straight." She handed CJ a picture she had cut out of a men's magazine. "Like this. Sort of like yours, wavy."

"Can I keep this?"

"Sure."

"So, he had dark brown wavy hair?" CJ asked.

"Yes. I'm certain of it." Lillie bit her bottom lip. She was about to cry. "Detective O'Hara, I hope this helps. I keep trying to remember details, but it's hard for me to think about it."

CJ covered her hand with hers. "I'm sure it's painful. I'm happy you're safe, and these new details are helpful."

Lillie finally smiled. It was a feeble smile, but she was doing her best. She checked her watch. "I need to go back to work. Thank you for coming."

"Lillie, before you go, I need to ask you about one other thing."

"What's that?"

"Sam suggested we have an officer monitor you. I agree."

"No! I want this behind me and seeing an officer will only remind me."

"But—"

Lillie's face was red. "I said no!"

CJ raised her hands. "Okay, but please call me anytime if you notice or suspect anything is off." When Lillie had gone, she shoved the last hush puppy in her mouth, left twenty dollars on the table for Lillie, and took her check to the register.

The cashier tore up her check. "The owner said your money's no good here. It's on the house."

The owner waved at her from the kitchen.

CJ mouthed, "Thank you."

He stared at her from across the street as she left the restaurant. She was a natural beauty. He couldn't believe she was a cop. Auburn hair wasn't his thing, but coupled with her brilliant green eyes, the shape of her face, and her fit body, she was just amazing. He felt his urges stir as she got into her truck and left.

He mumbled, "Now, where was I?" *Ah, there she is.* Lillie was laughing at a table of older women. Too bad he couldn't hear her. He had to stay in his truck. Well, at least for now.

He gazed at Lillie through the window for a few more minutes. He hadn't seen anyone watching. He was safe. He knew the damn camera the FBI had installed couldn't catch him from this spot. *Assholes!* He smiled as he left to go get into position.

CHAPTER

FIFTY-THREE

Tuesday, May 4
Downtown Charleston

CJ's night was all flips and flops—no sleep. She'd been haunted by the fact she hadn't crossed the street to check out the truck she'd seen when she left the restaurant. CJ had tried to put it out of her mind. She'd circled the block, but the truck was gone when she returned. It was an unusual place to be sitting—at the end of an alley. Was someone watching her, the restaurant, or Lillie?

She had called Lillie and made sure she got home, but she still couldn't shake her unease. She almost went to Lillie's apartment. Her roommate wasn't home, and that bothered her. Lillie had assured her she was home and her doors were locked. "I appreciate you being worried about me, but I'm okay. I want to stop thinking about this and put it behind me."

CJ rubbed at the knot in her stomach and mumbled, "I'm going to get her a gun for protection."

She finally got up and rode her bike for forty-five minutes before she ate part of a bagel. At five a.m., she decided she'd shower, dress, and walk down to Sal's and get a coffee. It was a beautiful morning. The sun was just coming up, and the birds sang. She was falling in love with Charleston, its rustling palm trees, cobblestone streets, and the breeze off the ocean. Almost all the buildings were old but well-kept.

CJ had grabbed a book on Charleston from a local bookstore. Bill's information had piqued her curiosity, and she'd wanted to know more about the city. It amazed her how it had survived the Civil War, numerous hurricanes, and even a 7.0 earthquake. The historic nature of the city was evident everywhere.

Sal looked up when she walked through the door of the coffee shop. "Good morning, my lovely. Your usual black coffee?"

"Yes, please."

"Would you like a fresh blueberry muffin? he asked. "I just took them out of the oven."

"I had a bagel, but can I have a dozen to go? They'll be a hit at the station."

He winked at her. "Yes, ma'am."

CJ watched as he packaged the muffins. Every time she came in, he seemed to be there. He had to be in his mid-fifties, but he constantly flirted with her.

He handed her the box and her coffee. "Here you go, pretty lady."

She handed him two twenties. "Thanks, Sal. That should cover it and feed the tip jar."

———

CJ entered the war room at six-forty-five a.m. Sam was already there and her eyes went straight to the box in CJ's hand. "You brought treats!"

"I did. My favorite coffee shop had fresh muffins, so I grabbed a few." CJ handed her the box.

"Yummy. Blueberry. I'll get some napkins, and we'll try them."

The two of them sat and ate a muffin each while Sam told her about more places in Charleston she had to see. The girl knew everything about Charleston.

CJ looked up when the door opened and Robert walked into the room. He said hello and joined them in having a muffin.

He shoved a piece of muffin into his mouth. "I tell you what, ladies. I'm going to gain twenty pounds eating all this good food here in Charleston. I must be eating every couple of hours."

They finished their muffins and got more coffee. CJ buzzed from all the caffeine she'd consumed.

Harry wasn't coming into the station today, and Ben and Christy would arrive after lunch since they planned to work the evening shift with the FBI agents, so CJ and Robert got started.

Robert pointed to the board. "We're waiting on the DNA results from the lab for vic seven, but I'd like to talk to them about our partial latent fingerprint. How about we get them on the phone and have them give us more details?"

Sam got up from the table and went to her desk in the corner. "I can call them and transfer them to the speakerphone."

"Thanks, Sam."

Sam called the Forensic Services Division and asked for the tech who had performed the analysis. She was in but unavailable and would call back ASAP. Within minutes, she had the tech on speakerphone.

Everyone introduced themselves. Robert asked the tech to go over the fingerprint analysis. They had the report but wanted to be sure they understood the significance.

"I'm happy to walk you through the report. The sample we pulled from the cooler top was only a partial print. It wasn't a great print, and it didn't help that someone had run over the top with a vehicle."

"You only found the one print, correct?" CJ asked.

"Yes. Only one usable print. Whoever dropped the top appears to have kept it clean. My guess is it was frequently wiped down."

Robert picked up the report. "Take us through the patterns, please."

"Sure. Fingerprints come in three basic patterns. The first one is most common, the loops pattern. About sixty to seventy percent of the population has this pattern. The second, which about thirty percent of the population has, is the whorls pattern. The last one, which we have here, is the arches pattern. Only about five percent of folks have this pattern."

CJ looked at the photo of the fingerprint. "So, our pattern is the least common?"

"Correct. Helpful, but it still gives us a long list."

The tech continued. "Once we had the print, we ran it through the state database. As expected, we got a long list of people who might match. It's long even for individuals who have been arrested for only violent crimes."

Sam handed them the list.

"At your request, we sent the print to Quantico, and they also ran it through their databases. We added anyone not on our original list. The list we sent over is our combined effort."

Robert was looking at the list. "This list is close to a hundred people. It will take a long time to work it. I'll get my researcher to see if she can group it by violent offenders in the Lowcountry that match our profile."

"Makes sense," the tech said. "The good news is we can compare this print to the suspect's prints when we find him. Alone, it wouldn't be enough to convict, but it could be part of the puzzle."

They thanked her and said they'd call with any other questions.

"Sounds good. Sam has my cell number. Good luck."

CJ got up and pinned the report to the board. She sat back down and looked at Robert. "Good news, bad news.

The good news is we have something to compare to suspects. The bad news is we can't use it to nail the unsub without more evidence."

Robert nodded and sighed. "Correct. Let's hope the DNA sample gets us further down the road. If we have a profile match, the person doesn't have solid alibis, and the print and DNA matches, we should have our guy. I'd think the DA would take it to trial, and we'd have a good chance of getting a conviction."

"If we have DNA, wouldn't that be the nail in the coffin?" CJ asked.

"It depends on how good the DNA results turn out. We have a hair strand but not the entire follicle, and the DNA sample may not be of the best quality. Any DNA result may not be at a high confidence level. A defense attorney will argue all we have is circumstantial evidence."

CJ looked down.

"Let's not get discouraged," Robert said. "We are making progress. We're going to get this guy."

"I know," CJ said. "I just hope we have no more lives lost before we catch him." She looked at Sam. "Can you give Robert and me a minute, please?"

Once Sam had left, CJ asked Robert, "So, where are we with Officer Parker and Ben?"

"They fit the profile and match the partial print. We're waiting on DNA, and then we'll approach them about their alibis on the dates of the murders. We know they were in town on those dates. For most of the critical dates, both were off work. For the others, it looks like they were on patrol alone."

CJ rubbed her neck. Ben's fingerprint pattern matched the partial print she'd found! "Okay. I assume you'll interview them?"

"Yes. Since they're Charleston PD, it's best if the FBI handles it."

"Does anyone else but me know you have them on your list?"

"No. Not yet. I've found that it's best to keep this contained with the FBI until we need to disclose it. It can cloud things if local law enforcement knows it. I trusted you with it so we could keep Ben at arm's length on certain steps of the investigation. I know this puts you in a tough spot, but it was needed."

CJ just nodded. She *knew* it wasn't Ben. Was she too close to him? Was her judgment clouded?

He could see she was struggling. "Like you, I pray it's not Ben. We have to follow the evidence."

Tears formed in her eyes. "I understand."

He got up, came around the table, and put his hand on her shoulder. "I'm sorry to have to do this to you."

"I know, Robert. I respect your judgment." CJ sniffed and wiped her eyes. "Let's talk about Ricky Floyd. Looks like the can Harry brought back gave us his fingerprints and DNA sample. We should hear today if his print pattern matches the partial print."

Robert went back to his seat. "If his prints match, we'll keep him on the list. The other three have dropped off due to their alibis checking out, and their print patterns aren't a match. We owe them a call to thank them for their cooperation and to let them know we have what we need to clear them."

"How about we do that now?"

He nodded.

CJ went to Sam's desk and got the file with their contact information. She called them on the speakerphone and advised them of their findings. All three were happy to be cleared. They all said they'd be glad to answer any more questions if needed. As for the investigation, there were still three suspects on their list.

Sam came back with lunch. She handed them each a box and brought them drinks. The three of them sat and ate. Sam told them about the construction of the Arthur Ravenel Jr. Bridge, so CJ asked if she was any relation to the man the bridge was named after. She chuckled and only said, "I wish." They had just finished eating when Sam's phone rang. She jumped up to answer it and tears immediately erupted. "Lillie's missing!"

"What do you mean, she's missing?" CJ asked.

"Sully's Restaurant's owner said Lillie didn't come in for her eleven o'clock shift. He called her cell and house phone and couldn't reach her. The owner went to her house and knocked, and there was no answer. He's called her parents and roommate, and no one has heard from her since last night."

CJ's eyes widened. "Oh, shit!" She got up and ran for the door, Robert hot on her heels. "Call and have an officer meet us at her apartment and have another go to the restaurant," she yelled as the door closed.

CJ sped through downtown to Lillie's apartment, completely terrified. "I spoke to her after she got home from work last night. She said she was fine and had her doors locked. Her roommate had gone to see her parents, so she was alone. I had a bad feeling. I almost went over and got her."

"It's not your fault," Robert said. "Maybe there's an explanation, so let's not jump to conclusions."

"Robert, she's a responsible girl. She'd never miss work and not call the owner. He's like her second father. I know the unsub's got her."

FIFTY-FOUR

Tuesday, May 4
Downtown Charleston

CJ skidded her truck to a stop. Lillie's car was in her parking spot. It was locked, and nothing looked out of place. CJ ran up the stairs leading to her door. She dug into her pocket and pulled on some surgical gloves. CJ's heart jumped when the knob turned, and the door opened.

"Lillie! It's CJ."

No answer.

Both officers drew their guns as they entered the apartment. They went room by room. There was no sign of Lillie. The second bedroom was Lillie's. There were pictures of her, her parents, and her friends. Her apron for the restaurant was thrown across a chair. Lillie hadn't made her bed. A bookshelf was lying on the floor, books spread everywhere.

"Detective?"

"Back here, Officer. Don't touch anything."

An officer stood in the bedroom doorway. CJ and Robert were on their knees looking at the bedroom window, which led to a fire escape.

CJ's face went pale. "It's been jimmied open from the outside." She slowly raised the window. There were scrape marks on the window seal. She grabbed her cell and called Sam. "Sam. She's not here. I need you to call the CSU and get them over here ASAP!"

Sam started crying. "CJ, please find her."

"We'll do our best."

CJ was numb. She just stared at the window. "Robert, he took her."

"Let's hope not."

He turned to the officer. "Officer, can you secure the scene?"

"Yes, sir. I've got some crime tape in my cruiser."

Robert added. "Secure the parking lot. Nobody comes in or goes out."

The officer took off for his car. "Yes, sir. I'm on it."

CJ was shaking. Why hadn't she come over last night? She'd had a bad feeling. Why hadn't she had Lillie stay with her? She had left her alone. *It's my fault he got her.*

"CJ, let's go down and see if we see anything at the bottom of the fire escape."

She carried her guilt as she followed him out.

They were inspecting the fire escape when the CSU arrived. It was hard to see from the ground, but marks indicated the fire escape had been recently pulled down.

Eddie walked over to them. "Where do you want us to start?"

Robert looked at him. "We have a young woman missing. We're afraid she's been abducted." He pointed at the fire escape. "It looks like someone pulled the fire escape down, used it to go up, and jimmy that window open. That's the young woman's bedroom. The entry door was closed but not locked. My guess is he went in this way and exited through the door." He turned and pointed at Lillie's car. "That's her car. I want you to get video of the area, dust everywhere for prints, and photograph every inch of the place."

"Yes, sir." Eddie turned to his team. "Okay, guys. We think a young woman has been taken. We're going to start at her car and cover every inch of the area. I want video and photos first, then let's inspect everything for prints and anything else." He pulled out his cell phone and dialed the lab. "It's Eddie," he said when a tech answered on the other end. "Get someone over here with a ladder. I need to inspect a fire escape."

Four more cruisers pulled up on the street beside the parking area's entrance. The officers got out of their cars but stayed behind the crime scene tape. One of them yelled to CJ, "We're here if you need us."

CJ looked at them. "Thanks, guys. Can one of you have hospitals checked for anyone who's come in since nine last night?" She had a lump in her throat. "She's twenty, five feet eight inches tall, weighs about one hundred and twenty pounds, blond hair, and blue eyes. Her name is Lillie Ferguson." Her voice caught, but she continued. "Have officers check marinas, docks, and marine businesses in the zones for a body."

"Got it." The officer turned for his cruiser.

CJ looked at Robert. "Sully's isn't far from here. While these guys process the scene, how about we go talk to the owner?"

"Good idea."

The owner recognized CJ as she came through the front door. He motioned them back to the office and asked anxiously, "Did you find her?"

"Not yet," CJ said. "We went to Lillie's apartment, and no one was there. A team of officers is searching for her."

He dropped down on a milk crate and put his hands over his head. "Please, God, let her be okay." Tears started running down his cheeks. "I walked her out to her car last night myself. She got off a little before nine. She called me when she got home. I wanted to make sure she was safe." He started shaking. "I should have taken Lillie home and made sure no one was around."

CJ put her hand on his shoulder. "No one had any idea she wasn't safe. Let's stay positive we'll find her and she's okay."

He just nodded. "I asked if she wanted to come home and stay with my wife and me. I knew her roommate was gone . . ." His voice trailed off. "I should have insisted."

CJ asked him who was working with her last night. The owner called two young women over. Neither said they'd noticed anything suspicious or out of the ordinary and primarily families had come in. There was only one man by himself—the older guy CJ had seen at the table when she arrived. The young women said he came in three or four times a week. CJ knew he wasn't the unsub. He couldn't have been more than five-ten, was in his sixties, and had gray hair.

CJ suddenly remembered the black truck she'd seen when she left. She asked the owner to follow her outside. She pointed at the surveillance camera on the corner.

"Do you know what those cameras capture?"

"Not sure. Why?"

"It may be nothing, but when I left at around eight last night, I noticed a black truck sitting across the street in that alley."

Robert called one of his agents. He gave them the camera's location and asked them to pull him a list of any vehicles there between seven-fifteen p.m. and eight-fifteen p.m. He also asked for a copy of the tape. "They're pulling the videos now," he told CJ when he finished the call. "I'm not sure if the angle will capture where you saw the truck, but it's worth a try. He had to come out of the alley."

CJ stood staring at the spot where she'd seen the truck. "Unless he backed up and went out the other side." She ran across the street to the alley to see what was on the other end. CJ looked up but saw no more cameras. She should have gone over to the truck when she noticed it. *This is a nightmare!*

CJ and Robert left the restaurant and returned to Lillie's apartment. The first officer that had arrived earlier was still there guarding the parking area. He said no one matching Lillie's description had been reported at any hospitals. He looked at the ground. "No one has reported any bodies either. I made sure the task force leads for all departments were alerted. Everyone's looking, and they know to call you on your cell with anything."

CJ went over to Eddie, who was coming down a ladder. "Someone pulled the fire escape down recently—see the recent marks in the rust?" He pointed to a spot about fifteen feet up. "The window seal was pried open from the outside. There are clear pry marks, and they're new. I didn't find any fingerprints on the fire escape railing or the outside of the window. My guess is whoever went in wore gloves and used a small pry bar to get in her window. He was strong enough to force the screws on the inside latch to pull loose. That's the problem with these older buildings. The wood isn't that strong. I'm done out here, but the guys inside are still working. They didn't find any fingerprints on the inside of the bedroom window or the doorknob."

CJ said they'd wait until they finished to get a full report. She stood there beside Robert in silence. *It's my fault he has Lillie. I should have made her stay with me, or at least had an officer assigned to watch her.*

CHAPTER

FIFTY-FIVE

Wednesday, May 5
Downtown Charleston

CJ got home at four a.m. It had been all hands-on deck when Lillie went missing. Law enforcement personnel canvassed every marina, dock, and marine business in the area. She'd spent her night driving all over Charleston and listening to the communications on the radio. Harry had come in and gone with her.

Once she finally got home, she laid down and tried to sleep. All she saw was Lillie's smile. She couldn't sleep thinking about where she was and whether she was being tortured. The photos of the other victims filled her head. She got on her knees and prayed. *Please don't let Lillie be added to the list.*

CJ gave up trying to sleep. She got up, took a shower, and dressed. The last time she'd eaten was lunch the day before. CJ should have been hungry, but she had no appetite. She took a bite of a bagel, but it was all she could get down. CJ tossed the rest of the bagel in the trash, grabbed her to-go cup of coffee, and headed to the LEC.

CJ walked into the war room at seven a.m. The room was empty—no Sam. She put on a pot of coffee and booted up her laptop. A copy of the fingerprint report for Ricky Floyd was in her inbox. His fingerprints had an arched pattern. She forwarded the information to Robert. She wasn't sure when he would arrive, but she expected Harry and Ben in by lunch. Everyone was running on fumes.

CJ picked up the phone and called Stan. He agreed she should send two officers to pick up Floyd. She wanted him detained until she could sort out Lillie's whereabouts. She knew it would be a risk, and an attorney would scream bloody murder, but she didn't give a damn.

Someone punched in the code to enter the room. The door opened, and Christy appeared. Her eyes had dark circles underneath, and the whites of her eyes were bright red. She hadn't slept either. She dropped into a chair. They gave each other a halfhearted smile.

"I couldn't sleep, CJ. I guessed you wouldn't sleep either and would come here, so I came to keep you company."

"Thanks. You guessed right. I can't get Lillie out of my mind. These cases are difficult, but I had a personal connection with her, so it's worse."

Christy stirred the creamer into her coffee. "I'm not sure how you're doing this. This case is making me question being an agent. I worked hard to make it onto Robert's team, but now I'm not sure. I'm barely older than these poor young women. I'm not sure I'm strong enough to chase monsters like this one." She looked down at her palms. A single tear ran down her cheek. She quickly wiped it away and sniffed. Barely audible, she asked, "How do you do it?"

CJ thought about the question. How did she do it?

Christy slowly rubbed her hands together.

When she looked up, CJ confidently replied, "I do this because I will not let anyone get away with these types of crimes. No way, no how. The bottom line is we need committed people to bring these criminals to justice. I'm not resting until we have this guy in cuffs."

Christy stared at her. "Do you think I'm as tough as you?"

"You are. I doubt my toughness at times. Low points are part of this job, and during those points, it makes you question yourself. That's normal. It doesn't make you weak. It makes you human."

Christy kept staring at her. "Have you ever shot anyone?"

"Yes. Unfortunately, I had to shoot and kill a man to save my partner. Being forced to kill someone is hard to live with."

They sat quietly for several minutes before Christy spoke up. "Can I ask you another personal question?"

"Sure."

"Are you and Ben together?"

CJ was shocked. "Uh . . . no. We're partners. We get along great and all, but . . ."

"I wondered," Christy said. "He's such a great guy. I've enjoyed spending time with him and—"

CJ's cell phone rang, and she flinched. She stared down—it was Sam.

When she answered, CJ heard the sadness in her voice. "I'm sorry I didn't make it in yet. I couldn't sleep. I'm so upset about Lillie."

CJ was again faced with being strong for another person. "I understand. I didn't sleep much myself. Listen, how about you take today off?"

Sam exhaled. "Are you sure?"

"Yes. I'm sure. Please stay home today."

"Okay, call me if you need me and if you find Lillie." She burst into tears.

CJ tried to be bright in her response. "Will do."

This case was taking its toll on everyone. Even Harry and Robert were exhausted. It wasn't the long hours but the mental wear and tear. It was the pressure of knowing someone was out there hunting to rape and brutally murder another young woman. It was the fear he already had another victim: Lillie.

CJ asked Christy if she wanted some fresh air. *Don't ask me any more about Ben.* She suggested they walk down the street and grab a cup of coffee. Christy agreed, and they headed for the door.

As CJ and Christy were returning with their coffee, CJ's cell phone rang. Her heart stopped. She glanced at Christy and sucked in a deep breath.

"Detective O'Hara."

"Hello, Detective. It's Helen. I'm sad to say it, but we have found a body near Folly Beach. I've dispatched the CSU and Medical Examiner Whitehall. An officer from the Folly Beach PD is on the scene. He asked for you. I'll text you the location."

CJ dropped her head. "I'm on my way."

Christy had been holding her breath. "We have another body?"

CJ slowly nodded—her eyes wet. *Please don't be Lillie.*

FIFTY-SIX

Wednesday, May 5
Folly Beach

CJ saw the flashing blue lights of a Folly Beach PD cruiser on a long stretch of road ahead of them. The road cut through the marsh to Folly Beach. A young officer stood just off to the side of the road when they pulled up. He had crime scene tape in his hand. The look on his face told CJ all she needed to know. It was Lillie. Every officer in the Lowcountry had her photo. She parked behind his car and walked over to the officer.

He pointed toward the marsh. "Detective O'Hara, it's a body. A jogger found her and called 911 from his cell. He's sitting in the back of my car. I didn't get close, but I saw the top of the person's head. The victim has blond hair. I'm afraid it's the young woman we've all been searching for, but I'm not sure. I didn't want to touch anything."

CJ told him to finish securing the scene. He nodded and went to the trunk of his car for cones.

CJ turned to Christy. "Can you help him with the crime scene tape?"

Christy nodded and went to the officer's car. "I'm Agent Ellis. Call me Christy. Let me give you a hand."

CJ steadied herself and stepped off the side of the road. Carefully, she approached the tarp. She didn't want to disturb the scene, but she had to see if it was Lillie. Using her gloved hand, she reached down and gently lifted the tarp. Lillie's frosted electric-blue eyes stared at her. Her heart sank as she dropped to a knee. *Oh, Lillie.*

CJ went back to the edge of the road. Neither the officer nor Christy asked her if it was Lillie. CJ was sure they knew as they worked silently, getting the area secured. CJ sat down on the ground.

"Is it the young woman who was on the news last night?" someone asked.

CJ looked up. The jogger stood there. He looked at least seventy and was wearing a T-shirt that read *The United States Marine Corps Retired*. CJ simply nodded and stood.

He said angrily, "There are some mean bastards out there. How could anyone harm a beautiful young woman like her?"

CJ didn't answer his question. The CSU and ME pulled up shortly afterward. Harry was close behind. CJ told the jogger to go back and wait in the car to make his statement later. He nodded and slowly turned to go back to the officer's car. Eddie and Thomas got out of their vehicles and walked over to her.

CJ shook her head. "Lillie."

Eddie dropped his head. "Let's go to work, guys. Work carefully and look for everything."

Harry walked over to her. "What can I do?"

CJ sighed. "We need to let the forensics team process the scene, and Thomas can do his field exam. If you wouldn't mind, you could take the statement of the man who found her. He's waiting in the back of the officer's cruiser."

"Got it."

Harry went to the cruiser and took the man to his car. The old marine was crying. Robert and Ben arrived and stood with CJ watching the CSIs work. Thomas had moved closer to the body. Other Folly Beach officers arrived, and Christy asked them to block the road fifty yards in both directions. The media would be swarming around them soon. She also asked them to walk the roadside looking for anything that needed to be collected. She handed them the numbered flags out of the CSU van for evidence collection.

A white crane slowly moved in the marsh beyond where Lillie was lying. It watched them. A mist from the rising temperature was slowly growing across the marsh. Under normal circumstances, CJ would have found it beautiful, but not today.

"CJ."

CJ turned, and it was Christy.

"We flagged a few items. A few bottles and cans. I'm not sure if any will be helpful, but the CSIs can take a look."

"Thanks."

Ben remained beside CJ on her left, Christy was on her right. The three of them were silent, watching the CSIs finish processing the body. Eddie walked toward CJ, and she felt a stabbing pain in her chest.

Eddie removed his gloves. "Detective, I wish I had something new to tell you. She has lacerations across her throat and down her midsection. Thomas can confirm, but it looks like she was raped."

CJ struggled not to cry. She worked not to scream. *How could someone do this?* "Any ligature marks?"

"Yes—neck, wrists, and ankles," Eddie said. "Same as before."

"Any visible fluids or residues?"

"No. No markings." He turned toward the body. "Let's hope Thomas can find something during the autopsy. I'll grab the team, and we'll examine what the officers flagged and collect anything that might have fingerprints or DNA."

CJ thanked him, and he went back down to where his team was packing up. CJ watched a clearly shaken Thomas inspecting Lillie's body. *I'm not sure which of us has the worse job.*

Thomas finished his field exam and motioned his team to come for the body. Everyone else stood together as he approached them. "Nothing new to report. The same cause of death and same mutilation. I estimate the time of death as six to eight hours ago. Do we know when he took her?"

"No. Lillie talked to her mother at ten p.m. on Monday. I spoke to her an hour earlier. The restaurant owner said he talked to her a little after nine after she got home. She was alone, but safe by all indications. But she wasn't at home when the owner called her around eleven-thirty yesterday morning. She was due at work at eleven a.m."

He checked his pad. "That means someone took her after ten p.m. on Monday and before eleven a.m. yesterday. My guess is he wouldn't take her during the daylight. Gives us a window of approximately eight hours. Coupled with the time of death, he held her longer than the last six victims. I'd guess about twenty-four hours. The only thing that appears different was the rape was especially ferocious. Like the first victim, she was raped more than once." Thomas fought back a sob. "I'll confirm it, but it appears she was a virgin."

Christy flinched and grabbed CJ's hand. CJ squeezed it. Hard. They both shook.

Harry had laced his fingers and put his hands behind his head. He exhaled loudly. Robert stood, rubbing his forehead. Ben stared blankly at the coroner's van.

CJ felt tears. She wiped her eyes and did her best to collect herself. "Thanks. Let us know what you find in the autopsy."

"Will do. I'm going back to start it now. I'll call you when I'm done and email you my report." Thomas glanced at his pad again. He had something else to say but was reluctant. He stared out across the marsh. "We need to call her parents. They live in Savannah, but came to Charleston yesterday. I expect they'll want to come in this afternoon."

It was the last thing she wanted to do, but CJ knew it would be best if she made this call. She had not spoken to Lillie's mother since she went missing. "I'll call her mother. We've spoken before, so it will be easier."

Robert spoke up. "I'll call them if you want."

"No, I'll do it."

Thomas reached out and rubbed CJ's arm. "I'm so sorry."

She wiped away tears. "Me too."

Once the coroner's van had pulled away, CJ told the officer he could clear the tape and open the road. She thanked him for keeping passersby and the media away from the scene. Everyone headed back, and Christy rode with CJ.

The two women didn't speak during the drive back. CJ drove, dreading the call she knew she had to make. She finally pulled her truck over to the side of the road and dialed Lillie's parents.

"Mrs. Ferguson? This is Detective O'Hara."

No response. All CJ heard was heavy breathing and Lillie's mother sniffing. She was struggling not to cry.

"Mrs. Ferguson, we found Lillie . . . I'm so sorry."

For the next several minutes, all CJ heard was loud wailing.

CHAPTER

FIFTY-SEVEN

Wednesday, May 5
Downtown Charleston

The two FBI agents, Harry, CJ, and Ben, sat around the table in the war room. To CJ's surprise, Sam was there when she arrived. She was visibly upset, but told CJ she was there to help them catch whoever killed Lillie. Lillie had become a close friend.

Robert added Lillie's name to the evidence board. Their list was growing longer, and their second evidence board was full.

- *Amanda ("Mandy") McCarthy*
- *Laura Perkins*
- *Kelli Simmons*

- *Kara Morgan*
- *Kathy Meeks*
- *Elizabeth ("Beth") Atkins*
- *Margaret ("Maggie") Bell*
- *Lillie Ferguson*

CJ watched Robert's eyes trail toward Ben. *He does think it's Ben. Does he know something he's not saying?*

Robert stared at the board. "Other than our profile, all we have is the latent print from the place of the abduction of victim number six. We hope we get DNA from the hair strand we found inside victim number seven."

CJ snapped her head to stare at him. He'd just mentioned the DNA in front of Ben. She caught Ben's look of surprise. She was glad she had told Harry about the hair. *Why did you mention it, Robert?*

Ben spoke up. "We might have DNA?"

Robert sat down and looked at his notes. He stared up at Ben. "Yeah. Maybe. I've called, and I expect the DNA result within twenty-four hours. The lab said there's a small portion of the follicle, so they hope to have some DNA. Let's hope the hair strand gives us something concrete. Once we have the DNA, it'll be run through our databases. We also have DNA from everyone on our potential suspects' shortlist."

There it is! He already has Ben's DNA.

Ben nodded. "DNA would be an excellent addition for us."

CJ watched him. He didn't seem concerned.

Robert kept staring at Ben, thinking about how he'd gotten his DNA from a coffee cup Ben left in the war room.

———

At four p.m., Thomas led Lillie's parents to the table to view her body. They were both inconsolable. Lillie's mother was crying hysterically. Her father seemed as though he would pass out at any minute. He was breathing heavily and moaning.

Harry and the two FBI agents had come with CJ. CJ looked at Harry, and they both stepped forward and took the parents' arms. When both were about to collapse, Robert and Christy also assisted. Harry and Robert each took one side of Lillie's father. CJ and Christy took her mother.

The six of them stood beside the exam table. Thomas looked at CJ and she nodded. *Ready as we'll ever be.* He pulled the sheet back to show Lillie's face. Her face, no more. He spared them from seeing the nasty gash across Lillie's throat. Lillie's father howled, and the two men struggled to keep him from falling forward on Lillie's body. Lillie's mom's legs gave out, and CJ and Christy gently guided her down to the floor. She sat there holding on to them and cried uncontrollably.

None of the viewings had been easy. This one was by far the worst. The parents were completely devastated. No one, not even Thomas, who did this for a living, had dry eyes. It was the first time CJ had seen Harry cry since her parents and sister died, more than twenty years ago.

CJ was thankful she had insisted Sam not come with them. She had been a wreck, and Ben had offered to take her home. She didn't need to drive in her state.

The four rode back to the LEC in stony silence.

It was after five when CJ knocked on Stan's door. "Cap, got a minute?"

"Yep. Sorry to hear about Lillie."

CJ nodded. "Yeah, me too."

She dropped into a chair and after a minute of silence, Stan asked, "Whatcha got?"

"We picked up Ricky Floyd and, at a minimum, he's going down for two rapes. We've tied his DNA to cold cases."

"DNA was at the scene?" he asked.

"Yep. Floyd didn't wear a condom, and fortunately, both women reported the rape and got rape kits. Semen was collected, and DNA run. Up until recently, he wasn't in CODIS, so we couldn't find him."

"Will the victims testify?"

"Yes. Both said it was dark, but both victims identified him in a lineup—said there was no doubt in their minds. The sketch we had before was pretty good, but not good enough to find him. The DA is going for the maximum sentence."

"Is he still a possible for the Lowcountry Killer?"

"He's still on our list for now. His physical appearance and fingerprint pattern match our evidence. We can't alibi him on any of the critical dates, including our latest victim. He didn't use a knife in his priors, so that makes us doubt him. We won't know until we get the DNA from the hair we found on one of our vics."

"Keep me posted. At least he's locked up."

CJ left Stan's office and walked back to the war room. She wanted to be optimistic, but her instincts told her Ricky wasn't their guy.

Except for Harry, who had gone home, the group gathered back in the war room. Ben had returned from taking Sam home. He'd talked her into going to her parents' place—she needed their support. No one had the energy to stay at the station, so they went for drinks. It was probably not the best idea, but an idea, nonetheless. She had to stay in control. Robert planned to monitor the other agents' movements throughout the night. He told CJ, Ben, and Christy to take the night off and go home. After several rounds of drinks—CJ was careful to keep it to two—they passed on dinner and went home.

Ben walked back to the LEC with CJ. She had kept thinking about Robert's belief Ben was their unsub in the back of her mind. She still wasn't convinced it was possible. She hadn't known him long, but she knew him. It couldn't be him. *Am I reading him wrong, or is Robert?*

Ben suggested CJ leave her truck at the LEC and he'd walk her home. "No need to drive after drinking and your apartment isn't far," he told her.

She agreed. They wound up sitting in her apartment, talking for a couple more hours before Ben took a cab home. CJ stared at Ben as he talked about growing up in Charleston. She noted that he, like her, was a bit tipsy. He talked about his football-playing days at the Citadel when his face twisted.

"Before when we talked about our sports careers, I left out that I had a chance to go pro. NFL scouts were really interested. That all died when I tore up my shoulder. To be honest, I don't think I've ever gotten over it."

CJ stared into Ben's amber eyes. She wanted to put her arms around him. He couldn't be the unsub. *Are my instincts totally wrong?* "I'm sorry that happened to you."

Ben smiled feebly. "Well, it's really late. I guess I'll go."

She came close to asking him to stay.

CHAPTER

FIFTY-EIGHT

Thursday, May 6
The French Quarter, Charleston

CJ sat at her window, watching the tops of palm trees sway in the morning breeze. It was only seven, and she had already showered and pulled on her favorite pair of jeans, a black blouse, and her comfortable black lace-up Oxfords. She added her Glock and badge and topped things off with a light gray blazer. *Gonna need some cooler clothes for this Charleston heat.*

Her head hurt, and her eyes were burning—too much stress and not enough sleep. Ben had said he'd take a cab back over this morning and walk her back to the LEC.

CJ's cell phone chimed. It was a text from Ben to say he was on his way. He'd be there in five minutes. Her cell phone rang—it was Robert. She heard the urgency in his voice.

"CJ, where are you?"

"I'm here at home. I'll be in shortly."

"Are you alone?"

"Yes."

"Where's Ben?"

"He's on his way to get me. We're going to walk over. I left my truck—"

"Don't do it. He's our guy!"

Her pulse quickened. "What?"

"The DNA results came in. It's Ben!"

She dropped hard on the floor. Her head spun, and she was dizzy.

"Did you hear me?"

"Yes. It can't be Ben."

"It's him. Don't be alone with him. I'm on my way."

CJ heard a knock and her door opened.

"Hey, it's Ben. Are you here?"

She stood and walked out of her bedroom.

Ben was in the doorway, looking at her. "You should keep your door locked. Anybody could walk right in."

She stared at him.

He was confused. "You look like you've seen a ghost. What's wrong?"

She was breathing heavily. *It can't be him.* She pulled her weapon and pointed it at him.

"CJ! What the hell!"

She struggled to get the words out. "Why?"

"Why what? Put the damn gun down."

"Why did you murder all those young women?"

Ben's eyes went wide. "What are you talking about?"

"The eight young women. Why did you do it?"

Ben put his hands out. "CJ, I'm not sure what's wrong with you. I have no idea what you're talking about. I haven't hurt anyone."

Sirens got louder, fast.

Ben started looking around. He pleaded with her. "Please put the gun down. Let's talk about this."

She wanted to put her gun down. This had to be a horrible mistake! "Ben Parrish, you're under arrest."

"CJ, Jesus Christ!"

Four uniformed officers rushed through the door and took Ben to the ground. Robert was right behind them. His gun drawn.

"CJ, my God, are you okay?"

Tears ran down her cheeks. Ben was lying face-down on her floor as two officers held him and a third handcuffed him. The fourth officer had his gun trained on him.

Ben had a horrified expression on his face. "Why, CJ?"

Robert read him his rights. The officers yanked him up and took him away.

Ben continued to plead with her. "I didn't do this."

CJ collapsed on the floor.

The rest of the day was chaos. The press got wind of the arrest of a police officer, and the news spread like wildfire. Local news channels cut into television programming, and the radio covered the story non-stop. The station was flooded with calls, and television crews blocked Lockwood Drive in front of the LEC. All were clamoring for the name of the person arrested, and it would only be a matter of time before Ben's name hit the press.

CJ, Harry, Robert, and Christy sat in the war room. Sam sat at her desk in silence. Walter and Stan entered the room. No one was sure whether to be happy they had their guy or sad it was one of their own.

Walter stood at the end of the table. "Special Agent Patterson, as requested, Ben has been booked and is being held in a cell downstairs. He's ready for you to interview him."

Robert cleared his throat. "Thanks, Chief. Under the circumstances, I'd like to interview him with Agent Ellis observing. Since he's Charleston PD, we have to make sure no one thinks there is favoritism being shown."

Walter nodded and exhaled. "Agreed. Ben has always been a damn good cop. To be honest, I'm struggling with this whole damn thing. I wish the media circus hadn't started before we completed a full investigation, but we are where we are."

Robert could tell he was irritated. "Understood, Chief. The whole city has been on pins and needles. In a small town, news travels fast." He got up and started for the door.

Christy trailed behind him.

Walter watched them leave and turned to CJ. "Let's talk in my office."

She got up and followed him. They went into his office, and he closed the door.

"Have a seat."

She sat down. "Yes, sir."

He sat down behind his desk. "This is unbelievable. One of the leads for the investigation is the perp."

She wasn't sure how to respond, and he hadn't asked her a question—yet.

"How could this happen?"

CJ bit her bottom lip. "I'm not sure, sir."

He got up, walked to the window, and stared out at the chaos. "Do you believe he's our guy?"

She felt a wave of nervousness. If she said yes, she'd be lying. If she said no, he'd ask her why. She struggled to find a response.

"I tell you what, don't answer," he said. "I want to see what the interview tells us. Fair is fair, and Ben at least deserves to be heard. Everyone's innocent until proven guilty."

"Yes, sir."

He stared back out the window, talking to himself. "Part of me wants it to be him, so we can solve this case and make sure no more young women die. The other part prays it's not him." He turned to her. "That's off the record and between us." He sat on the end of the desk and leaned down close to her. "Go and sort this mess out. If it's him, I'll drag his ass to the trial myself. If it's not, we still have a monster out there we need to catch."

CJ stood. "Yes, sir."

FIFTY-NINE

Thursday, May 6
Downtown Charleston

Robert and Christy entered the interrogation room where Ben sat, forehead resting on the table. Ben's puffy, bloodshot eyes rose as they sat. His usually vibrant face had been replaced with paleness, and his lips protruded as he fought tears.

Robert acknowledged Ben with a slight head tip. "Ben, we'd like to talk to you and sort things out. Make sense of all this."

"There's nothing to sort out," Ben said. "I didn't kill anyone."

"Here's the deal." Robert leaned forward. "You match the physical description we've seen on the video and that a witness observed. Your fingerprints match the rare pattern on the cooler top, and your DNA matches that taken from the hair inside one of the victims. We can't confirm your alibis when the victims were taken. You received accusations of sexual assault in college and the military." Robert knew the facts would be challenged by a decent defense attorney, but all the facts mounted to a solid conclusion. "Help us out here. The facts tell us you're our guy."

Ben pulled in a deep breath and slowly let it out. "First, there are lots of people here that resemble my appearance. Lots have my fingerprint pattern, and the DNA isn't as solid as you'd want me to believe. As for the alibis, I was home or working on the dates in question."

"We can't verify that."

"What the hell do you want me to say? I live alone. I wish my dog, Jake, could vouch for me, but he can't. He'd tell you I was there with him. The other nights I was on patrol hunting the real killer. There's evidence to prove it if you look at the records."

"Ben, we have. There are gaps where you were silent or your location couldn't be verified. You could have easily taken a victim in those windows of time."

"Bullshit!" Ben screamed. "You're spinning it the way you want. Meanwhile, the real killer is out there. You wait and see, he'll kill again while my ass sits here in a cell."

"What about the prior accusations?" Robert asked.

"That's all they were, and both got resolved. I was innocent."

Robert watched Ben closely. *What am I reading?* "Ben, you're a cop, which in this case, works against you. Who better than a cop to know how to beat the system?"

Ben's fight was gone, and he broke down in sobs. "All . . . all I can tell you is I didn't do this. You have your facts, but they're telling you the wrong answer. Give me a lie detector or whatever test you want, but I'd never . . ." He was broken. Defeated. "There's no use talking anymore. You've made up your mind. Get my attorney here."

Robert and Christy got up and closed the door.

Christy's mind was spinning. *I had a crush on him. Oh, God.*

CJ went back to the war room, where she found Harry looking at the board.

Harry pointed at a list of dates the young women were taken. "Based on his shift schedule, Ben was off work on several of these nights. The others he was working but alone out on patrol. The key is matching the windows when the young women were taken to his availability to take them." Harry looked at Sam. "Do you have the DNA report?"

Sam shook her head. "No. Not yet. Robert said the lab called him. I'll call and have them send it over."

Harry nodded. "Thanks. I want to see exactly what the report shows. I want to match up Ben's alibis with the windows in which the young women were taken. Robert may already have done this and not shared it, but I'd like to make my own decision after I review the facts."

Robert and Christy returned about an hour later. They sat down with CJ and Harry at the table.

Robert shook his head. "He's adamant he's not our guy." He pointed to the board. "He fits the physical profile. Strike one. He provided alibis for the windows when the victims were taken, but he doesn't have anyone to verify them. He was at home or on patrol. Either way, he was alone. Strike two.

"The latent print matches his fingerprint pattern. Not conclusive, but it is the type of pattern only found in a small percentage of people. Strike three. The DNA results from the hair are better than I thought, as the lab found a bit of the follicle. It gave us a partial profile. It has a high-probability match with Ben's DNA. Strike four."

The weight came down on CJ. *If they have DNA and it matches Ben, he's our guy.*

Harry asked, "On the DNA, how high is the probability match?"

"Not one hundred percent, but a high probability," Robert said. "If we had a full DNA profile for the sample found at the scene, we'd be absolutely certain."

Harry nodded. "Wouldn't Ben's brother have the same DNA? He fits the physical description on the tape, and the witness wouldn't know the difference."

"He would, but we've confirmed Will was out-of-town when two vics were taken," Robert said.

The group reviewed the file again until lunchtime. The two FBI agents would brief the other agents and work on their files during the afternoon. Harry and CJ decided to leave for the day as well.

CJ's mind was still racing about Ben being their unsub. She knew the evidence pointed that way, but it didn't feel right. "I've got a few things to take care of this afternoon. How about we have dinner tonight?" she said to her uncle.

Harry smiled. "I'd like that. Would you like to come to my place or go somewhere?"

"Let's go somewhere, and I'll buy."

"This sounds better and better." Harry was trying to cheer her up, but his voice was flat.

"Okay. I'll call you later." She hugged him as her tears fell to the floor.

CHAPTER

SIXTY

Thursday, May 6
Johns Island

CJ sat in her truck—she was numb. She had to come to grips with the idea Ben was the unsub, but first she had to convince herself. She called Ben's father, Bill, to see if he would meet with her and answer some questions. She wasn't sure if he would talk to her, but she had to try. He picked up on the third ring.

"Hello, Bill, this is CJ."

Silence at the end of the line.

"Bill, are you there?"

"Yes. I heard you. I was trying to decide if I should hang up or not. You arrested my son." There was tension in his voice. He was angry.

"I know," she said, flatly.

"Why the hell do we need to talk, then?"

CJ hesitated. She had to be careful how she phrased her response. "I want to be sure Ben is the right guy."

He laughed sarcastically. "You didn't know he was the right guy, but you arrested him."

Uh-oh. Here's that dilemma again. CJ couldn't say what she wanted to say. *I don't think Ben did it, and that'll be replayed in a trial, but I need answers.* "Cases like this are always complicated. Let's say I want to give Ben every benefit of the doubt. Any suspect deserves that, don't you agree?" She heard him shuffling something in the background.

"I suppose. Tell you what, I'll talk to you only because we had a wonderful day together and you seem genuine to me. I won't talk to you just because you're a damn cop."

"Fair enough. Can I come over now?" she asked.

"Yeah, but just you."

"Agreed."

She hung up and took off for Johns Island.

———

Thirty minutes later, CJ pulled into Bill's driveway. She sat there for a few minutes, working up her courage. Then she exhaled and got out. She knocked on the front door. No answer. *Maybe he changed his mind.*

She saw his boat on the dock, and his pickup truck was in the driveway. She walked around back and found Bill sitting in a chair down by the edge of the water. Jake was lying beside him. As she walked across the grass, Jake came to meet her, his tail going a mile a minute. She rubbed his ears—they were baby-duck soft. "Bill?"

He turned around and wiped his eyes. "Looks like you found me. How long do you need to grill me?"

CJ stared at a man who loved his son and had no idea what to do to help him. "Bill, I don't need to grill you. I just want to talk to you. As a friend, not a cop."

He looked at her and spat on the ground. "Friends don't put a friend's son in jail."

She grimaced. "I know. Please talk to me."

He stared at her. It was clear he was trying to decide if he should talk to her or tell her to leave. "Shit! Okay. I'll talk to you, but only if we can go for a ride in the boat."

Should I be scared of him? "Okay, let's go for a ride."

He led her to the boat, and she dropped into the seat across from him.

"I won't go too fast," he said. "I ain't going for a long ride, either."

"Sounds fine."

Bill steered the boat into the middle of the Wadmalaw River. "What do you want to know?" he asked.

"Tell me about Ben."

He stared straight ahead and started talking. "Ben has always been a kind soul. Killing these young women would be out of character for him. When he was small, I used to take him and his brothers out fishing. My other two boys would catch fish and have no problems getting them off the hook. They never had any issues cleaning them. Take the knife, gut 'em, and cut 'em up. Not Ben, though. He ain't no sissy. He just didn't like the blood and guts."

"Did he ever do anything violent growing up?"

"Nope. Not Ben. He got into a small scrap or two on the playground, but it was mostly two boys wrestling around, getting their pants dirty."

"How was Ben with the girls?"

"He's had girlfriends throughout the years. He's always been respectful. I've never seen or heard of him doing anything rough with a woman."

"Did you know he was accused of sexual misconduct at the Citadel and in the marines?"

"Hell no!" he spat. "That's a crock of shit."

CJ checked her notes. "Ben's right-handed, correct?"

"Yep. Just like me. His mama and Will are left-handed."

"Have you ever seen him use his left hand for anything?"

"Like what?" He turned and stared at her.

"Oh, say, cleaning fish?"

"I already told you, he hated to clean fish. I used to process them after I caught them years ago. Will or I would clean and cut them up. Ben would package and vacuum-seal them, and we'd sell the packs to local restaurants. The big guys pushed us little guys out and I closed the processing shop."

"So—"

He cut her off. "He wouldn't clean them with his left hand, anyway. He tore his shoulder really bad over at the Citadel in a football game and no longer has full strength. Couldn't even use his left arm for the longest time."

CJ's mind raced. *How much strength does he have? Would he be able to cut someone up?* She stared at the note she had written. "Did you process the fish at your house?"

"No. I had a building where we did the processing. You need room to do it. Cleaning tables, sealing bench, and a large freezer for storage."

She jotted down more notes. *What else?* "Did his time in the service affect him?"

"No. Ben never served in combat. It made him proud of his country and made me damn proud." He turned the boat around and headed back to the dock.

CJ sat there quietly and left him alone. They pulled up to the dock, he jumped out, and tied up the boat. "Let's have a beer."

"Okay. I'd like that."

CJ stood in the doorway as Bill got their beers. She noticed a photo on the wall. "Is this your family?"

"Yep," he said as he glanced up. "Well, that *was* my family."

"Can I see the photo?"

"Sure. Come on in and look away."

A photo of him with a young woman and three boys was on the wall. The young woman was beautiful. CJ guessed she was five feet six inches or so. She had blond hair and blue eyes. One boy was older than the other two. She assumed it was Will. The two smaller boys were spitting images of each other.

"Is this your wife?" she asked.

"It was. Mary Beth. She was beautiful, wasn't she?"

"Yes," she said as she leaned closer to the photo. "Absolutely."

Bill handed CJ a beer and took a sip of his. "I'm not sure how she wound up with me. She worked at a restaurant where I'd sell fish with my dad. We talked, and next thing you know, we're married with Will on the way." He stood there looking at his wife. "She was a natural beauty. Didn't wear makeup, didn't need it."

"Ben told me she left," she said.

"Yeah. After we lost Bryan, she couldn't take it and left us. Been twenty years now. Always blamed me."

"Bryan?"

"He was my third son. We lost him when he was ten."

"Ben told me he drowned."

He stared at her. "Yeah. He did. A bad storm came up, the sea got rough as hell, and he fell over and drowned. It's one of the reasons Ben gets so pissed at me when I go out too far."

"I'm so sorry, Bill."

Tears filled his eyes. "I hope I don't lose Ben, too."

CJ put her hand on his arm. "I'm sorry for this."

He wiped his eyes.

"Bill, I'm going to go. I appreciate your time and that you answered my questions." She glanced at the photo again. "Do you mind if I get a copy of this?"

"No. Go ahead. Take it. It only makes me sad, anyway."

"Thanks, Bill. I'll bring it back." She took the photo and left Bill standing in the kitchen.

CJ sat in her truck. *What are the key takeaways?* She wrote down the following bullet points:

- *No record of violence*
- *No joy in gore*
- *Two accusations of improper conduct with women*
- *No other issues over military service, no combat, so no PTSD*
- *Right-handed and weak in his use of his left hand*
- *The unsub is using his left hand when he cuts*
- *A brother drowned at ten*
- *Mother left*
- *Mother and older brother are left-handed*

She stared at the points she had written. Something else was bothering her, but she couldn't put her finger on it. Will was left-handed, but he was out-of-town. *Think, CJ, think!* She started her truck and headed back to her apartment. She needed to sit quietly and think through everything she had learned so far. There were still holes. What were they, and how could she fill them?

At home, CJ sat going through the case file. She still had questions, although she wasn't sure exactly what they were. Hopefully, Harry would have ideas over dinner. She called him and gave him the name of the restaurant where she wanted to meet, the Boathouse at Breach Inlet.

Harry was sitting on a bench out front when CJ walked up to him in the evening sun. He got up and hugged her. "I got here a little early. I'm excited to have my favorite niece buy me dinner."

She kissed him on the cheek. "I'm your only niece."

He stepped back and spread his arms wide. "And thus, my favorite."

CJ had called ahead to arrange a table for them. She'd asked for a table in a quiet area. When they walked in, the man who worked the host stand looked at her. He seemed puzzled, and then his mouth dropped open.

"You're her," he said.

She wasn't sure who he was talking about. "Excuse me?"

"The detective on TV. The one who got the Lowcountry Killer."

Several people who were waiting to be seated snapped their heads around. Some of them pointed and whispered. A couple told her, "Nice job."

Damn it! So much for a quiet dinner.

SIXTY-ONE

Friday, May 7
The French Quarter, Charleston

CJ had spent another night staring at her notes and the ceiling. She had lain in bed thinking about Ben in a jail cell. It made little sense to her. *Did you do this, Ben?*

She rolled over and peered at the reddish-orange digits: 4:35 a.m. She pulled herself out of bed and went to start the coffeemaker. While she waited for coffee, she showered, dried her hair, and put on her robe. She got a cup of coffee and sat by the window. The sun's rays were just beginning to peek above the horizon. Strands of dark clouds streaked the sky, and there were low rumbles of thunder in the distance.

She got dressed and walked down to her favorite coffee shop to grab something to eat. To be honest, she wanted to see the barista, who always made her smile. The door chimed as she entered the shop.

"Good morning, beautiful."

She smiled. "Hi, Sal."

"I have some cinnamon muffins today. Fresh out of the oven!"

"They sound delicious. Give me one of those and my usual, please."

"Anything for you, darling."

He got her muffin and a large cup of black coffee. She paid him and found a spot at a small table with a forest green umbrella. She sat, ate the muffin, and watched Charleston wake up. Numbness gripped her body.

She picked up her ringing cell. "Good morning, Robert."

"Hey, CJ."

"Are you still at the Regency?" she asked.

"Yes. I was about to go grab some breakfast with Christy. Want to join us?"

"Sure. I'll be right over."

CJ joined Robert and Christy at their table in The Bistro twenty minutes later. Christy was pale—shocked the guy she was interested in was a serial killer. Robert clearly hadn't let her in on the fact he had been a suspect for a while.

"Robert, I know we have the press conference, and the chief wants you and me at the podium with him," CJ said. "We have to tell the public what they already know.

They've heard the rumors. We have someone in custody and it's someone on the force. But do we have to give them Ben's name yet?"

"No. We can delay giving out his name. Why?"

CJ steadied herself. "I'm still not convinced Ben is our guy. I'd like to make sure we exhaust our investigation before we convict him in public."

He sat and considered her request. "What does Harry think?"

"He agrees with me that being cautious can't hurt us. If Ben is indeed our guy, he's in a cell. Why give a defense lawyer anything they can use against us?"

He nodded. "That's a fair point." He leaned back. "I tell you what. Out of respect for you and Harry, we'll leave out Ben's name. For now. I'll keep the agents out on the streets for the next two nights." He leaned over and looked her in the eye. "But by Monday morning, we're going to have this wrapped up."

CJ nodded. "Fair enough. I have forty-eight hours." She got up from the table. "I'm heading to the station, but can I ask one more favor?"

He eyed her.

"I'll stand with you and the chief in front of the press, but can you do the talking for the both of us?"

"You'll miss your time in the spotlight, CJ."

"I don't give a shit about that. Let's have Christy stand with us, too. Give her some credit." She saw Christy's head snap up.

He smiled and nodded. "Okay, you got it."

The press conference was a total circus with media present from all over the country. First, the chief briefly discussed the case's circumstances, his appreciation for the FBI, and Charleston's first female detective's hard work. Then he asked Robert to talk about the suspect they had in custody.

CJ was happy with how Robert covered his part. As he'd agreed, he didn't mention Ben by name. He talked about the process they had used to apprehend him and echoed the chief's appreciation for all law enforcement who had helped. CJ could tell he was experienced with press conferences. Like a politician, he said a lot without saying much. He closed by indicating his agents would spend the weekend in Charleston out of an abundance of caution.

As Robert stepped back from the mic, the room exploded with reporters screaming for more. While Ben's name was not officially released, it had undoubtedly already leaked as the press was yelling it during their questions.

CJ's eyes caught Wendy Watts in the front row—screeching, red-faced, and arms flailing. *Not for long, bitch. I'm about to deal with your leaker.*

After leaving the press conference, CJ found a small conference room. As her invited guest entered, she motioned to a chair. "Officer Parker, how about you have a seat?"

Jared smirked. "What's going on, City Girl? You need me to solve your case for you? I think I'll stand."

The smirk left Jared's face when Chief Williams walked in. "Officer Parker, sit your ass down in that chair."

"Uh, yes, sir. What's this all about?"

CJ almost laughed. *Is that a look of panic, you cocky son of a bitch?* She leaned forward and stared Jared in the eyes. "Did you think no one would notice?"

"Notice what?" he asked.

"That you removed information on the Lowcountry Killer case from the war room and probably leaked the name of our suspect."

"What the—uh—what are you talking about?"

"Your fingerprints were on the door. Can you explain that?"

Jared squirmed.

The chief leaned forward. "Officer Parker, answer her question."

"I don't know," he said. "Maybe I touched it by accident or something. I've never been in the room."

CJ rubbed her chin. "Never?"

"Nope, never."

"We also found your fingerprints on a file cabinet. The same cabinet where the files are kept. The same files Wendy Watts used for her story."

Chief stood up. "Parker, effective immediately, you're suspended. Now, bring your ass with me." He grabbed Jared's arm and said, "CJ, I'll give Art Smith a call over at News 4 and make sure he understands that if he allows Wendy Watts to use any more stolen confidential information, there'll be hell to pay."

She watched as the chief escorted Parker to Internal Affairs. *Not so cocky now.*

CJ walked down the hall to the war room. She had less than forty-eight hours to address her nagging concerns. She had a copy of the entire case file. What was she missing? Maybe nothing. Was it time for her to defer to the FBI and get on the bandwagon? Life would be easier. *But if we're wrong, the unsub's still out there and my instincts tell me it's not Ben.*

CJ sat alone at the large conference room table and flipped through the file. She stared at the profile and ran the facts through her head. In the end, she knew a jury would hear Ben matched the profile, had no alibi, and his fingerprint and DNA matched—it would be a done deal. She rubbed her eyes. In her gut, she still doubted it was Ben, but with the evidence, it appeared clear. *Oh, Ben. Am I defending him because I care for him, or worried we might let the real unsub get away?*

She picked up her notes from her conversation with Ben's father. Suddenly, she noticed something. She grabbed her cell phone and dialed. *Come on, answer!*

She heard his voicemail message. "Hello, this is Bill. I'm not here and won't be back any time soon. You jackals can go to hell!"

CJ hung up. What the hell was he talking about? Oh shit, the media had found him. No doubt they'd be camped in his front yard. She called Mount Pleasant PD and asked the officer covering Shem Creek to call her. Within five minutes, an officer called her, and she asked him to go by the Shem Creek dock where Bill kept his bigger boat and see if he was there. It had room to sleep, and he might have moved there to avoid the media. Twenty minutes later, the officer called back. The boat was in the slip, and the media was camped out. There was no sign of Bill. She hung up.

Where is Bill? She had a question that needed to be answered, and she only knew one way to get it.

CHAPTER

SIXTY-TWO

Friday, May 7
Downtown Charleston

Ben's hair was tangled, his face stubbled, and his eyes glassy. He clearly hadn't slept or eaten since he was arrested. He sat slumped in his chair in the interrogation room where CJ had asked that he be placed.

"Ben?" CJ asked.

He exhaled and slowly gazed at her, but didn't speak.

"Ben, I'm sorry this is happening. I don't want to believe you could do such a thing, but you're a cop—look at the evidence."

There was no response. He just stared at her.

"I'm giving you the benefit of the doubt until I review and re-review everything," she said.

His mouth twisted, and he pursed his lips. "You've already arrested me. The deed is done. Everyone has already convicted me." He squinted. "For the record, I'm not guilty of harming anyone."

"What happened at the Citadel and in the marines?" she asked.

Ben's eyes were like fire. "Jesus Christ! A girl who I thought was a friend lied and said I raped her at a party. She told her boyfriend, and he went nuts and reported it. They called her and me in, and she admitted she lied. She screwed some random guy and knew her boyfriend would lose his shit. I wasn't even at the party, for what it's worth.

"As for the marines, some guy tried to rape a girl. He wore a mask and had a knife. She didn't see his face, but gave three or four names. I was one of them. Fact was, I was on exercises forty miles away that whole weekend." He grunted and said sarcastically, "But hey, all of us serial rapists and murderers lie, right?" He gave her a shooing motion with his hand. "Now go and leave me alone."

CJ got up and was about the leave the room but turned back. "Ben, I do have one question. Your brother who drowned, Bryan. You looked the same age in a photo your dad has in his kitchen. How old were you when he died?"

He just stared at her.

"Ben, please answer me."

She showed him the photo.

He rubbed his face. "He was ten. That photo was taken a couple of months before he died. We were twins. My mom left because of it. Anything else painful you want to talk to me about?"

"No. I'll go and leave you alone." She turned and left.

———

As she sat alone again in the war room, something continued to bug CJ. Frustrated, she called Sam.

"Sam, I need you to find out some information for me."

"Sure. What do you need?"

"I'm not sure exactly where the information is kept here in Charleston, but can you find out if a Bryan Parrish drowned twenty years ago? He would have been ten years old. He was Ben's twin brother."

"I didn't realize Ben had another brother," Sam said. "I'll do some digging. There should be an old obituary or newspaper article. I have a friend who can help. Anything else?"

"Actually, yes. Can you see if Bill Parrish owns any other properties besides his home? I need to find him."

"Sure. I can get that from records. I'll text you what I find ASAP."

"Thanks, Sam."

CJ went back to her apartment. A tragedy involving Ben's brother's death could be a contributing factor to explain why he'd done what he had done. If he had done it. If Bill had another property, maybe he was hiding out from the media there.

It was late afternoon when Sam called CJ.

"CJ, I'm sending you a text with an attachment. I found the obituary for Bryan Parrish. Death by drowning at ten. I found a short newspaper article on it, too. Second, Bill owns another piece of property. At one point, he had a license to operate a fish processing business."

"Thanks, Sam, you're the best."

CJ hung up and her cell phone chimed. She scanned the information from Sam. There wasn't much else confirming Bryan had died by drowning. She copied down the address for the other property Bill owned. She dialed Bill—she got the same voicemail message. Where was he? CJ paced in front of her picture window. Bill was probably being hounded by the press. The media were a bunch of jackals, and Bill was going through enough. *To hell with it, I'm going to go find him. I owe him that much.*

CHAPTER

SIXTY-THREE

Friday, May 7
Wadmalaw Island, South Carolina

The sun was setting as CJ drove to Bill's house on Johns Island. She had to go east anyway, since his home was on the way to his old fish processing site. The Ashley River sparkled in the last rays of the setting sun. Seagulls hustled to their nightly resting place as the breeze kicked up white-caps. The horizon began growing darker as the sun peeked over it for the last time.

CJ imagined Bill had hunkered down, hiding in his home. Perhaps Will was with him and both men were hiding in some back room. Or they might have simply left town if they weren't on Johns Island.

She pulled into Bill's driveway and found two television camera crews lurking in the yard. They stormed her when she got out of her truck. *This is the downside of being in the spotlight, right, Robert?* She waved them away. "No comments. I'm on duty. This is private property, so I'd suggest you leave, or I'll be forced to arrest you." This wouldn't deter them, but CJ felt better.

She knocked on the front door—no answer. She crept around back and yelled at the reporters to stay away. Neither Bill nor Will were anywhere to be found. The sun dropped further on the horizon, and darkness fell. The house was pitch black, and there were no signs anyone was hiding inside. She knocked on the back door again. Still no answer.

CJ walked to the small dock on Wadmalaw River. Bill's boat was gone. Had he and Will taken their boat to hide away from the press? It was possible, but the boat was too small to sleep on, and there was no cabin. She left a note on the back door if Bill returned.

Bill. I'm sorry I missed you. I'm sorry the press is hounding you and Will. You don't deserve this. Please call me. CJ

CJ took a right on New Cut Road to the address Sam had given her for the location where Bill had run his fish processing business. The site was near Johns Island, but in the middle of nowhere on Wadmalaw Island. The road twisted and turned. Blackness had taken over, with no streetlights and no houses.

She flew by the entrance to the property the first time. The trees had almost overgrown the access and an old metal sign was the only marking, nothing else. The sign had worn letters reading *Parrish Processing*. A picture of a fish was underneath the words.

CJ eased her truck into the entrance. A gate stood twenty yards away, and there were no signs of buildings or the presence of anyone. She put the truck in park and climbed out. Recent tire tracks were visible under her headlights. Someone had driven down the road. *Found you, Bill!*

The swinging gate had a massive chain and padlock. CJ grabbed the chain and realized the lock was open. She removed the chain and swung the gate open. If Bill wanted it locked, she'd do so on her way out. She peered into the blackness and blew out a breath.

CJ drove slowly for about two hundred yards through the trees until the silhouette of an old building appeared. It was dark and hulking against the dim sky. The building was dilapidated and clearly hadn't been used in a long time.

The truck's headlights gave the metal structure an eerie glow. The lower windows were boarded up, and the front door appeared unused. An oversized metal garage door, painted white, glistened. CJ stared at a faint glow in an upper window. She hadn't seen Bill's truck but guessed he'd parked inside to keep from being seen by any media snoopers. The media would find the place soon.

He watched the vehicle coming down the road with curiosity. He should have locked the damn gate, but he'd planned to leave soon. The gate and chain should have scared them off. *Who in the hell has come here?*

He peered through the small hole in the board covering the window. The headlights blinded him to whoever was coming through the darkness. It was an SUV, but he couldn't tell much more. He kept staring—waiting. *Who has come to my safe place?*

———

CJ cut the engine and sat in her truck. She thought about honking, so Bill would come out, but she was afraid he'd be pissed off. He was no doubt trying to hide. *Come out, Bill. Shit!* The interior lights lit up her face as she opened the door and stepped outside.

———

He smiled wickedly. *Well, well, Detective CJ O'Hara in the flesh. How nice of you to come alone.* He stared as she approached the building and whispered, "What a lucky man I am. Another one walks up and begs me to take her."

He suddenly panicked. What if others were coming? Who knew she was here? He worked to calm himself. It didn't matter. He was leaving town, but he'd have one last treat. *I'll really show them how stupid they are.*

———

CJ knocked on the front door. Nothing. She pressed her ear up to the door, but no sounds came from inside. She tried to see in the window, but the boards blocked her. It was dark, but there was some kind of light inside. The only sound was the song of crickets and katydids.

She traipsed back to the truck for her flashlight, and was digging for her Maglite when someone grabbed her from behind. A rag was pressed over her mouth. She twisted and tried to pull away, but his grip was too tight. She kicked as her world went black.

SIXTY-FOUR

Friday, May 7
Wadmalaw Island

CJ's eyes fluttered open. She struggled to focus as her vision cleared. A faint glow revealed the ceiling. Anxious, she jerked her head right and left. A workbench was to her right, and to the left through a doorway, a black SUV. No one was around.

Where the hell am I?

CJ tried to sit up; her hands were above her head, and her arms wouldn't move. Her legs were locked. She raised her head as far as she could. Her feet were tied, and she was lying on a metal table. CJ twisted her body. She was stretched out and tied down tight, and now wore only her panties. Her heart started pounding. She knew was in trouble.

No one knows where I am!

Her clothes were on the end of the workbench. Her cell phone was in her back pocket, but her cell was no help if she couldn't free herself. Suddenly, she realized something important.

Ben isn't the perp.

CJ breathed heavily. She didn't know what was coming next, but knew it wasn't good. Tears ran down her cheeks.

———

Harry checked the clock on his kitchen wall. He tried CJ's cell phone and got the damn voicemail again. Where was she? She always called him if she was running late. He dialed Robert. "Robert, is CJ with you?"

"No. I haven't seen CJ since the press conference. Have you tried her cell?"

"Multiple times. I keep getting her voicemail."

Robert grew concerned. "It's not like her to not answer her cell. Give me a yell if you don't reach her soon. I'll send an alert out."

Harry hung up. Where was CJ? He called Sam. "Sam, have you seen CJ?"

"No, Harry. Not since earlier today after she visited Ben. She went to check if his father was home. I'll text you his address."

"Okay, thanks."

Harry ran for his jeep. He looked at the address Sam had texted him and took off. Thirty minutes later, he ran to the front door and knocked. No answer. He ran around back. A man was on the dock cleaning a boat.

"Excuse me. I'm looking for Bill Parrish."

Bill stared at him. "I'm Bill. You a damn reporter? I just ran a bunch of you bastards off."

"No. I'm Harry O'Hara, and I'm trying to find my niece, CJ."

"She's not here," Bill said. "She left me a note to call her. I tried and got her voicemail."

Harry grew more frantic. "Yeah, me too. Where else would she try to find you?"

"She may have gone to my other boat at Shem Creek. I showed her where it was when Ben and I took her for a boat ride."

As he ran, Harry yelled back over his shoulder, "Thanks. I'll try there."

Bill watched Harry tear out and tried CJ's cell again. Voicemail. "Damn it!" Where was CJ? He went back to his boat and started cleaning it again. He liked her, but she wasn't his problem. Where was she, though? He turned off the hose. "Shit!" He went to the house and dug through his drawer for the card Ben had given him. He found it and called the number on it.

Sam answered.

"Hello. This is Bill Parrish."

"Ben's dad?" she asked.

"Yes."

"I'm sorry about him. This must be difficult for you."

Bill didn't want to chitchat, but he held his impatience. "Listen, Ben gave me your number. He said you worked together and I could call you if I ever needed him."

"But he's in jail," Sam said.

"I know. I'm looking for CJ. Any ideas where I can find her?"

She was concerned and remained quiet. *Why is Ben's dad looking for CJ?*

Bill realized she was stalling. "I'm trying to help Harry find her. I'm here at my house, and Harry's checking my boat at Shem Creek."

"Yeah. CJ said she was going to both those places."

"Did she mention going anywhere else?"

She exhaled. "She mentioned going to your old fish processing location. I gave her the address."

"Thanks, Sam."

Bill hung up. He was puzzled. Why would she go there? *Hell, let me go find her. She's probably lost on that shitty road or had a flat.*

SIXTY-FIVE

Friday, May 7
Wadmalaw Island

Bill pulled into the driveway to his old fish processing site half an hour later. The gate was wide open. *What the hell?* He drove up to the familiar building. It brought back memories of him and the boys and the days they'd spent processing their catches. His headlights reflected on CJ's truck. *She must be here, but where?*

Bill sat examining the scene. A flash of faint light appeared in the building. *CJ must be inside with her flashlight.* Bill grabbed his light, got out of his truck, and went to the front door. The door was locked, and he'd forgotten to bring his keys. He went around to the locked side door. *How the hell did she get in?*

He banged on the door—there was no response. Did CJ fall and hurt herself? The damn building was a death trap, and when this was over, he'd knock it down. He grabbed a crowbar out of his truck. No keys, no problem. He pried the latch on the side door loose and pushed the door open.

A black Ford Bronco sat in the garage area. *What the hell! Who's been using my place?* No one was in the truck. "CJ, are you in here?" Bill called.

A muffled noise came from the processing room. A faint light showed through the crack under the door.

"CJ, are you hurt?" Bill called again. He shoved the door open and walked in to find CJ lying on the table he'd once used to clean fish, half naked. Her feet and wrists were tied to the table with rope. Who the hell would do such a thing? *No way. He couldn't be here. Oh, God. The monster is back.*

CJ's eyes went wide when she saw him. *Bill is the Lowcountry Killer!*

Bill ran to the table. "Oh my God, oh my God."

He yanked the tape off her and she screamed at him, "How could you do this, Bill?"

"No, no, no. It's not me. It's the monster inside. It's the monster inside!"

She didn't understand. *What is Bill talking about? What monster inside? Inside of him?*

Bill ran to the workbench and grabbed a knife. CJ panicked and fought hard to free herself. "Stay away from me!" she screamed.

She prepared for him to attack her, but instead, he started cutting the ropes from her wrists. CJ was confused. "Bill, if you're not the killer and Ben is in jail, who's the killer?"

A tall man with dark brown hair stepped from behind the door. "That would be me, darling. Hello, Daddy. Wonderful of you to join us."

CJ stared at the man . . . *Ben?*

Bill angrily glared at him. "You were born bad, and I should have drowned you when I had the chance."

CJ suddenly realized the man standing there was Bryan. Ben's twin brother was alive!

Bryan crept toward Bill with an evil smile on his face. "Yes, you should have. Condemning me to that shithole only made me more determined to return one day."

Bill stopped cutting the ropes and stared at Bryan. "You're a monster. I won't make the mistake of leaving you alive this time."

In a flash, Bryan slammed into Bill and knocked him backward. Both men hit the floor hard. Bryan was on top of Bill, pounding him with his fists. He pulled a knife out of a sheath on his belt and stabbed Bill in his stomach. Bill fought hard, but Bryan was younger, stronger, and in a frenzy.

CJ realized Bill had freed her hands, but her ankles were still tied. She frantically tried to untie the ropes. She had to get her gun, which she hoped was on the workbench with her clothes. Bryan stabbed Bill again and straddled him, smirking.

"Not so tough, are you, old man? You're a worthless piece of shit."

She saw it! Bill had dropped the knife he was using to cut her loose. It hurt like hell, but she twisted her body and reached the floor. Almost. Almost. She had the knife! She pulled herself back onto the table and cut the ropes from her ankles. She jumped up and raced for the workbench. Her gun was so close—she didn't make it.

Bryan tackled her and took her down. A searing pain ran through her when he stuck the knife into her side. She kicked him off, but Bryan was quickly back on top. Stars swirled when he punched her hard in the face.

"Fight hard, bitch. I love it!"

Bryan slammed CJ back onto the table. The force of the blow to the back of her head almost knocked her unconscious. She tried not to lose focus. She'd be dead if she did.

Bryan stood over her. Through her foggy eyes, she watched him pull his shirt off over his head. He started unbuckling his pants. She tried to move, but he hit her again. Her face exploded with pain. *Don't black out, CJ!*

With a flick of his knife, he cut off her panties. He smiled wickedly at her. "You're a natural beauty, although I like blond hair the best. I think we'll pass on the condom this time. No one is going to find your body, anyway. Let the cops keep it all pinned on my stupid brother."

She struggled to escape as Bryan forced her back down and started to climb on top of her.

Bill growled loudly as he struggled to his feet. "Get the hell off her!"

Bryan screamed in rage. "Damn it, old man, you're spoiling the mood." Zipping up his pants, Bryan winked at CJ. "I'll be right back, sweetheart. I need to finish something."

He stood in front of Bill, who swayed back and forth. Bill's once white shirt was stained crimson. Bryan stood laughing at Bill with his knife in his hand.

CJ's head was spinning, but she knew it was now or never. She took a deep breath, quickly rolled off the table, and sprinted toward her gun. Bryan turned to grab her, but Bill lunged and grabbed his leg.

Bryan wheeled around back and stomped Bill in the face. "Get off me, you bastard!"

He turned back to find CJ facing him. Blood ran down her side, and her bloodied right eye was swelling and closing fast. Her Glock was trained on his face.

Bryan spread his arms. "Well, well. Lookie here." He threw back his head and roared with laughter. "I love fighters. Damn, you're turning me on." He stopped laughing and smirked at her. "You don't think I left the gun loaded, do you?"

Her heart sank. Had he unloaded her gun?

He suddenly lunged at her—there was a glint of silver. She squeezed the trigger and prayed. The gunshot was deafening, and a red mist appeared. The tall man staggered backward and crumpled to the floor. Blood drained from the gaping hole she had put in his forehead.

CJ collapsed to her knees, but she crawled to Bill, who lay on his back. She had to help him. Blood was everywhere. What could she use to stop the blood? She grabbed her shirt off the workbench and pressed it against the worst of the wounds.

"Please, God, don't let Bill die. Please help us."

Suddenly, the door slammed open against the wall, and Harry and Will entered.

Harry was already talking into his phone. "I've got an officer down and a man severely injured. We need medical now!"

CJ was crying and squeezing Bill's hand, telling him to hang on.

Harry found the tarps Bryan had used to wrap his victims and used one to cover CJ. Bryan had cut off her jeans and shirt, so they were useless. Tears ran down his face as he held CJ. "Help is coming, sweetheart."

Will kneeled by his dad. "Hang in there, Pop. You'll be okay."

Less than fifteen minutes later, more than a dozen of Charleston's finest roared through the gate. Robert, Christy, and the other FBI agents arrived and began scouring the building and surrounding area. A life-flight helicopter landed in the clearing behind the building.

CJ held Bill's hand as they lifted off. The lights of Charleston sparkled in the distance as she closed her eyes.

CHAPTER

SIXTY-SIX

Sunday, May 9
MUSC, Charleston

CJ blinked. Startled, she looked around to see where she was. She was lying in a stark-white room with a hanging TV, lots of gadgets in a console next to her, and a damn tube in her arm. The hospital. *I remember now.*

Harry was asleep in the chair beside her bed. Her mouth felt like sand. *Water.* The nurse answered the pushed button.

"Good morning, Detective O'Hara. How are you feeling?"

Harry suddenly had her hand. Immediately, tears appeared in his eyes.

"Dry," CJ said. "My mouth is dry."

The nurse smiled. "I'll bring you some water."

Harry kissed her hand. "Thank God. If I lost . . ."

CJ shifted. "Ouch."

"Don't try to sit up!" Harry said. "You have a nasty wound."

She patted his hand. "Okay, okay. I'll be fine."

The nurse helped her sip water, and CJ smiled feebly. "Thank you. You're Abby, right? Mandy's friend."

Abby smiled. "Yes. Good memory." She adjusted CJ's blanket and set her cup with a straw on her bedside table. "I'll leave this. I'm going to get the doctor."

CJ looked at Harry. "Did we get him?"

He nodded. "You got him."

She shook her head. "It was Ben's twin brother." Her heart jumped. "Oh my God, where is Ben?"

Harry took her hand. "Ben's been released, and he's at home. I spoke with him, and he's doing as well as one might expect. He's trying to wrap his head around all this. I can't imagine what it's like for him dealing with the fact his twin brother was alive all these years and returned to commit such awful acts, including killing their mother. He's also struggling to understand why his father sent Bryan away instead of getting him the help he needed. There's lots for him to process."

CJ's eyes filled with tears. "Can I see him?"

Harry patted her hand. "Give him some time. Focus on getting well right now."

"I need to apologize to him. I arrested him."

"Ben told me he knew you were doing your job, and the evidence pointed at him. He'll forgive you if he hasn't already. Let him deal with all this first."

CJ sniffed and slowly nodded. "Okay. I really want to see him, though."

Harry smiled. "I know. Patience."

CJ suddenly remembered Bill had been seriously injured trying to save her. "Is Bill . . . okay?"

Harry smiled. "His injuries were pretty bad, but his surgery went well, and he's going to be fine. He's a tough old bird."

Tears filled her eyes. "If he hadn't come, I'd be dead. He got my hands loose and fought Bryan, which is why I was able to get to my gun. I want to see him."

"You will, but not today. You both have to rest."

She slowly nodded.

Harry was busy fussing over her blanket. He was obsessed with making sure she was comfortable.

"Uncle Harry, what day is it?"

"It's Sunday. You were pretty out of it yesterday. They had you on some strong meds. They wouldn't let me stay with you until I threw a fit. They finally gave in last night."

"When can I go home?" she asked.

"Not today. The doctor said he'll keep you a couple of days. The good news is the knife didn't do too much damage. No major organs were hit. The doc repaired you, but you have to stay still."

Sam entered the room and joined Harry at CJ's bedside. "Glad to see you're awake. You gave us quite a scare. Can I get you anything?"

"Thanks for being here, Sam. I think water is all I need right now."

Sam whispered, "Harry, I'll stay while you take a break."

"Thanks. I'd like to have someone here with her. Knowing my niece, if we're not watching, she'll get up and go to the station."

Harry quietly left the room, and he and the doctor talked briefly in the hall. The doctor said he'd come back later.

———

Late in the afternoon, Chief Williams, Captain Meyers, and Mayor Sellers came to see CJ, who was now fully awake. Her meds had been decreased, and her fog had lifted. Nevertheless, she wasn't too pleased when the mayor announced she had brought a camera crew to interview her for the evening news.

CJ was horrified. "I look like shit! Can't we wait until I'm out of here?"

Mayor Sellers smiled while she shook her head. "The doctor said a short interview would be okay. The press wants to get a shot of our new heroine. I promise I'll keep it short. You look fine."

Harry, who was back, wasn't happy. "Come on, Mayor, can't you wait?"

"Only two minutes, I promise. I'd like you to be in it, too."

"Nope. I draw the line there," he said. "Besides, I promised my girl some hush puppies."

CJ croaked, "And some key lime pie."

Harry chuckled. "Whatever you want, sweetheart."

Sam pushed her way between Walter and Stan. "CJ, I'll wash your face." She glared at the mayor. "Not sure why it would hurt to wait a day or two for an interview."

"Thanks, Sam. Just be careful with my left eye. I hope it looks better than it feels."

The mayor got her way. The interview lasted longer than CJ wanted, but she survived it. Fortunately, the mayor talked most of the time. *Politicians!*

Walter hung back as the entourage left. He smiled at CJ. "I had a great call with your former captain. He said to tell you hello. I also got to rub it in."

"Rub what in?" she asked.

"He told me you struggled with trusting your instinct, and I told him he was crazy."

"Thank you, sir."

"I'm gonna head out and let you rest. Take your time getting well. Once you're ready, I plan to hold a press conference and present you with commendations. Hell, you've been here eighteen days, and we've taken two serial rapists and a serial killer off the street. Lots of families now have justice for their daughters."

"How about Ben, sir? He helped me, plus he's the one who got Elrod Harris."

He smiled. "Okay, I'll include Ben, too."

CJ saw Detective Vincent Jackson peek around the door frame as Walter left. He gave her a sheepish smile. "Detective O'Hara, is it okay for me to come in?"

"Sure, Detective Jackson. Please come in." *This should be fun.*

He came in but stayed near the door, staring at his shoes. "I, uh . . . uh, wanted to come by and see how you were feeling."

"Much better. Thank you."

"That's good. I'm happy you're okay. I also want to tell you I was wrong about you. You're a damn good detective, and I shouldn't have given you shit. You deserved to have this case. I'm sorry."

CJ smiled. "It's okay. No harm done. I appreciate you coming by."

He smiled. "Well, I need to go. I just wanted to see you. Hope you feel better soon." He turned and hurried away.

———

CJ was enjoying her hush puppies when Robert and Christy arrived. Robert filled her in on the investigation of the building where Bryan Parrish had raped and murdered his victims. The CSIs had collected lots of evidence that would link him to all eight young women.

"He kept souvenirs—small jars of the blood of each of the victims. He also kept their underwear. They were all labeled with names he'd given them." He looked at his notes. "Nurse, Flat Tire Girl, Cheerleader, Bartender, Jogger, Pickup Girl, and Waitress."

CJ grimaced.

His face was grim. "He had a jar for you, too. He labeled it 'Detective.'"

CJ's stomach lurched. "Do we know why he started killing?"

"Twenty years ago, Bill sent him away to live with a friend who was a commercial fisherman in Sitka, Alaska. After the old man died, Bryan came back to Charleston. He somehow found out where his mother lived, and lured her back here. We found some letters he'd written her. Bryan wanted revenge for her deserting him." Robert stopped. "We could talk about this later."

CJ shook her head. "I need to know. At least the headlines."

Robert exhaled. "He lured her back here and killed her. We found her body in the freezer. He wrote 'Deserter' on her forehead."

CJ's eyes went wide. "Did he . . . did he . . .?"

"He didn't rape her, but he mutilated her the same way as the others," he said. "Psychological profiling in similar cases suggests this could have triggered him to hunt young women who were his mother's age when she married his father. He had a photo from their wedding day. She was gorgeous."

"Oh, Jesus." CJ sat there trying to absorb what Robert had told her. She ran through everything in her head again. She must have missed something. "Robert, the list of jars. How many jars were there?"

Robert frowned. "There were eight." He started going over the names again. "Yes, there's eight, but that includes you. Unfortunately, we're missing one jar of the eight young women. Christy, what do you have in your notes?"

Christy read out the seven names again, not including CJ's empty jar. "I have seven plus the empty one intended for CJ, but I remember we found two jars with no labels."

Robert slowly nodded. "Okay, we need to check and make sure the two unlabeled jars account for the eighth girl and the mother. That should match everything up." He turned to CJ. "Damn, girl, you had me for a moment. Nice to see that brain is still sharp."

The doctor walked in and cleared his throat. "Okay, time to let her rest. Visiting hours are over. Everybody out."

Harry wasn't happy. "Can I stay?"

"I suppose, but no more shop talk. None," said the doctor firmly.

Robert, Christy, and Sam said their goodbyes.

Robert winked at her. "See you tomorrow before we leave, Detective CJ O'Hara."

Harry excused himself and went into the hall. CJ watched him whisper in the doctor's ear. The doctor smiled and held up five fingers. Her uncle came back inside.

"CJ, I have a surprise for you," Harry said, and pointed behind him.

A man appeared. He was the spitting image of her father—six feet tall with dark brown hair and the same chiseled face. He stared at her as he slowly approached. His eyes glistened under the bright lights as he leaned down and took her hand. "I'm your Uncle Craig. You look just like your mom. I'm so sorry I . . ."

CJ threw her arms around his neck, ignoring the pain. Harry wiped his eyes as he watched the two of them.

EPILOGUE

Sunday, July 4
Downtown Charleston

The sun was warm on CJ's face. She leaned back and soaked it in. Charleston was beautiful. A clear blue sky and white puffy clouds created the perfect backdrop for the green, yellow, pink, and various other pastel-colored buildings. The ocean breeze caused the palm trees to rustle. Seagulls lazily circled overhead. It was in the nineties, and the air felt damp, but the breeze and broken shade made it bearable.

"I'm happy we're doing this," she said.

Harry leaned back, arms behind his head. "Yeah, me too. I make a good tourist, don't I?"

Harry's procedure for his prostate cancer had gone well—brachytherapy. He had surgery at the Crosstown Surgery Center and was in and out in one day. He had his energy back and looked great.

CJ smiled at Craig. "Uncle Craig, having you here makes it perfect. I'm so happy to have my two uncles in my life."

He hugged her. "I was an ass for waiting so long."

The man who drove the carriage looked back at them. "Y'all having fun?"

CJ threw her hands up. "Absolutely! This is wonderful."

"General Lee is happy you're here," the driver said. "He likes you."

CJ, Harry, and Craig got out of the carriage by the dock. CJ caressed General Lee's nose, and he bobbed his head for her. He nibbled her ear. She kissed his nose and slipped him a small carrot.

CJ waved at the two figures coming towards them. "Hey, Bill. How do you feel?"

"Hey, everyone. I'm feeling much better. I'm damn glad to have all the stitches out and the cuts are pretty much healed."

Ben stood behind him. CJ was happy he'd said he'd forgiven her and agreed to go out with them for the day. He was also slowly forgiving his dad. It had taken her a couple of weeks to get them together to talk. *Maybe I should counsel men on getting along more often.* "Hey, Ben."

"Hey, CJ. I figured someone needed to come to make sure we didn't get lost."

He shook hands with Harry and Craig and gave CJ a hug. Ben's smile wasn't overly bright, but CJ had to give him credit for trying. He even managed to provide Bill with a "Hey Pop" and pat his shoulder.

Bill broke a moment of silence. "Okay, I think we're ready to go." He took CJ's hand and helped her down the steps. "How are you feeling?"

"I'm feeling great. There are a couple of scars to add to my collection, but I'm all good otherwise. So, I guess I'll pass on my bikini today."

Ben laughed. "Damn! I was hoping for that."

CJ plopped down beside him and grinned. "I thought you'd have a date today." *I'm sure Sam, Christy, or Melissa would love to be here with you.*

He laughed at her again and she wanted to kiss him, but thought better of it. She did arrest him, after all, and he needed some time to truly forgive her.

Bill eased the boat away from the dock. He jammed the throttle forward as he cleared the no-wake zone, and the boat surged.

———

Rumbles, booms, and whistles preceded the multicolored lights that lit up the night sky. CJ had seen the firework shows in the Boston Harbor, but this one was the most magnificent she'd ever seen. Maybe it was because she was on the water. She felt like the shower of lights engulfed her. The cheers, oohs, and aahs of those on the boats surrounding them made it even more special.

Bill dropped CJ, Harry, and Craig off at the dock a little past ten.

Harry smiled at CJ. "A pretty great day, wasn't it?"

CJ put her arms around her two uncles. "Absolutely, the best day!"

———

A man watched from the shadows of a magnolia tree as they pulled into the dock, and she and her two uncles said their goodbyes. His eyes were fixed on CJ. He'd always been partial to blond hair and blue eyes, but she was an exception. Her natural beauty captured him. He smiled. Patience and self-control were his strengths.

THE END

ACKNOWLEDGMENTS

First and foremost, I'd like to thank my readers. I hope you enjoyed the first novel in the CJ O'Hara crime thriller series as much I enjoyed writing it. My goal was to provide an interesting plot with a fast pace, and intriguing characters while weaving in lots of information of the Lowcountry.

If you did enjoy the book, I'd be grateful if you'd write a review. I'm also always happy when readers reach out on my website, Facebook page, or on Instagram, Twitter or Goodreads. Please see the About the Author page for details.

———

A special thanks goes to the numerous restaurants and local businesses who graciously agreed to be included in my books—Poogan's Porch, the Boathouse at Breach

Inlet, Vickery's, The Wreck of the Richard and Charlene, Coconut Joe's, Henry's on the Market, and Dunleavy's Pub. If you make to Charleston, I highly recommend you give any or all of them a visit.

It takes a village to publish a book, and I owe a giant thank you to all those who pitched in beta reading, editing, and designing. Thanks to those professionals and special people who helped me produce this book—James Osborne, Aja Pollock, Kelly Lydick, Joanne Lane, and Danna Mathias Steele.

Finally, thanks to my wife, Lisa, who supported me throughout this journey.

UNDER A BLOOD MOON

A homicide with a mutilated corpse. A policewoman facing extreme pressure. Can she end a spree of savagery?

Charleston, South Carolina. Detective CJ O'Hara feels the strain. Juggling multiple tough cases and still tormented by her past, the hunt for a serial rapist stirs up even more demons. And the dedicated cop fears a new killer is only just beginning when a young woman is found in bed with her heart removed.

Pulling apart bizarre clues, CJ believes the evidence may point to hoodoo rituals connected to the full moon. And with this lunar phase bearing down as she races to solve three major investigations, she struggles with her personal troubles while trying to prevent a close friend's grisly demise . . .

Can CJ keep her focus on the murderer before the moon turns dark red?

Under a Blood Moon is the gripping second book in the CJ O'Hara crime thriller series. If you like driven heroines, powerful psychological tension, and Lowcountry folk magic, then you'll love this page-turning dark mystery.

ABOUT THE AUTHOR

 John grew up in the South and currently lives with his wife in the California Bay Area. He lived and worked in Charleston for ten years and fell in love with the Lowcountry. Connect with John on his website, www.johndealbks.com, or via social media:

- www.facebook.com/JohnDealBooks
- www.instagram.com/johndealbks
- www.twitter.com/JohnDealBks

Made in the USA
Monee, IL
27 July 2024

62759787R00233